BELVIDERE.

III

X
Sans Nom

Title: **Belvidere.**

Summary: *A mysterious man is sent to a dead-end town; to do what, and to whom, he simply doesn't know. It's all part of a game he neither understands, nor controls. He befriends those he will likely betray; there will certainly be trouble if he does not. A fantastical, mysterious journey; an ephemeral olla podrida of raw erotica, graphic violence, racism, heathenism, bigotry and vulgarity, all buoyed by the providence of friendship, love and kindred souls.*

1.   Fiction-General.   2. Fiction-Fantasy.
17 18 19 20 21   j i h g f e d c b a
First Edition - American

Warning:

This novel installment contains adult-directed narrative and dialogue not suitable for children, including, but not necessarily limited to:

racism, bigotry, heathenism, vulgarity, graphic violence and raw erotica.

Proceed at your own peril....

TABLE OF CONTENTS - III

CHAPTER 66 – HE CHANGED, JUST A BIT. AND IT WAS GOOD

Cord placed his hand heavy on his knee and pushed himself vertical, brushing the grass residue from his bare skin. He looked toward the three pin oaks just inside the wrought iron fence along Oxford, about one hundred yards ahead of him, where he first began his graveyard crawl.

He walked slowly in that direction; he didn't bother to read any of the headstones he now passed.   There was no need.

He stopped where he started, in proximity to his first run of stones, but this time he was focused on the grass.

Beck
Pursell
Pierson
Stuart
Hicks
Bell
Whitmore

There wasn't much room between, but he looked anyway; he was near where he and Lillian fell off their bikes, a mere twenty-five feet off the concrete sidewalk along Oxford Street, which was now quiet, and empty.

Nothing.

Stopp
Bossard
McFadden-Handelong
Armstrong
Gardner
Beers
Thatcher

Again, nothing.

He switched back and walked closer to the wrought iron fence, just alongside and under the trio of spreading pin oaks. The grass was sparser here, thinned by the lack of sun and the steal of water by the countless veined tree roots. He was walking in the checkered shade, under a canopy of intertwined oak branches; he raised his eyes to see the speckled evidence of blue sky, spied through small wormhole openings, corkscrewed through the dappled overstory.

A lone crow lit in one of the oaks and let a low growl, followed by a click and clipped cackle. C couldn't see it, hidden in the leafy collage, but it was there, talking to him.

He came upon a group of headstones closer to the road that he didn't notice his first two passes; he wasn't sure how his eyes missed this isolated group.

 It was the *Pierson* family plot. He had seen other scattered *Piersons*, but not this one.

The main stone held a simple two-word epitaph, one of the few he saw, even in the old section. It was the only one he noticed at this end of the graveyard, by Oxford.

Perpetual Care

Father Miller 1867 – 1940
Daughter Mabel 1892 – 1940
Mother Luella   1872 – 1950

He kicked about looking in the grass, sparse and thin due to the abundance of shade, which made the grounds much easier to dissect. The crow unleashed a loud guttural call; it seemed directly overheard.

His heart stopped. There, just ahead of the *Pierson* plot, was a small bronze, *bas relief* plaque, flush with the ground, slightly askew.

He found it!

He rushed to the spot, scurried around it, and fell to his knees, knowing the words he longed to read would finally greet him.

But they weren't the right words. Instead, it was a quiet memorial to a name he did not know.

Gladys A. Greene
May 24, 1906   +   September 27, 1960

He rolled over onto his butt, grabbed his knees and pulled them toward his chest; a feeling of utter sadness enveloped him. He felt upset, empty....more than he really should have. He raised his head and looked into the overlapping tangle of sunlit leaves, colored in a dozen shades of summer green.

Where are you? He whispered aloud.

The crow clicked and loudly cackled overhead, twice, far up toward the top of the tree; still sight-unseen. It was mocking him.

And in a flurry of gnashing leaves and twigs, it took flight, cawing loudly as it flew away; he heard its raspy voice fade as it flew to the west. He never did see it, and now it was gone.

He got up, brushed himself off once again and headed toward the gate, head down in defeat. He decided he wouldn't tell Earl and Lilly he was here, unless they already knew by now. Maybe he would try and find her again some other day.

Maybe.

In this section, in the shade, the ground was cool and moist, even though they were in the middle of a June dry spell. The oak's roots snaked along the ground surface; half-buried, half-exposed, spreading like the bulged veins on the back of one's hand. He picked up an old acorn, probably from the year prior; how it escaped the squirrels he didn't know. A simple tiny white mushroom cap caught his eye; as he focused on it, he soon saw a whole sentry of them, maybe a half-dozen count, in a lazy, curvilinear line, hiding in toto amongst the shade.

He picked the first one and spun the stem between his thumb and pointer, the umbrella top snapped off, leaving him holding the skinny stem. He walked along, guided by the toadstool road, back toward the main gate, to hop onto Earl's bike, and head back to work.

And somehow, this time, it caught his eye.

It was set off to the right, at the periphery, alone in a patch of thinning, brownish-green grass, the ugliest patch of grass he saw in the whole Cemetery. As he saw it, his eyes welled and he cracked the faintest hint of a smile; it was a good smile.

And on that day, Friday, June 23rd, although Cord didn't realize it, he changed, just a bit.

And it was good.

CHAPTER 67 – A LONG-WAY BACK-ROAD HEADWORK

He walked slowly, respectfully; he didn't have to look - he knew it was her.

And she looked up at him.

Carol Liddell
1945 + 1981

He couldn't believe it was really her; he couldn't believe he was this close; Carol Liddell was only six feet away. And it was *really* her.

All the stories he heard from Earl, from Sam, others, yet she was still just this figment in his mind, a vision that somehow knew him, according to Earl, at least. For fleeting moments here and there he believed it too, the balance being more than skeptical.

But now, she was finally *real*.

He knelt down and gently ran his hand across her name on the ground, barely touching the metal. He had a connection to her, and it felt so real, even though it made no sense.

The plaque didn't denote any months, days, or anything, just a simple cross separating the years of birth and death; it was a standard funeral home marker that comes with the basic burial package. The marker wasn't even bronze, but rather an imitation, bronze-colored spelter, a cheap zinc knock-off. The name of the funeral home was embossed at the bottom – an advertisement in perpetuity.

The funeral home in Town, over on Hardwick Street, a block from Carol Crowe's house, off the Park.

Cord shook his head; he felt sad, and mad. She was lying less than twenty-five feet from the sidewalk, in a shady area with the worst patch of lawn, all by herself, surrounded by ugly, gnarled oak roots, spindly mushrooms and last year's acorns. She was too close to the road he thought, too much noise. And why did she have such a shit marker? Where was the headstone? Why did Earl and Lillian think this was okay?

It wasn't okay, not by a long shot.

First thing tomorrow, he would order a beautiful marble stone, to rival the best the Cemetery had to offer, to a height greater than twenty feet, towering into the canopy of oak leaves above. He started to design the garniture in his head, sketching the shape in a dozen incarnations, rapid fire between his ears.

Then he looked up at the leaves of the regal oak, gently turning in the faintest wisp of a summer breeze; he felt the cool, moist soil on the heel of his palm. He took a long, deep breath; maybe, things were okay just as they were. *Life is always better lying under a tree*; he said that to himself time and again over the years, on his many travels around the globe. No matter where he wandered, life was always better on your back, gazing up into a canopy of green. And right here, Earl and Lilly's mom was doing just that....forever.

He smiled, just a bit, to himself; maybe Carol was just fine, right where she was.

He turned to the marker, placed his hand gently on it again to feel the *bas relief* of her name, rubbing it softly with his pointer. He introduced himself in a whisper.

"I've heard a lot about you, good stuff. I'm just gonna sit with you for awhile; hope you don't mind."

C sat, legs to his chest; he closed his eyes and began his familiar ramble – a long-way back-road headwork.

CHAPTER 68 – AT SEVEN, I WROTE HIM OFF FOR LIFE

It was a ritual he practiced for years.

He would unlock the vault, walk in, alone, pull up a chair, and stand against the massive, speckled orange and brown granite wall, adjacent to a towering twenty-five foot marble etching of a humbled Jesus, and run his finger gently along the gilded lettering spelling out his mother's name.

Lillian

He never told Lilly that little tidbit, nor Earl, nor anyone else for that matter. Not that it really meant anything, just a backstory quiddity he kept to himself.

His mother was never called Lilly; it was either Lillian or Lil, that was it. To his father, it was always Lillian….always formal; there was no deviation.

He despised the color of the granite facade; he didn't think they particularly liked it either.

He would lightly run his finger backward, right to left, once, over her name, feeling the gilt, grooved letters; he never did it for his dad, just his mom. He didn't know why that was the ritual - it just was. Then he would take his open hand and, in what might seem to be a fit of rage to others, would slam it violently against the granite wall, right on their names, in a series of three or four thunderous claps, reverberating the shock wave of air in the mausoleum atrium. He never said a word; he didn't have to; it was simply meant to wake them up, to let them know he was there. He thought it worked.

As the mausoleum returned to silence, he would quietly, gently, sit in the same chair that always rested beside their spot in the wall, drop his shoes, and prop his bare feet against the cold-stone granite just below their names and simply begin to *remember*; anything that swam into his head at that moment in time was good enough.

They were the snippets of life that formed the memories of his parents, in no particular order, in no apparent queue of importance; a streaming video of conscience pulled from points unknown in his brain. A chaos of memories.

He would sit in utter silence, barely breathing, and think, for twenty, thirty minutes, eyes closed, with a juvenile smile plastered on his face most of the time.

That was the best.

He would end as he started, with a wicked slam of his hand against the wall three or four times, then he would walk out in silence, till he came again, months, years later. He couldn't remember the last time he made it back, but it mattered little; they always waited for him.

Now, as he sat next to Carol, he slipped off his shoes and dug his bare toes into the moist soil beside her grave, to get just a bit closer.

He turned to thoughts of his mother.

C closed his eyes and began to wander, as he did when he visited the mausoleum, through long-past years in his life, the respite of better times, sandwiched between the torture.

- Sunday morning at the dining room table, with a pile of newspapers stacked between them, silently reading and eating bakery crumb cake and donuts with thick crackled glaze – her perfect penmanship on letters written to relatives between reading sections of the local and national news, and the comics, always the comics;

- Napping on her bed after *Kimba,* the smell of her perfume on his worn, white baby blanket;

- The sweater she wore, the orange one, which was a harbinger of trouble whenever she slipped it on – he seemed to always find himself in trouble whenever she wore that sweater….that was his memory anyway; years later, she would laugh whenever he reminded her of the bad omen;

- The crispy tails of sunnies she grilled in butter after he caught and brought them up from the lake – half the time he would feel guilty about hurting the fish, so he would rush back down to the water to save them….the unfortunate ones who didn't survive while his conscience changed went down tail first – shared with his best childhood companion, his cat – *Midnight*; and

- The God-awful smell of cocoa butter at night on her cheeks when she kissed him goodnight, a small peck on the forehead or cheek. He hated that smell, and she knew it, so she would kiss him extra-long, just because.

He smiled and tried to remember more of that, more of when she hugged or kissed him in other than a formal, perfunctory act….a heartfelt contact. He thought, and thought some more. But there were no memories of that; despite his close relationship with his mom, his love for her and her love for him, there was none of that wanted warmth floating in his head.

He remembered when she was stricken with cancer, yet again in 1998; it was lymphoma, her third tussle over the years, the round she finally lost.

He recalled he was driving, and the woman he was with at the time, her name escaped him - lost in his memory, told him to call her and tell her how much he loved her.

He hesitated; it was not something he would ever think to do, nor she would ever expect to hear.

Upon further prompting, he reluctantly picked up the phone and made the call; when she answered, on the second ring, C felt awkward....foolish.

He loved his mother, he always had, but he was thirty-five and never once had he said those words to her, nor had she to him. She knew things were bad, but couldn't have realized it was so close to being over. She was dead less than two months later.

"Hey mom, just wanted to call, just to say....I love you."

That was the first and only time he ever uttered those words to her in the thirty-five years they spent together. An awkward silence greeted him on the other end of the line.

"Okay."

Was all she said, before moving on to some trivial topic at hand, something he couldn't remember, something that had no meaning at all, forgotten before she finished her sentence. The entire call lasted thirty seconds, tops.

He hung up, feeling both foolish and like shit. He just stared hard at the girl beside him, mad at himself that he even considered her ridiculous suggestion, let alone following it. He didn't say a word to her, and she responded in kind. The silence lasted for ten long seconds, eyes locked, until he turned his head in disgust, back toward the blacktop disappearing under the wheels. A week later, maybe less, he ended whatever he had with that nameless face beside him in the car, and never saw her again. Good riddance.

And C had never thought about that dismal incident again, that ill-omened phone call, until, for some reason, now.

That was not how this process usually worked, Cord thought as he opened his eyes and was back in the now, in the Cemetery, beside Carol. Those weren't the parental memories he usually roused. It was usually only good stuff, not lousy recalls like that. He shook his head, as if to wipe the slate and change the subject....a clean *Etch A Sketch*.

He turned his head slowly and gazed down at Carol, starting a rambling dialogue, without opening his mouth nor uttering a word.

C had a lot to say and a lot to ask, in no particular order, with no particular plan.

And so it began.

Are you reading my mind, right now? It feels like you are, like you're hiding in my head, somewhere.

I'm not a good person, never in the end....sometimes not right from the beginning, but you should know that, right? Especially in the past, especially the bad, bad times – those memories are hard to digest. I'm not sure you know all about that; I can't imagine you really do....I can't imagine you could, and have me anywhere near Lilly and Earl. But there was always a reason, a method to the madness – if you know about any of it, you must know that. But enough of the past; nowadays, I'm kinda good, sometimes; well at least it starts that way, like when I helped out Earl, when you told him about me.

And why did you really tell him to talk to me that first time? That very first day?

I haven't figured out the whole ' kindred' thing, that's the only one that doesn't make a lot of sense....well, certainly not the only one, but a big one. How did Earl come up with that word? Out of all the words in the world, it's that one, and he doesn't even know what it really means....and it's the word I was just thinking about regarding him, and me, us. Just perchance? Really? Come on.

This is stupid.

I don't know why I'm sitting here next to you, or why I even think I'm talking to you. I'm talking to myself, or to whomever lives in my head – and there is more than one, for sure. This is a private conversation in my noggin, with whomever chooses to listen. Maybe you live in there too, maybe you always have, and I just never knew it. Welcome to the neighborhood.

You think I'm some sort of angel? Here for Lilly and Earl? But it can't be good, not a good one, not the good kind. No way I'm that. Then what am I? An ame damnee? Fallen for sure. And you should know why I'm here, the whole story, the whole game, right? Did you throw that last dart? I doubt it, maybe, but I doubt it. It would answer a lot of questions though, it certainly would. Do you know Jenny? Does she talk to you too? Are you some sort of new player? If so, why now? Why so late in the game? You're decades late.

You simply don't make any sense.

You told Earl I'll tell him, something, 'when I'm ready'? How did you know that line? How did you know I wrote that on my box, years ago? And why is it your line too, about your note, to Lilly? Why do we own that, together? Is that just another strange coincidence?

Nothing in my life is a coincidence; I learned that a long time ago. So you mean something, for some reason. I just haven't figured it out yet. Maybe this is the start of that figure-out.

And what story am I supposed to tell Earl? Which one? There are so many bad stories....and he doesn't need to hear any of them. Bad things done to so many, I've long since lost count. I have so much empathy it's debilitating....just not for humanity. Since I was a kid, people have been a throw-away as far as I'm concerned. At least they always were until I got here. Maybe they still are, but I'm thinking that maybe some aren't. That's a new one.

Earl said to ask you if you know my mom? Well? Give me a sign; show me something. Are you the one that made me remember that stupid phone call I made to her? Why?

[Cord picked up his shirt and stared at his midsection, scanning the countless scars marring his chest, his belly]

I'm sure you know all about this too; the story behind each one, and you know the latest story too, the ones that are waiting, patiently....the ones that are next. Well, I say 'fuck it', I'm done. But, of course, you know that's not really up to me, as much as I'd like to think it is, right?

And you must know I'm not afraid of dying; for all I know, I'm dead already. Maybe my life, the last thirty-odd years, is what dead really is. And maybe those thirty years have been just a minute in my mind, stuck on that fence. And if not, I couldn't give a rat's ass if I died today; to me, life isn't about living as long as possible, it's just about living, day to day, a page at a time; when your done, you just put the book down.

Most people spend a lifetime worrying about making whatever they're doing last longer, just for longer's sake, rather than just accepting the cards they're dealt; what a colossal waste of time and energy.

If I died today, right now, it would be cool if I could just dissolve into the ground, disappear, shoes and all, no trace, no mess, no fuss. And then I'd be lying right next to you, wouldn't I? That would be kinda cool.

Why'd you do what you did? What is in Lilly's note? How could you do that to Earl and Lilly? Especially Earl....especially Lilly.

I don't care about anyone, and I don't have anybody that really cares about me. I like it that way, it makes my life simple, and clean.

The Pont Champlain, crossing the St. Lawrence River in Montreal, heading south, has a big fucking sign; a giant inculcation in red lights that flashes a warning every second or so, just to jam the point home as you cross the bridge:

Drive Carefully - Someone Loves You

Doesn't apply to me, and I like it that way.

Stupid fucking sign.

But they cared about you, and you still checked out. You fucked up Lilly, but good, that's for sure, and she's a good girl, she really is. I guess you know that, if you really know anything.

Cord's stumbled back to Montreal.

He remembered shuffling into the Cathedral Basilica, the church on the corner of Rene Levesque Boulevard, downtown.   And he always, for some reason, remembered the name.

Basilique – Cathedrale Marie-Rene-du-Monde

'*Mary, Queen of the World*' Yeah, that was it, stupid stuff like that, he somehow always remembered. It was a beautiful church.

He remembered walking the City all day, his feet and legs were killing him, and it had sprinkled on and off for hours, just enough to be annoying. Then, whipped from nowhere, came a wicked storm, an absolute downpour. The wind wrenched his umbrella inside out and broke it less than a minute into the mistral – he slogged through the City streets soaked to the skin, looking for refuge. Not a building nearby was open; not a cab to be found. He remembered it sucking pretty bad.

C directed his thoughts, his conversation, back to Carol.

So I eyed the Basilique across the way, and made a mad dash for her. It looked abandoned, but its doors were unlocked. I slipped in and shook off the weather, trying to quell a shiver. It was dim, and my eyes took a bit to adjust. I shuffled along and quietly slid into a pew about a third of the way down the main aisle, toward this massive altar; the endless envelope of gilding, garniture, dossals - the whole package - was pretty over-the-top, even for the Catholics.

I felt out of place; I really didn't want to be in there. And I certainly didn't want to get too close to the front. That wasn't unusual.

But it was dry, so I stayed, to wait out the storm.

The cathedral was a half-scale replica of St. Peters Basilica in Rome, Vatican City, at least according to the promotional pamphlet shoved in the pew slot next to the verse books, Kumbaya and the like.

Kumbaya was my favorite as a kid, actually. "Someone's singing Lord, Kumbaya...." That's all I remember, and who the fuck knows what kumbaya means anyway - singing it never changed a damn thing. Stupid fucking song.

Anyway, there I was, drying out, resting my legs, and drinking in the impressive architecture; a tremendous waste of resources, funded by countless Catholic saps looking for some ticket to a better place. But it was pretty to look at, and the view didn't cost me a dime.

As I quick-counted, there were about fifty-odd people scattered in this enormous cavern of a building, sitting quietly, praying for who knows what, when this guy shuffles in, alone, and noisily parks two pews behind me, just off the center aisle, oblivious to me or anything else in the church.

He was soaked, just like me, but it didn't seem to faze him in the least.

This guy was a stereotype if I ever saw one; mid-forties, with '80's style hair, a bit longer in the back, like a little rat-tail. He wore a wrinkled tee-shirt with some inscription on it - NASCAR race memorabilia, or the like. Picture a beer-guzzling, wife-beating, blue-color prole. And he looked worn, rough....haggard. This guy was the last guy who would ever step foot in a fucking Church, or even believe in God. Any other week this bum is hung over on a Sunday morning, sleeping it off, and much too busy in front of the tube for the Saturday afternoon option.

Stressed was an understatement; this guy was a walking mess.

It was clear he'd been crying; his eyes were watered, red and swollen – and guys like this don't cry in public. He immediately knelt down while clutching a long strand of black rosary beads in his hands, rubbing them hard between his fingers, too hard, as if he was trying to squeeze the beads away, mouthing unknown verses of unheard prayers to himself and whomever else he thought was listening in his head. I remember wondering where a guy like that even found rosary beads to begin with.

I remembered smirking to myself in mock of this clown; how pathetic, clinging to some black plastic beads in a place he probably never visited before, the last guy you would ever expect to see in a church, mouthing forgiveness, grasping for help and hope to empty air, air filling a ridiculous temple to man's fear of dying, fear of the unknown.

I spun a half-turn to watch the spectacle; the guy was oblivious to me and everything else around him.

And I remember chuckling, a bit.

This guy bought the whole package, lock and stock; he figured mumbling and blubbering in that church would help, make some sort of difference. Yet he was just mouthing to empty space. He might just as well pissed in the wind, it would mean just as much.

Pathetic.

Then I remembered that somehow, my derision turned to a tinge of envy; what must it be like to believe, to really believe in the nonsense known as religion. For this guy, on this day, he believed, and to him, I guess it helped. And my chuckle stopped, and my wry smile faded away.

I slid out of the pew and left; the storm had stopped, and what I did the rest of that day in Montreal, I simply can't remember.

What does that delusion called faith feel like?

I was brought up Catholic; what a joke. What does that even mean, 'brought up'? Regardless of the weekly indoctrination, even as a child, the whole process was lost on me as nothing but an incredible waste of time, and an insult to intelligence.

In fact, the only memory of real faith, the sole, was when I was seven. I think I had done something wrong, but I can't remember what. It doesn't really matter for the purpose of this story, all I remember was telling God to turn a glass of water I filled in the upstairs bathroom cup on the sink to the color blue. If he turned it blue, I promised not to tell anyone, and I would believe - I was in for life - a card-carrying member of the flock....a true sheep.

I remembered walking from the bathroom back to my room, giving God some extra time to complete the task; an extra five minutes past the five minutes a seven-year old thought it should take to perform some sort of miracle, even though this was pretty low on the miracle scale. I remembered laying fetal on my bed in the late afternoon; the sun hung heavy in the sky - I could see the orange disk out my bedroom window, sliced between the slats in the Venetian blinds. And I remember I was crying; yeah, I remembered crying, about what I don't know. But I remember hesitating before rising from the bed and slowly creeping down the hall, afraid to interrupt the pious process, afraid I hadn't given God enough time to turn the water blue. But I was tired of waiting, His time was up. I was impatient, even at seven.

When I got to the sink I tentatively peeked into the cup to witness the miracle.

The water was clear as crystal; at seven, I wrote Him off
for life.

CHAPTER 69 – SHE SMILED SAD AND DIDN'T SAY A WORD

Mother-fucker, mother-fucker, mother-fucker, mother-fucker.

The broken record rang his head. Actually, that was the de facto phrase....*mother-fucker*. It was kind of a placeholder, an echo that danced in Cord's head till he moved onto the next thought.

The words often occupied his mind.

[Cord lightly rubbed his chin, running his left fingers across his upper lip, over to his cheek, up either side, feeling the short, coarse scrub of hair from a several day shadow. He turned his thoughts back to his guest]

I'm forty-three years old, and until two months ago, when I showed up here, I hadn't gone a day without shaving. Never missed a day, not one, till I came here. Now it's once a week, more or less. Don't know what changed, just don't seem to care, I guess. I guess that's the change.

C thought of an old power-lifting partner, a hold-em poker pal, from a prior life....Vito, Vito from Staten Island. Jesus, that *gumba* could grow six days of stubble in about six hours; he was hair front to back, top to bottom. He even shaved his knuckles. He was a straight-shooter, a good man, one of the few C met, one of the few he actually remembered, or cared to. God he hadn't thought of Vito in years. Another abrupt end, collateral breakage, and that was a fucking shame; C whisked the dreadful memory away.

Lilly likes the stubble, so does Mae, so does Carol; they all like that just-over-the-edge, bad-boy scruffy look. Guess I should have done it years ago.

C looked down at his belly; it was noticeably flatter than that first day dogging it around the Park. His face was more angular, thinner – chin chiseled, like it once was as a younger man. He felt better about himself; he didn't shy from the mirror without his shirt on, and didn't need to worry which clothes fit - they all did - at least the new ones he bought. The old wardrobe that he packed in his boxes, limited as it was, were now too large and clown-like, which begot a new wardrobe, to fit the new physique. C wasn't where he wanted to end up, he was likely still in the low 190's; but out of the 210's, that's for sure. Maybe that's why Lilly started to notice him more, to pay attention....not certain, but maybe. He cracked a small smile.

He had heard all about Lilly's past *men*, mainly from Frank talking loud to others in the store, trying to get C worked up. It was one of the few weapons Frank had, and he used if often. He would describe how they all had the same killer body style, and it certainly wasn't Cord's. Especially this dickhead Button, he seemed to be the thoroughbred; C wondered if he would ever meet that clown. He hoped not; things seemed to be okay right about now, and this guy was surely trouble waiting to happen. Why was Lilly so into that guy?

A crow, maybe the one from before, maybe not, landed in the pin oak overhead, cackling and growling in a low rumble, talking to itself. Cord strained to see it through the overstory of rustling leaves, but there was nothing he could make out.

His eyes traveled down the trunk; the base was covered in a montage of gray lichens and patches of dark green moss, from grass level up about three feet. A flimsy, rusty fence post was partially enveloped by the pin oak, slowly being absorbed into the trunk; just the top third remained, the rest of the post was long-buried under the bark, slowly being swallowed. He lazily looked to his side at the adjacent oak; it was also eating an old post, the two rusted sticks the last remnants of a fence long gone.

He laid back prone and stretched his arms out, like an iron cross, his right arm resting across Carol's name. He arched his back a bit to stretch.

You know why I'm a vegetarian? Of course you do. You know, I don't ever tell anyone the real reason, too long an explanation, and usually the beginning of an argument. Sympathy for shark fins was the final blow, the cruel finning of sharks for Chink wedding soup; makes me out to be some sort of freak, like the worm thing.

Shark fins....that revelation came in Panama, many years ago.

You know all about Panama too, I guess. I told Earl we would go; I hope to keep that promise. I want to go with him, but will it ever really happen? Don't know, part of me thinks not, but I hope that part is wrong. Earl needs to see it, all of it; he needs to see lobsters outside of the supermarket tank, and the little blue fish that circles the coral; it's as if I only found that place and kept it till he could go, like it was really meant more for Earl than me. That's how it feels, anyway.

What do you think?

'The hours are long, the pay is short, all deliveries are carried on foot.'

That line is great isn't it? I've always loved it. It was written in a diary, in 1938; it was one of only two entries in an otherwise blank book – tucked in one of the estate boxes – written when my father was a teenager, just eighteen years old, his first job in a food market downtown. He lasted all of six days. The second entry in the diary was simply: 'Quit.' And that was that, and the journal was forgotten, never another entry made. Kind of sad, don't you think?

[Cord rubbed his forearm back and forth against Carol's marker, feeling the raised letters on his skin]

You know how long it takes for the last of the heat to leave your body? About eight minutes.

I was holding her hand the minute she died; I saw the last faint rise of her chest. It's amazing how quickly the hands go cold, within thirty seconds, a minute tops. The heat recedes like the tide, up the forearm, to the shoulder, then the neck. I remember cupping my hand gently on her neck, trying to stop the heat from leaving. The cheeks were next, the warmth backing its way up to the brain; that's the last to go you know, the last defense, the last part your dead body tries to protect....but I guess you would know all about that. How does it feel when the heat recedes, and you turn to forever-cold? I wonder if I know.

I cradled her forehead with my palm and slowly felt the temperature fade, like sand slipping between your fingers. Even when her head turned cold, I kept it there, moving it gently up over her scalp, running my fingers through her short salt and pepper hair, searching for any faint remnant of warmth. But it was gone forever, a one way street. Nothing left but stone cold.

I wonder if Lilly felt it when she curled up next to you on the floor, the inevitable retreat. Did you feel it? Did you feel her heat against the cold of your skin?

I cut some of her hair off; it was super-short, growing in after the last wave of worthless radiation. I told her I liked her hair that way, she looked Parisian, even though she had never been. I'm sure she didn't believe me, but it was true, amidst the frailty and the sickness that consumed her, her regal profile, and that fashionable hair, an accidental byproduct of the malignancy, let her hold onto a bit of dignity....a small fuck-you to the inevitable. I still have it, her bit of clipped hair, it's back in the apartment; I brought it along, with some other things. It reminds me of her, not so much then, but of better times. It's in a little plastic bag, which is wrong....I need to find an appropriate Limoge, or some such sort.

C turned his thoughts inward.

He thought about the tide, sitting in that brown chair, the front legs slowly sinking in the bathwater surf, cupping a *Maduro Macanudo* to protect the tip from the constant breeze, hunched over, waiting for the sun to set behind him. The cigar was slightly stale, with a hard draw....not a good stick.

A line of buoys, tinged orange-red and covered in a green algal film, bobbed in the surf, a line of dots which receded into the water and curved down the beach, thirty-three in all. There were exactly thirty-three. He could barely see the one at the far end of the line. He thought about walking that buoy line right then and there, just walk out, to the end, and quietly slip under the surf....go out with the tide, unnoticed. It was taunting him, teasing him to join.

But thought remained just that, a thought. Jenny, rather the voice that spoke her warning words, wouldn't have any of that....it simply wasn't the way the game was played.

He looked down the beach; there were a line of palms at the edge of the sand, crooked trunks, but upright nonetheless, except the last one, the only one that wasn't above the high tide line, the one that had the misfortune of taking foothold and living on the part of the beach that was exposed, vulnerable. It sat at a forty-five degree angle to the ground, slowly succumbing to gravity and the effect of the surf on it roots, slowly being pulled into the ocean. How did it hang on? Why did it try? It looked like it would topple at any moment, yet for now, it stood there, alone, close to the others, yet a world apart. Unsafe.

It was him.

He cocked his head toward the sky and dug his toes into the sand. He spit lazily at his feet; the saliva seeped between the grains and washed away with the next lick of water. A Zydeco band, with a Dominican twang, played in the background, just off the edge of the beach, out of sight. He was sure there was dancing, lots of dancing. He saw the bride and groom mosey down the beach and stand in the water, down toward the tilted palm, barefoot, collecting photos to fill an album neither would want when they divorce.

The horizon was bumper full of cumulus clouds, the kind that take on the shape of whatever is dancing in your head, but he didn't see an elephant, or the masts of a sailing ship, his *Rorschach* was a set of brass knuckles - it looked just like a set sitting in the sky, knuckle loop up. And he never even used them, not once. No need.

He didn't know why those first came to mind; a bit odd to see something like that in the clouds. That must mean something, right? He didn't have an answer.

A distant fisherman was waist-deep in the surf, lazily casting a line toward the horizon. He came up empty, cast after cast.

He remembered feeling the intense heat from the end of the cigar against the skin of his palm, as he shielded it from the constant buffet of wind. It was barely a quarter-inch from his skin; he felt like driving it in, burning a whole clear through to the other side. But he didn't.

The edge of the surfline foamed around his feet; as it receded the air pockets in the sand bubbled and popped. He always thought they were from tiny crabs when he was a kid, and furiously dug in the surf sand to find them. He never did find a one.

The cigar eventually extinguished; he was a bit nauseous from the heavy drag. He sat back and wondered why he was even there; if he didn't have the balls to walk into the surf, then it was time to go - he wasn't waiting for her to talk to him any longer – he was bored and done. Fuck it - time for a break of the rules. He stood up and looked out over the water; it was a half dozen shades of blue….absolutely beautiful.

He wouldn't bother telling anyone; they'd figure it soon enough, and be safe. By tomorrow, he would be gone. He set his mind and this time, he would stick with the decision. Fuck them, fuck them all.

But in the end, he didn't break the rules, and he didn't go the next morning. He waited for Jenny's words, like he always did. Rules are rules. And she whispered soon enough, and, unfortunately, he left the island alone; another mess for others to clean.

C didn't realize his eyes were closed, till he felt the pelt hit him in the chest.

"Hey, do I have to call 911? No mouth-to-mouth buddy, if that's what you need, sorry, but you're a goner."

The *DeMuth*, a candela, rolled off his chest and settled in the sparse grass by Carol's plaque.

"Figured you were out by now; have a couple more in my pocket, if you're interested."

He paused a bit, then continued.

"Hey when are my *quid pro's* gonna yield a *quo*? My kids gotta eat; right now, all you're doing is costing me cigar money. Tired of that apartment yet? You sticking around? Got a great house out on Fourth I could show you, closer to the Cemetery, if that's what floats your boat."

Cord turned his head the slightest of cocks to look; he was still prone, barely moving, except the swivel of his neck.

"What's the matter, fallen and can't get up?"

He smiled at his own, stupid joke, typical Woody.

Of course, we knew *exactly* who was buried immediately beside where Cord lay, yet he didn't figure any connection, not then anyway. Plus, he knew just about everyone else buried around Carol as well – he sold most of them their houses, or his dad did. He figured it was just a guy he didn't know much about lounging in the Cemetery, for some odd reason. The location of the lay was not as puzzling as the lay itself, but Woody long ago figured it wasn't worth trying to sort those things out, he was too busy trying to sell….something, anything, to somebody….anybody. He woke and slept each day to that same goal.

Cord sat up and half-heartedly brushed the dry grass off himself, never looking back at Carol's grave. He sauntered over to the gate, met W and shook his hand, grabbing the other two candelas from him. They walked over to the bike, passing small talk, then parted ways. He never did ask why C was laying there, and Cord never offered.

Ay mounted Earl's bike and slowly pedaled toward Sam's to finish the day; he turned to look back at the Cemetery once, one last look. His thoughts turned back to Carol.

You know, that fourth drunken dart, that's got me stumped....but I said that already, and you know that already, don't you?

Can you really talk to Al? I hope so. That would be pretty cool.

You know, I don't even know what you really look like?

"Lilly's sister' is as close as it gets, that's what Sam says, anyway. They don't have a picture of you out in the apartment – not a one. Lilly won't let him, and that's a shame.

See ya.

Carol watched him leave; she smiled sad and didn't say a word.

CHAPTER 70 – WHAT A FUCKING LIFE

Saturday, June 24th; day sixty-six.

Cord never did go back to Mae's the night before; nor did he call. Shitty, yeah, and he missed out on a for-sure bang, but the complications that would invariably follow worried him; he didn't want to deal with all the strings attached to that pussy. Since his dick was the only one protesting, he jerked-off to fucking her hard from behind, standing in the kitchen, and that settled that. When he saw her next, he'd throw up some excuse, apologize profusely and self-deprecate as needed – it usually worked like a charm. He'd figure out the details tomorrow.

Well, today was tomorrow. But at this point, Mae wasn't on his mind. Cord was slowly, gradually, picking up the pace, wondering if Earl would even notice.

Earl was busy yapping about Carol, like usual, asking the same questions three and four times over again, just so he could get Cord to talk about her, especially the parts about how Cord thought she liked Earl. Now that running was easier for C, Earl was allowed to talk again.

Those were his favorite parts.

Cord was feeling pretty good about the run. This was lap seven; they were going to go for ten today – first time. That was a shade over three miles; not bad for a guy who passed out after one lap two months ago. And although he could talk a bit more when running, he still preferred to breathe....just breathe.

Earl finally noticed what Cord was up to.

He just smiled and kicked the pace up another notch, and looked at Cord, smiling the whole time. In no time, Cord was huffing.

"Okay, okay, you win; slow the fuck down."

Earl just kept smiling, and then asked for the seventh time in seven laps.

"Do you think she's gonna come out and say *hi*? She always does; why is she waiting to come out?"

"I told you six times already, and now I'll say it again, number seven, she saw your sister riding her bike behind me yesterday and thought we were together; you know how she gets mad about stuff like that."

"Yeah, but you weren't riding together."

"Well that's not the point, now is it? *I* know we weren't, but *she* doesn't know that, and close proximity equals guilty, at least in Carol's mind."

"Well, you gotta tell her; I don't want her to be mad at us, do you?"

"She's not mad at you."

Cord was thinking about his planned rendezvous with Carol tonight; actually, he had been thinking about it nonstop. And to have Lilly come up and ride with him was something he never expected, a truly pleasant surprise, and a nice time to boot, but why did it have to happen right when Carol pulled into Town? Shit like that always happened to Cord….*always*.

Why? Because that's always what happens when a guy is playing with more than one girl, or at least trying to play more than one girl. You could hardly call what he was doing playing; both of them had hints of interest, between bouts of disdain. And he really wouldn't do anything with Carol anyway, knowing how Earl felt about her, would he? No, probably not. No, he wouldn't. But it was still be nice to know she was interested, a nice ego boost.

"Well then let's just keep doing laps till she comes out; she's gotta come out sometime."

Earl decided.

Cord answered that one quickly.

"NO! Ten and *I'm* done! Unlike you, Earl, this isn't easy for me; I'm done in three more laps, then we can go knock on her door, or you can go knock on her door, if you want, and I'll go home."

"NO! I'm not going over alone!"

"Well, then you better hope she comes out in the next three laps."

Please, please, please, please, please, please, please, please....Earl chanted aloud a monologue loop, willing her to come out.

Cord looked at him, annoyed.

"No way Earl, am I listening to *that* for three more fucking laps."

Earl never looked at Cord, but he stopped saying *please* out loud; C could see his lips move as he said it silently to himself, over and over.

Carol stood in the dining room, velvet drape partly drawn, pissed off. She had been standing there for all seven laps; she hadn't moved, just watching them endlessly circle the Park.

That bastard, making a fool out of her. She thought somehow he was different – on *her* team, but they're all alike in the end. Fucking snake.

She never unpacked the chit supplies, she left them in bags. She wasn't sure if she should return them, or just throw it all away. While she thought about it, they waited warm in the trunk.

She saw Earl spy the house like a sad sack every time he went by. Actually, she had her binoculars out; she kept them in the server by the window. Earl had been looking over his shoulder all the way around the Park, watching her front door like a lost dog.

She felt bad; even though Cord was an asshole, she couldn't be mean to Earl. She was a big enough girl to walk out on the porch and greet them, Earl, at least; otherwise, he would probably circle all day and night.

*Please, please, please, please, please, please, please….*Earl prayed harder as he turned the corner of Mansfield and headed down Third, on his way toward an eighth pass of Carol's porch. He squeezed his eyes shut and prayed harder as he got closer.

Carol put her head down and skulked into the foyer, opened the inside double-door, and grabbed the lion-head knob on the left side, big, black outer door, opening it inward, the hinge squeaking its trademark twang, which Earl picked up like a bird-dog.

"It worked! The doors opening!"

Earl screamed as he pushed on Cord's shoulder in excitement, to get his attention. The shove was a bit too hard; Cord flew off the sidewalk like a shot and landed in a heap on the grass in the Park.

"Oops, sorry."

"What the fuck Earl, I saw the God-damn door!"

Cord said in a puff of dust, mad at getting pushed down, but more so at how easily he went down, like a sack of potatoes, from a pretty mild push by Earl. God help the man that ever got Earl truly mad.

Usually Earl would get upset when someone yelled at him. But it was Cord, and they were best friends, and the door was open and Carol was standing on the porch….all good things. So it was okay.

All Earl could do was smile a goofy grin and extend his hand to help Cord right himself.

At first he wasn't going to take it, but of course he did. Earl yanked him up like Ay was springing from a *Jack-in-the-Box*.

"You okay?"

Earl said as Cord rubbed his dislocated shoulder.

"Yeah, just fine."

Cord looked up and saw Carol laughing her ass off; she saw the whole episode. And the ice was broken.

"Thanks Earl, that's great; now I'm gonna have to hear about this one from her for the next year."

Secretly, Cord was happy she saw the shove; a little humility in front of her right about now would go a long way toward the bike incident….the start of his penance.

"Hey C, you wanna stop at seven and a half? Huh? Huh?"

"Sure, I'll race you to her front sidewalk."

Now Cord was only kidding, but before he finished the sentence, Earl was a slingshot, running at a full gallop; he was on her sidewalk in less than thirty seconds. Cord had barely run thirty yards and was still half a block away.

Carol greeted Earl and he followed her in to get a drink; if he had thought about what he was doing, going in her house alone, without Cord glued to his side, he would have froze, but he was so giddy at seeing her, his prayers answered, that he lost himself.

As Cord limped into the finish, the two walked out with tall glasses of iced tea; Carol wasn't carrying Cord's glass. Cord noticed, as he was supposed to.

Carol just looked at him with a furrowed brow, and didn't say a word.

"I'll get myself a glass….thanks."

C said deadpan.

The sarcasm hopscotched Earl; Carol watched as he walked by her and headed into the house.

"It's all gone."

She said indifferently as he passed, which made him stop, shake his head and huff.

"Well, maybe there's a little left."

She added.

Cord snorted air with another head shake, and continued inside; Carol followed him.

"I'll be right back Earl, have a seat and relax. You look really good Earl, *real good*."

He just smiled; Cord just shook his head in the negative.

He walked slow, just to annoy her, she was right behind him.

"I can manage."

C said, sarcastic.

"I'm not getting you a drink, asshole. I only came out for Earl."

"No shit. Why are you mad at me? Are we dating? I feel like I'm in high school, grade school in fact. I didn't even know she was behind me till I saw you give me the evil eye, and almost swerved onto the curb. And I saw you tweak that wheel, I know you did."

"You don't know how close I came to jumping that fucking   curb,   let   me   tell   you;   that   little fucking….wave….of hers. I swear I'm going to kill that bitch some day, I really am; tire tracks right over her God-damn smirk."

"Woah."

Cord said as he held up his hand.

Carol let out a deep, frustrated breath.

"Well, for the record, I was making a delivery up to Brookfield, when she came up behind me; I swear I didn't know she was there."

"Why should I care what you do?"

Carol snapped.

"Well you obviously do."

"I just don't want to be made a fool, is all. Do you go telling her all the things we talk about? Like a little girl? You better not; I swear, Cord, you better not!"

"Please, take a fucking breath. Are you kidding me? Earl and I don't even mention your name to her, for fear of getting stabbed; and Earl runs faster than me, so I'd be a goner. You think we would tell her about stopping here when we go for runs? *Are you kidding*? She'd have a fucking coronary. Actually, I think she knows about it from other people, but it's a topic no one brings up. Believe me, *no one* utters the C word around Lillian."

"Why? Are you embarrassed to be around me? Is it some sort of problem?"

"Would you take it easy, for Christ sake; it's a matter of survival and sanity.

First you say don't talk about you, then you're mad when I tell you we *don't* talk about you. I swear, you're just as bad…."

Cord stopped himself mid-sentence.

"That was very smart; don't you *ever* finish that sentence!"

She said as she poured him his drink. The fact that she poured, without being asked, meant the worst of it was over.

"I thought you'd be modeling that skirt you're supposed to wear tonight; it is the 24th, isn't it?"

She didn't answer or even look at him; that was either a good bluff, or maybe he wasn't quite out of the woods yet. The discussion ended, and they joined Earl on the porch.

"Al's gone."

Earl said, dejected; his head dropped.

"Earl, you know Al's gone, he's been gone a month, no big deal, he always goes. In fact, he stayed longer this year than ever, you know that. He'll be back in the Fall, like always; you'll see him again, like always."

"How do you know for sure C? How do you know he'll come back?"

"Because if he wants to see you, he's gotta come back, right?"

"No, what if he's waiting for us in Panama?"

By the strained look on Cord's face, Earl immediately knew he said something wrong. And he got scared.

"Uh, uh."

Cord jumped in.

"When you gonna let Earl take a spin in the *Spider*? He can't stop talking about it."

"Panama? What's in Panama?"

Carol wasn't letting *that* one go.

Cord looked her in the eyes, and it was clear he *wasn't* up for a discussion on the subject.

"Nothing."

He said abruptly, in a way that meant the issue was dropped, end of story.

An awkward silence followed. Carol wisely let it go, for now.

"Tell Carol about the cows!"

"Not now Earl, she isn't interested in the cows."

"Sure I am; if Earl is, I am too."

That just about bowled Earl over; his smile was pretty much set for the rest of the night with that one line. Cord was sure he would have to repeat it to Earl at least a dozen times before he went to bed that night: *What did she say again about the cows?* would be his constant refrain to C.

"Okay, okay. I was telling Earl about the cattle, cow and steer, that graze right along the beach, and sleep in the sand, and I said that sounds like a great life, doesn't it?"

"Yeah, until they load them up on the truck and…."

Cord cut her off, annoyed.

"It's a great life for them *on the beach*; the beach is what we were talking about."

Carol was a bit ashamed of herself for not thinking before she talked, but Earl didn't pick up on it, which made her feel relieved.

"Is this the beach in Panama?"

Carol asked, reeling the topic back in, since they opened the door.

"No, *not* Panama; this is a *different* beach."

"There seem to be a lot of beaches you know about. Where is this one?"

"It doesn't matter where, just a beach I was at once."

"Right, just some beach."

Carol snapped sarcastic.

"Tell her about all the colors! And the ones with the big horns staring at you; oh boy, that must have been scary!"

Earl's voice was getting excited. Carol dropped the beach talk and just waited to hear the rest, with a small smirk on her face.

"Pray tell, Mr. Brin, please share your cow story."

He ignored the snide, and proceeded to weave a tale.

"Well, there were two dozen of them, untended, stretched out over a hundred yards, the kind with a hump on their back and lots of hanging skin on their necks; I don't know the variety, but not like the cattle around here, for sure.   Each one or two had a cattle egret nearby, pretty skinny white birds that follows the cattle around, eating bugs stirred up when they walk.   The cattle were all different colors....there were white ones, and tawny, some a splotchy mix of white and tawny."

Earl butted in, voice rising.

"And black ones, and brown ones too!   And tell her about the black one with the big horns snorting at you, staring you down!   You were afraid it was gonna chase you into the water!   Hah!   That would have been so funny! Bet you would of run real fast then, huh C!"

Earl was rubbing his hand together excitedly telling the story; God, Cord just looked at him and smiled.   He couldn't believe how much he cared about Earl; he would do anything for that guy, anything.   And there was no one else he could say the same for....no one.

He loved Earl, he really did.

"You bet, my ass would have been in that water in no time. But he only snorted once, chewed his cud, and walked away; guess I wasn't worth a charge to protect the ladies in the herd."

Earl laughed aloud thinking about Cord running into the water, bullhorn right on his butt.

"Tell her about the cave! The one I wouldn't fit in! I bet she would….she'd fit!"

Carol was smiling broadly, thinking about how happy she was that she finally met Earl and got a chance to actually know him. What a shame she lost all that time, him dropping off the check with nary a word, for years. But now, he had become a good friend, a true friend, probably one of the best she had. And she had Cord to thank for that. She turned and smiled silent at C.

Ay continued.

"Well, along part of the beach, near where the cattle were grazing, was a whole run of lava rock, which ran from the high tide line straight into the surf; jagged black lava, full of holes and crags. You couldn't walk on it barefoot, it would tear your feet to shreds.

Well, out of nowhere, up by the edge of the field, is this hole, about four feet across, and about seven feet deep. There were all flowering vines around the edge, which hid it, unless you walked directly up to it. You'd be in trouble at night; you'd fall right in, sliced to pieces on the jagged lava.

Anyway, I'm on the beach, alone, and I stumble on this hole, so I decide to climb down, explore a bit. I'm about fifty yards from the ocean, and there's water running in the bottom of the pit, about a foot deep or so. So I get down inside, and the water is crystal clear and cold; I dip my hand in and run it across my lips….fresh water! It's a spring, running down through the lava.

I crouch down and see that it's not just a hole, but a sort of cave, that turned sharp to the right, whatever was beyond was out of sight. Now it was tight, and the upper rocks razor-sharp; I could barely move around, but it looked as if it got bigger as you went in.

I crouched there for awhile, and I noticed the water level rose every time the tide came in; I could hear the waves crash outside the hole. As the fresh water rose in the cave, all the holes in the lava hissed, burped and gurgled, like it was alive, breathing and talking. It was very cool….primordial.

I kept looking up out the hole at the sky, waiting for someone to walk by, but where I was, the beach was deserted for a good half-mile in either direction; I was utterly alone out there, just me and the cattle.

Anyway, after a bit, when my eyes acclimated, I slowly inched and squeezed my way to the corner and peered around the edge. It was dimly lit; light was coming in from somewhere else down the line. And the cave opened up into a little ante-room, maybe ten by five, where I could stand up. Earl couldn't, but I could, and down there, the lava rock was smooth as silk, from thousands of years of water running through it, slowly erasing the edges. I was seven feet below the surface, about thirty feet from the opening, and it might has well been another world; an escape from the real world.

I just stood there, enjoying my find, enjoying the solitude, standing in water up to my thighs, when I casually placed my hand on the lava wall next to me.

All of a sudden the whole chamber erupted in bedlam, right at the level of my ears, the rasp and chir of something unknown, scurrying about the darkness all around me.

Holy shit, I thought, what the fuck is in here with me? There's no getting out quickly; I'm stuck. What the fuck am I gonna do? So what did this brave explorer of the deep do?

"You froze! Hah! You got so scared you didn't know what to do!"

Earl yelled, as he laughed out loud, clapping his hands in the excitement.

"Yeah, fucking-A right I did! And you know what it was after all? Damn crabs on the walls! God knows how many, probably all of one or two, but man did they make a lot of noise scurrying away; scared the shit out of me! Anyway, I guess I know what I'd do under pressure….freeze. I told Earl maybe some day I would show it to him, show him the crabs, although I actually never even saw the bastards."

"And where was this?"

Carol figured she'd try again; to her surprise, he answered.

"*Hispaniola.* Punta Cana in the Dominican Republic; far eastern shoreline, as far east as you can go before you run out of room."

"Why were you there? Getting chased by bulls and scared by crabs."

"Funny. Hey Earl, you ready to go? Or, do you want to stay here all day and night; maybe Carol doesn't have any plans."

Earl sat up, mulling the real possibility of a sleepover party.

Carol leaned toward Earl and gave him a big, friendly smile.

"Hey Earl, I was thinking; what do you think about helping out Ji-Sue when she feeds the cats when I'm in the City, would you want to do that for me, maybe? Would you like that? I know Ji would love the help."

Earl just looked at her with glazed eyes; he didn't have any idea how to respond to that question. He just stared and stared, with his mouth slightly open, like he saw a ghost.

Cord smiled.

"I think that's a *yes*."

And with that he gathered up a stunned Earl by the arm and led him off the porch. Good God, how many times was Cord going to have to relive that line with Earl today, tomorrow and the next day, for the rest of his life?

But one thing was for certain, C would be seeing Ms. Crowe again later that night, and he couldn't wait.

As they walked down the sidewalk Cord looked back and Carol was smiling, a good smile. All was forgiven, for now.

Two of the black cats were on the porch roof, he could never remember which was which; their paws were dangling over the edge in utter repose, soaking in the summer sun, barely paying attention to his passing. Sheer indifference.

What a life he thought to himself. What a fucking life.

She slowly turned the knob till the latch clicked; she knew it wouldn't be locked, it never was. She peered in, around the door; no sign of him. But she heard the water running….the shower.

She smirked to herself and tip-toed through the kitchen, peeked down the hall toward the bathroom – the door was cracked open.

She decided to take the risk; she scampered down the hall, grabbed a chair and stood frozen. Water still running.

She opened the closet and flipped the switch, climbed up and moved the box to see the aluminum packet where she erased the dozen or so dots on two of the amoeba designs. Still missing.

Hah! She thought to herself, he still hasn't found it!

But wait, if the packs aren't touched, and she had gone through every inch of that apartment, which she had, then where did he get that wad of money for the black girl? She was sure the foil packs would have been disturbed....but they were pristine.

Where was he hiding the dough?

He must have some other secret place she hadn't found yet; that was probably where his wallet, and phone, and everything else was! *Oh my God, if she could only find his phone and look at the contacts list, his whole life would unravel in a scroll of names. She would call every one of them, and all his stupid little secrets would melt away!*

She had to find that phone! She had to find that secret hiding place! She thought of Earl and his stupid kid's mystery-detective books; maybe she should have read them after all. She certainly couldn't ask Earl for help; he would rat her out in a second.

And what would she say when C finally noticed someone messed with the red ink and asked her if she was touching his foil packs? She had it all planned out; she would innocently say:

What foil packs? Do you have foil packs? Of what? Show me these foil packs you speak of....she snickered to herself.

She wasn't afraid of him or the packs, and she wanted him to tell her what they held, which she already knew....*money!* Lots and lots of money!   Then she would ask him about the secret hiding place, and he would tell her, of course; she could always get guys to do anything she wanted, if she really wanted them to, even Cord. He wasn't immune to her charm; to the contrary, he was probably the easiest of them all, he fawned all over her all the time. He was in love with her, more than most. He would marry her if she wanted to....she was sure of it.

She smiled in awe of herself, standing on the dinette chair, half-buried in the hall closet.

She stopped and strained again to listen. No water!

Fuck, fuck, fuck!

She jumped off the chair, flipped the light and dashed as quietly as she could down the hall.

She heard the water again; it never went off. False alarm.

'Shit!'

She said to herself, heart pounding.

She didn't know why she was so scared; it's not like Cord would do anything anyway….she was reasonably sure of that. It was just the thrill of not being caught.

She stopped at the head of the hallway which ran to the bathroom, the last, the only, door on the left. The layout was a mirror of her and Earl's apartment. She tip-toed down toward the shower to catch a glimpse; she couldn't believe she was going to peep in on him; a voyeur.

It was kind of fun.

She got to the door jam and pressed her nose up to the sliver of an opening….listening. Holy shit - Cord was talking to someone! He was having a conversation!

Who could that be? Who is he talking to in the shower? Who the hell is he in the shower with? She perked her ears, but the words were drowned in the heavy shower spray.

Good God, it had *better* not be Carol; Holy Christ, she hoped it wasn't Mae! That's a wrinkly sight she *definitely* didn't want to see.

She had the urge to run; whoever it was, she didn't want to see who he was sharing a shower with, did she?

But she didn't leave; and as much as she hated to admit it; it turned her on, being so close to them. God, she wanted to know who he was going to fuck in there, and at the same time, for the first time, she felt a tiny pang of something, not huge, but definitely there, nonetheless.

Jealousy?

Lilly jealous of Cord, of who he is with? *No way* she said to herself, no way, not that guy….no way.

Yes way.

She stayed glued to the door trying to peek through the sliver-opening and see the sets of clothes on the floor, but all she saw were his black boxers; the ones that sometimes peeked just below the hem of his shorts. That was it. His little slut must have stripped in the bedroom!

She scampered back to his room to check the evidence; she was a good detective after all!

But the bed was made and the floor was neat; in fact, not a thing was out of place, just like it never was, neat as a stupid pin. What kind of guy is like that? She thought to herself; he's weird - way too neat and anal.

But who's in the shower, and where are her clothes? Then it hit her; she *hoped* it was a girl!

Oh no! If she walked in on some gay-sex thing, Christ! Of course she had nothing against being gay; she was bisexual herself, and had *way* better sex with girls! But seeing C in that way, seeing him in the shower humping some guy? Or getting boned? Jesus, on so many levels that wouldn't be good; that just wouldn't be right. It would change everything.

She rushed back and slinked down the bathroom hall again, and then she heard it. It startled her, stopping her dead in her tracks.

Bang! Bang! Bang! **Bang**!

A body was slamming up against the side of the plastic shower stall, rocking the whole enclosure.

Oh my God! He's banging another guy in the ass against the side of the shower! Oh my God! Maybe some guy's banging *him* against the side of the shower!

Cord getting corn-dogged, that was a vision she *definitely* didn't want to see in her head! He's gay! They were right! Cord *is* gay! How could she not have seen it before? Hey, then why was he interested in *her*? Maybe he never was! Maybe it was all just a clever ruse, to get at….*Earl!*

Holy shit, this is a *mess!* I gotta get out of here! I gotta….

Then just as abrupt as it started, the banging stopped; Lilly froze. Then the talking started again.

Funny, she never seemed to hear the other guy talking, just Cord. It was like he was talking to himself.

Hey, wait a second….

She inched in closer, and gently grabbed the knob, to crack the door just a bit more, to whittle her nose and left eye in a fraction closer to the action - it was the only way to be sure.

She could only see half the shower through the opaque shower curtain; but there was no one there, best she could tell; he must be in the other corner. She hopped across the door and peeked through the crack in the door hinge. And she saw him; his back was to her….thank God, as best she could tell through a labored squint.

And he seemed to be alone. She breathed a sigh of relief.

Then the banging started again; and she jumped back, startled. Luckily, she didn't make a noise.

He always had a troubled mind. He thought too much, too fast, and when he did, he'd pump himself full of adrenaline and hate. That's usually when the trouble came, the real trouble, when he'd lose track of where he was, who he was, and what he was doing. He'd lose reality, ending up somewhere else, in a bad place, until he somehow came back, and had to deal with the mess. As the scalding hot water cascades around him, reddening his skin, those thoughts circled C's brain over and again – a random medley of past mistakes – each with dire results, haunting him, taunting him. Before he realized it, he started knocking his forehead into the shower wall harder and harder, till he noticed the vicious blows, became self-aware, and stopped, temporarily, until the perverse cycle repeated.

It didn't happen often, getting caught in this viral loop, but sometimes. The trigger was never the same; and it usually came when he was alone….usually. Hopefully.

Those morbid thoughts would ultimately morph to the terminal thought, which typically would be fleeting.

But not today. Today, he felt like having a conversation about it.

He looked down at his chest and stomach; they were looking much healthier, trimmer, after two months. But honestly, why did he bother?

He said aloud, but not loud enough for her to hear.

'You think I fucking care? Why in the world would you think that? Because I do something about it? About you? Not my choice asshole; not my choice....just another stupid contrary rule in a stupid fucking game I'm forced to play. So go ahead, sit and fester, you fucks; take a day, take a year, I don't give a flying fuck, because I'm done looking for you, searching you out, slicing you up. It makes no sense to do it; never has. I'm tired of playing; whatever will be, will be. I refuse to play any longer; you heard it first here....I'm done! It's all the same in the end; I didn't give up, I won! Because I have control, not you, mother-fuckers, I can end this game any time I want; not you, me! And I have the balls to do it, anytime I want, I'll simply pull the trigger, my terms....easy.'

Cord punched himself hard in the stomach, again and again and again and again, harder with each blow. Then he threw himself into the side of the shower like throwing a block, and then full force into the other wall, rocking the entire shower enclosure in its wooden frame. Trying to escape something that simply won't let go.

In the background, they all smiled at the exercise, knowing, once again, it meant nothing.

And then C stopped, exhausted, breathing heavy through the sound of water streaming from the shower, landing on his head and splaying his crown. He stood there, motionless, mouth slightly open, letting the water engulf him. He slowly turned the knob to the left, till the stream was above a scald, and stood statue, head cocked down, his skin slowly turning a bright vermilion, shrouded in a cloud of thick steam, which filled the bathroom in a thick, humid haze.

The burn hurt like hell, but he refused to move an inch, or make a sound. He needed to feel the pain, to absorb it without complaint; it was one of the few things that made him feel good….alive.

Lilly couldn't hear half of what Cord was saying, not even a third. But it was obvious C was in a violent rage at something or someone, and had no problem in telling himself so.

Was it Carol? Mae? Her? It couldn't be Earl, could it?

But when he started hitting himself in the abdomen, hard, and slamming into the side of the shower stall, and kept doing it, it more than scared her; she had never seen him, seen anyone, do something like that before. That couldn't be normal, for anyone….ever.

Suddenly, from nowhere, a general fright gripped her.

In a strange way, she felt as if she had always known Cord, from childhood; when she told him stories of her youth, it was as if C already knew the players, knew the outcome, like he had always been just outside the frame of the shot, but still there, in her world, Earl's world, her mom's world, from the beginning….it just *felt* that way. Even though he never said he was, nor even hinted it. It just had that kind of feeling, an odd familiar feeling; one she had never felt with anyone else she had ever met. That had to mean something, right?

But now she realized she only knew him since April 20th, two months and four days, and she still knew next to nothing about him.

Except Seattle, worms, and now this – not good.

774

CHAPTER 74 – HERE WE GO: AN IMPORTANT NOTICE

Earl was already out of the shower and sitting at the dining room table, in gym shorts and a ribbed, white guinea-tee. This was one of his favorite parts of the day.

He had on his favorite pair of wire-rim glasses, the ones he bought for $11.36, with tax, at one of the antique vendor booths years ago, during *Victorian Days* in Town, up in the Park.

The spectacles had clear glass in them; a theater prop, not prescription. They looked a bit funny on Earl's big noggin; he had to bend the arms a bit to stretch from ear to ear. But looking beyond the minor flex of the frames, he looked positively collegial.

On occasion, for no particular reason, he would look over the top of the glasses at the wall and cock his head, pretending to ponder some deep thought, or alternately, grab the right lens frame between thumb and forefinger, and slightly pull them down, exposing a naked eye at someone, like they were in for a scolding or a nugget of advice.

He liked to do that; just like Mrs. Gregson always did to him when he acted up in the second grade.

He always liked Mrs. Gregson, and would fester just so she would pull down those glasses at him. Once she did that, he was happy, and would stop whatever it was he was doing and smile at her, with that big toothy grin that no one could ever be mad at for long. And she would smile back at Earl, knowing she was part of his little game.

He laid the thin pile of mail on the placemat next to him, wooden opener in hand.   He was somewhat disappointed; today's mail was light, only three pieces, but they were all addressed to him.

The first piece he selected arrived in a light tan envelope, mailed from ZIP code 11101. He slowly sliced it open, a clean, crisp cut. He cracked the envelope and carefully emptied the contents in a neat pile in front of him, ready to absorb the important news at hand.

*Mmm....*Earl mumbled to himself, *This is very interesting.*

Apparently, Earl had been specially selected for an exciting offer. In fact, he had already been, by persons unknown:

Pre-Qualified to Refinance at 5.875% (6.10% APR),
and this was a 30-Year <u>Fixed</u> Rate!,
Based on Earl's Actual Credit History....*

Mm; Earl pondered the offer.

Earl –

*If you've received a proposal from another bank or
broker, please reconsider!
With our rate and service guarantees, why not let us
provide you with an offer,
you have nothing to lose!*

Mm....nothing to lose, sounds promising; Earl peered over his glasses at the apartment wall, deep in thought.

Nothing to lose; sounds pretty good. I'll have to talk to Lilly about this important offer he whispered aloud.

It went on:

Tenemos Oficiales Que Hablan Espanol!

Earl skipped over that one; he had no idea what all that meant.

Bad Credit OK!

Sincerely,

Harvie Crane
Vice President
BettenCourt Star Funding

The Vice President sent it to Earl personally!

Earl carefully set Harvie's letter aside for a later discussion with Lilly after dinner. This was clearly an important notice, and bad credit was okay; that must be a good thing, since he didn't know what kind of credit he had, or what that even really meant, but even if it was bad, Harvie was still okay with that. He liked Harvie; it even sounded like Marty, and he liked Marty a *real* lot.

On to the next one. It was a bi-fold flyer, held together by a sticker; not as fun to open as a sealed envelope, but it would do.

Uncle Ferd's Tire and Auto Center
Kick-Off Fall Savings!
It's A Trust Thing....

Mm; trustworthy, that's good. Now, let's see what kind of tires we need; Mm.

Right Tires! Priced Right! Right Now!
Come See Us!

There are an awful lot of exclamation points, Earl thought; that must be a good thing too.

No Appointment Necessary! Your Car Is Ready When Promised!
10% Off Anti-Freeze Fluid Exchange!
$20 Off Brake Service ($10 per axle)!
We Look Forward To Serving You!

Walter McLeod
Manager

Now, Earl probably wouldn't need this service information just yet, since he didn't have a car, nor did he know how to drive, but he set it aside, just in case. He looked back to be sure Walter had a phone number handy; yep, he did. He wondered if Uncle Ferd worked there too. Probably. And who's Uncle was he anyway? He didn't know anybody in Belvidere with an Uncle Ferd. Hey, this guy sounds kind of fishy! He better talk to Bibby about this guy pronto; he doesn't sound like he should be trusted. Plus, *Ferd* was a funny name; Earl snickered to himself as he whispered the word to himself, over and over, mixing it in with *nerd* and *turd....Ferd the nerd....Ferd the turd.* He cracked himself up, especially saying *turd.*

The last piece of mail was the thickest; Earl knew it had to be the most important of the three, so he saved it for last.

It came in a big white envelope, all the way from Phoenix, Arizona.

Dear Earl Liddell:

Earl looked cross; they spelled his last name wrong - it had two *d's*, not one. Despite his displeasure with the writer, he decided to read on; the package was simply too thick to ignore.

Enclosed is an *Important Notice* of....

Lilly swung open the apartment door and quickly shut it, running down to the front room. She flew into the seat beside Earl, slightly out of breath. The whoosh of wind from her sprint flitted his papers in disarray, landing half on the floor.

"Hey! You're messing up my mail! This is important stuff!"

"It's junk mail Earl, nothing is important; it's not even for you."

"What'ya mean? This is **all** for me! This is **very** important stuff here! I get mail every day, real mail, addressed to me!"

"Really, like what?"

Lilly snorted, sarcastic.

"I'll tell you like what; like this letter here from Mr. Crane; Harvie is a Vice-President, you know....and....and....bad credit is okay with him. And how about this letter from Walter, about the important fluid exchange available to me; this is important stuff Lilly; we need to *talk*.”

“Whatever Earl, just be sure to throw it all away when your done playing. Hey, I got something important to ask you; now, you gotta be honest, okay? I know you and Cord like to keep your little gay pinkie secrets from me; I swear you two are the girliest girls I know.”

“What? What?! I'm busy here!”

Earl was getting mad, his mail time was being interrupted by Lilly. He needed to finish reading about the **Important Notice** in the fat white envelope, which was now half-scattered across the floor.

“Did C ever, like, punch himself, or talk to himself, when he’s around you, kind of like yelling and stuff? You know what I mean? Angry, kind of crazy.”

Earl just looked at her, then he slowly, carefully grabbed the lens of his glasses and pulled them slightly, deliberately, down his nose, giving her the *Gregson eye.*

“Oh, cut it out! I know what you’re doing, with the stupid *Mrs. Gregson* eye.”

She pushed back from the table and huffed her way back to the kitchen.

Earl snickered at her - she was so easy - and went back to the task at hand. He bent over, picked up the scattered pages of the letter, and delved into the minutia.

Ah, here we go:

An Important Notice

CHAPTER 75 – IT WAS THE WRONG ANSWER

Cord partly dried off outside the shower; he never really did too good a job of it - he was always putting on clothes half-wet. He shuffled down the hall toward his bedroom, and noticed the hall closet door ajar.

Lilly; he smiled, whispering to himself.

He walked down to look at the foil packs; he knew she was probably fingering them again, to see if he noticed the missing dots, and wondering where, oh where, he hid the money he gave to Selena.

Selena, he just shook his head; that didn't even seem real anymore. He was surprised she was still alive; and the little girl? He quickly pushed the thought from his head – now was not the time to dwell on *that* subject. He turned back to Belvidere, to Lilly.

Lilly was so predictable; it made him smile. Well, his payback would have to happen soon; he just needed to pick the right time.

It was a little after eight in the evening; two hours to kill. He didn't dare go down to their apartment and hang; that would set him up for having to leave and explain where he was going. No way could he admit he was going to see Carol in front of Lilly; that would prompt anger….violence. And no way he could say he was going to see Carol in front of Earl; that would prompt him wanting to come along, or questions and sadness if he said he couldn't.

So it was best to go elsewhere and kill time.

He decided to smoke one of the new *DeMuths* Woody gave him; it was a nice night for it. Then he thought of the stale breath he would breath on Carol; it was one thing to smoke with her, and stink together, it was quite another to show up smelling like an ashtray.

So he shelved smoking, but put the cigar in his pocket, two in fact; no, better bring all three, just in case he was there awhile and she doesn't buy any, even though his email explicitly stated *DeMuths* and *Davidoffs* were to be provided as part of the chit.

He laughed to himself about that email; he doubted she would do any of the things he demanded, but it was fun to ask.

So what to do for two hours, what to do.

The apartment door burst open, which gave him his answer.

It was the wrong answer.

"Hey watcha doing? We're gonna watch *The Blob*; wanna come? We rented it on DVD."

Cord's stomach fell; he never lied to Earl before, but in less than a minute, he wouldn't be able to say that anymore.

"I thought you just rented that two weeks ago."

"We did! And I rented it again! It's *The Blob;* you can never get enough of *The Blob!*"

C stumbled.

"Um, I was thinking about just reading, or maybe going for a walk, maybe smoking some cigars in the Park, or something, I don't know."

"Really? Let's go! Maybe we can see if Carol's home? Wouldn't that be fun? We could just kind of sit on the bench and see if we see her way off in the windows, walking around – I betcha you couldn't see that far, but maybe you could! And maybe Eda, that's what I call Edamame for short, and Maguro will be sitting on the porch roof – she lets 'em out after dark you know, but only sometimes. Oh, boy, I can't wait to start helping watch the cats! I can't wait, I really can't! There's only one boy, you know; his name is Wasabi....I like him a lot! He's got a funny white nose with a wrinkle in it and he's really scared of everything and runs away from everything, all the time – but I would too if there were only girls around! He's surrounded by girls - he's got no boys to play with! But I'd play with him, if he'd let me, all the time – he'd be my second best friend, you know, right after you....but don't tell Marty *[Earl whispered the last part]*. Hey, you wanna go see if they're on the roof right now, huh?"

Cord just looked at him; his thoughts went to Carol, as in Liddell.

She must have something to do with this, for sure. It was too cruel; he was getting punished for something he said in the Cemetery, he knew it; he should have never talked to her in the Cemetery, spilt his guts; he even caused trouble with dead women.

Think, think.

"Of course she's home Earl, she's here for the weekend, like always. But she's probably had enough of us for one day, right? We'll see her again tomorrow for breakfast, after running. That's always the best, right?"

"Yeah, yeah, we'll see her tomorrow, I guess. Breakfast….tomorrow."

Earl paused.

"But it *would* be nice to see her tonight too, especially since I'm gonna be helping with the cats and all."

Earl stood there like a lost dog, staring at C, waiting for his best friend to agree; to say yes, let's go see Carol, because seeing Carol was even better than watching *The Blob* again, and watching *The Blob* was just about as good as it gets, as far as Earl was concerned.

But Cord didn't answer; he left his friend hanging. He had to cut this conversation off, it was killing him.

Maybe Cord shouldn't go; maybe he should do the right thing, for once. And for a second, he believed he would. But it was just a second. In the end, C knew he would go; he would shake Earl, and he would go see Carol, alone.

"Earl, why don't you go watch *The Blob*; I'm gonna read for a bit on the couch, and if I don't fall asleep, maybe I'll come down and watch the end with you, how's that? But I'm pretty tired, just so you know."

"Well, okay, but the beginning's the best part; well the end's good too, and so is the middle. Okay, come down soon – Lilly said she'd make us all popcorn!"

"She's watching *The Blob* too? I don't believe that."

"She said she would if you would; that's what she said. She's making popcorn and everything, for all of us....even you, she said."

Lillian making popcorn? For a Blob-fest? Are you kidding? He looked out the window, down Market Street, in the direction of the Cemetery, and shook his head. *Definitely* the doings of Carol Liddell, stirring this fucking pot; she was testing him, or mocking him, or both.

Now how the hell was he going to get out of this? And should he be giving up a movie date with Lilly – the first time she actually agreed to watch one of Earl's B-classics with Earl *and* him – for the Carol meeting. If Carol *ever* found out he blew her off for a movie with Lilly, he was done for life – that was for sure – no more chances. He might as well write her off for good.

Fuck, why does this shit always happen to him? This is the story of his fucking life.

"Okay, I guess I'll see you later...."

C said, not-so-convincingly.

"Don't forget! I'll tell Lilly were all watching *The Blob* together! I'll get out my favorite blanket and everything, and put some candles on, like the scary-story-night….remember? With the scary puppet, crickets and flies? Yikes! Oh, boy, this is gonna be great, this is gonna be the best night ever!"

Earl bounded down the hall and out the door. Cord closed his eyes and rubbed his temple hard….*fucking Blob.*

CHAPTER 77 – THIS WAS DEFINITELY A TEST, AND SHE WAS WATCHING

He was laying on the couch, book on his chest, eyes closed; in the last hour and a half he read a whole four pages. He was mainly staring at the ceiling, ruminating a hundred-fold on what to do and how to do it with the least collateral damage. And he was quickly running out of time. He didn't hear the door open or the footsteps come down the hall.

"Hey, you awake?"

She whispered.

Cord pretended to be startled and turned his head to greet her.

"What happened? I thought you were coming down; I had to watch that stupid *Blob* again with Earl all by myself."

Lilly sat down next to him on the couch, a bucket of popcorn balanced on her right thigh; only the half-burnt kernels remained. She never sat this close to him before. Actually, her whole upper leg and the curve of her hip pressed against his right thigh. He felt her warmth; he couldn't believe how good it felt. How can something so insignificant feel so good?

For now, Lilly forgot about the shower scene; she compartmentalized people and events – she was good at that. Out of her mind truly meant out of her mind; she would think about it again later, not now. Besides, Cord looked so peaceful lying there, a book on his chest; bare feet and dress shorts, with a button-down, white short sleeve Oxford, untucked, wrapping his upper half.

"Want some? Chewing on these and trying to crack 'em are the best part of popcorn to me, as long as you don't break a tooth."

She tilted the bucket to expose a whole handful of kernels waiting to be tested; to see if they were teeth-crackers.

"Sure."

"Whatcha reading?"

"Aesop's Fables"; I loved them as a kid, I'm trying to see how many I can remember, and how many morals I actually follow. So far, not too many, in fact, none....yet. What's Earl up to?"

"Oh, he's asleep on the couch; never made the end of the movie - usually he doesn't. He's done for the night. He's awful happy today; what are you two into now? He wouldn't give up a word – believe me, I tried, which means it's got something to do with you, and it's probably trouble."

Cord just smiled wry and didn't respond.

"I figured as much."

She resigned.

Earl's asleep, and done for the night – *golden*, Cord thought to himself. Now, what to do about this gorgeous woman sitting on his sofa, next to him, sharing popcorn and making pleasant conversation. Only a lunatic would try to shake out of this situation.

"Well, I just came up to see if you were okay and say goodnight; Earl missed you at the *Blob* viewing, but it isn't like he doesn't rent it once a month. Surprised you have avoided it so far. Do you want me to leave the rest?”

As she tilted the bucket at him.

“No thanks, you work on them.”

And just like that, Lillian had made the decision for him, and was pleasant about it to boot. He was just waiting for the shoe to drop. But it didn’t.

“See ya.”

Was all she said, in a positively perky tone; no hint of sarcasm, or anything – just nice. A moment later, she was gone; the hallway light went out and he heard her apartment door quietly click shut.

It was 9:48pm; and he was a leisurely ten minute walk to Carol’s front door. It couldn’t have worked out better if he tried; all was right with the world. Now whom did he have to thank for that?

He looked out the window a second time, down Market Street, in the direction of the Cemetery, and shook his head in the negative.

This was definitely a test, and she was watching.

CHAPTER 78 – THE CHIT HAD DEFINITELY BEGUN

He actually had butterflies in his stomach, he really did.

And honestly, once C hit the Park, and started to cross it on the diagonal, kicking along the gravel, he didn't think about Earl, or the guilt in lying. It was for the greater good, he told himself….and it was, for the most part. And he chose not to think about the other part.

The night was silent, eerie silent. No cars circled the Park and the benches were empty; the small pack of troublemakers who regularly hung around this time of night, early teens in rut, marking territory, and generally making a minor ruckus, were nowhere to be found. The sky was clear and lit with stars; a quarter moon, waning, hung behind him. The only sound was the crunch of gravel beneath his feet. He quickened his pace.

As he approached the house, he could see a set of candles flickering on the porch, near her favorite chair, the throne he was supposed to assume tonight. He squinted, but didn't see her. All he could think was what would have happened if he hadn't showed up.

He looked up on the porch roof, but couldn't see any cats in the night sky; if they were there, they were camouflaged, and quiet.

He climbed the steps and walked over to the candles; no Carol. The glass table was set with sliced white cheese, *Pitchounet*, a bottle of Fonseca Port – he didn't see the date, but knew it had to be 1963, stood nearby, along with a dish of fennel crackers and a mass of champagne grapes on the stem.

A small white *Post-It* was stuck to the glass tabletop, illuminated in the glow.

Mr. Brin:

When the cherubs kiss, your chit begins
As long as it stays between us.

Ms. Crowe

Holy shit, this was really happening.

He walked over to the large black double doors; the right one was slightly ajar; he peeked in-between and saw the large cherub newel post light lit in the central hall, which cast the main staircase and the landing in an amber, incandescent glow. The space was empty.

He slowly touched the bronze cherub, tilting her forward, till she gently touched the cheek of the waiting male. At the far end of the hall, out of sight, the door chime rang a deep double-gong.

He stepped to his left and waited for the show to begin.

Ten or fifteen seconds passed, then he spied two stand-up thighs turn the corner of the landing and slowly make their way down the main stairs. Those legs went on forever, till they disappeared beneath the skimpiest, sexiest black mini-skirt he had ever seen. If the light had been better, he swore he would have seen clear up those legs, right to her ears.

Good God, the chit had definitely begun.

CHAPTER 79 – AND HE WAS CRYING

She spied him eyeing her through the double-door glass; she felt on display, which was wholly the point.

She came face to face with him at the inner door; he was like a little kid, ogling her and making no attempt to varnish it.

Carol leaned toward the glass, she was the thickness of the pane from his lips, and smiled a small tick for an extended moment, for effect. She gently grabbed the lion knob and slipped past him, never making contact, but coming as close as one could without doing so.

He followed her like a puppy.

She walked by her chair, spun and sat gingerly on the loveseat, careful to cross her legs, using the minimum amount of fabric she had covering her midsection to its fullest advantage. He sat in the master chair, as was part of the deal, turned to her, and waited for her to begin the dialogue.

"Care for a drink?"

She purred.

"I'm not sure, what do you have?"

"A *Fonseca, '63,* but I'm sure you knew that. A fine port if I do say so; fancy a taste?"

"Certainly."

She pulled the stopper and emptied the rich, ruby syrup into an ornate port glass; first for him, then for her. She sat forward a bit and raised her glass toward him; he reciprocated. They both took a taste, and commented on the texture and flavor in elegant terms.

She next picked up a small cluster of miniature grapes; the clusters had been precut to allow for full insertion and stripping with the teeth. Holding it a-high, she gently proffered.

"Some grapes, perhaps, Mr. Brin?"

"You know, I never expected you to be a good loser, but I figured you would make a feeble attempt, more to the fact – a rebellious attempt, just to save face. But this, this is over the top, much appreciated nonetheless, but wholly unexpected. I'm waiting for the shoe to drop."

"I take my bets seriously, and I rarely lose. I just wanted you to know I can hold up an end of a bargain, no matter how painful."

"Is this painful?"

"We'll see."

She whispered.

"Let's push the envelope just a bit, if you don't mind."

And with that, Cord leaned forward in an attempt to be fed the grapes; she leaned toward in slow motion, ready to deliver. He closed his eyes and slightly opened his mouth; ready to receive; she responded by dropping the lot on his upturned face.

"*That* was a bit much."

She said, sitting back and smirking.

"I figured as much, but worth a try."

Carol took a piece of the *Pichounet,* placed it on a cracker, and settled back in her seat, careful to keep her crotch covered from Mr. Brin's eyes, which he tried to keep focused on her face. But it was hard not to look south, very hard. And she knew it. He grabbed some crackers and several pieces of cheese and rounded them on a small serving dish, sat back and let out a sigh.

"You have one of the best seats in Belvidere right here....beautiful."

"I bought this house on the spot, based largely on the vantage you see. Day or night, you can't beat it with a stick."

She continued.

"So, are you impressed?

He looked at her, as he leaned forward, reducing the air space between them to the outer edge of somewhat intimate.

She added.

"I mean with the spread. I think you will find it satisfied all your requirements."

"I'm impressed with the entire package, and I'm most impressed with your humility, certainly unexpected, and a pleasant surprise; an admirable character trait....congratulations."

She answered with a small smile. And, more importantly, Carol didn't change the spacing; she neither advanced closer to him, to complement his move, nor sat back, a retreat in response to his offense. He noticed the lack of movement with interest, and continued his pursuit.

"I see just about everything I mentioned in the email, except one. Is it safe to assume you fully satisfied the stage set?"

She just tilted her head in mock confusion.

"You know the condition; well it was an option actually, if you want to be technical about it."

She now leaned ever-so-slightly toward him, almost imperceptible.

"Some things are best left to the imagination, Mr. B, don't you agree?"

"Some maybe, but I would certainly like to know this *particular* one, without having to guess."

"Really? Interesting. And why is that? Do you think it will have any effect on our social meeting tonight? I mean, this meeting had something to do with Earl, did it not? And I certainly don't believe the answer to that question has any bearing on that topic, since he isn't here to join us, correct?"

Cord was all about control, he always was. And the fact that Carol played his game, however she spun it, revealed gads about her, and how she viewed him. She played as if she was in charge, that was her usual role in business, and probably in past relationships, but Cord knew he was really in charge, that she acquiesced to him, and that turned him on. Her going pantie-less would just add sweet icing to an already decadent dessert.

He decided to let it go, for now, lest he appear a bit too obsessed, with all its downside potential.

"You're right."

Was all he said, as he resettled in his chair and sat back, away from her, putting a dampening amount of space between them, a sign that the intimate encounter he thought they were sharing would be shelved, for now.

She responded appropriately by continuing the topic of Earl. That was the point, right?

"So, what is it that you wanted to talk to me about with regard to Earl, that you felt the need to fly solo. I take it he doesn't know you're here? That was the plan, right?"

"Right on both counts."

"Well?"

Cord's chair backed up against the front parlor window; as he was about to speak, he heard a long, loud meow through the glass. He turned to look.

"Hey Earl."

Carol said gently, looking at a large black cat with the white nose and white breastbone, which was pacing back and forth on the inside sill behind Cord.

"Earl? You have a cat named *Earl*?"

"Well, his given name is Wasabi, but about a month ago, I started calling him Earl, because, in so many ways, he reminds me of your Earl….our Earl. He's lean and strong, and doesn't know how strong he is….a true scaredy-cat. And he purrs with the slightest touch of your hand as loud as an engine, and he's surrounded by three sisters who constantly pick on him, and he is about the most gentle and loving creature you could ever know. That's not a Wasabi, that's an Earl."

She finished her soliloquy and just smiled and waved to Earl. He kept meowing, never breaking his eye contact with her.

"And he's so cute and sweet, you just want to hug him to death. But if you do, he'll wig out and run. I'm surprised he's actually that close to you, even through the glass; he pretty much only comes out when it's safe….you must be safe, Mr. Brin."

"Remains to be seen."

"Lately, since I changed his name, he seems to be happier, purring more, laying against my chest and cuddling in the evening in bed. Guess he didn't like the sound of Wasabi; Earl has such a good sound to it, doesn't it?"

"Smart cat. When are you gonna tell Earl that Earl gets to sleep and cuddle with you every night? That should just about give him a cardiac, in a good way, of course."

"I didn't know how he'd take it; I thought he might be mad, calling him a cat, or a cat him….whatever."

"Earl? Mad at you? Come on! If you stabbed Earl in the chest, he'd still be the happiest guy alive; are you kidding?"

She smiled. Cord continued.

"So, how does it feel to have Lilly's little brother stone in love with you? Bit of a coup, I'd say; *nice move*."

Carol's smile disappeared in an instant.

C saw it and immediately retreated. What a fucking idiot he was! Why did he even say that? He didn't think before he spoke; it just spilled, out of nowhere, like diarrhea of the mouth.

"Hey, I'm sorry; I didn't mean to bring that up, or imply something....anything about, you know; that was a stupid thing to say – don't even know why I said it. Sorry about that, really."

Cord held up his hand; it was amazing how open a wound that was, to the both of them.

But it was clearly too late; no putting that bullet back in the gun.

She spoke in a strained tone.

"It's Saturday; I'm spending a nice summer weekend at my favorite retreat from the real world. It's a beautiful night, good food, fair company, and I get the chance to talk about Earl, one of the most favorite men in my life, and a good friend, with **no** ulterior motives. There is no man I'd rather call my friend than him....period. Let's keep it at that; there are no **nice moves**."

Wow; talk about a bullet to the heart. *'Fair company....Earl, one of the most favorite men in my life....I know of no man I'd rather call my friend than him*; he replayed the snippets in his head immediately after the words left her lips. It stung, and he deserved it.

All of a sudden, he felt like a heel, and fumbled to get out of the spotlight.

"Well, there's a couple of things I wanted to talk about, not a big deal really, but to Earl it would be."

She looked at him, impatiently waiting for him to continue. Her arms weren't folded in front of her chest, but they might as well have been. Suddenly, he didn't feel so confident; in fact, he was stumbling a bit, like he was exposed as a fraud, with insincere intentions. Spot on.

"Well, first, having him watch the cats is great; I assume that was…."

She got up in the middle of his sentence.

"Excuse me, I have to go inside and take care of something. I'll be right back."

And just like that, she was gone.

And she was gone for as long as it took to walk upstairs, put on her underwear, which were sitting on the dresser, and come back down; he didn't know that's what she did for sure, but that's what he suspected….that's *certainly* how it felt.

This went to shit in a hurry, one stupid line, and right to shit.

Now he started thinking about how he left Earl watching the movie by himself, and how he lied to him about going out, and how he didn't take advantage of his opportunity with Lilly and the tub of unpopped kernels. He got a pang of anxiety in his chest; he wanted to get up and run.

Carol emerged from the house and sat hard in a formal, matter-of-fact manner; any innuendo was clearly gone - he knew that was the unspoken message. He didn't dare ask her what she had to do inside so suddenly; he could imagine the sarcastic answer he would get, the one he knew she was waiting to skewer him with.

So he was silent.

He clumsily grabbed his plate of cheese and crackers and fingered them, then put a small hunk of cheese into his mouth.

He liked *Pitchounet,* but it didn't taste so great right about now.

"Hey, all joking aside, I really appreciate you doing up the night; it was meant to be a fun joke and you were a good sport about it....thanks. I'll make this quick, so you can enjoy Saturday night on your porch, in your favorite seat. Saturday night is always the best part of the weekend, right?"

She didn't answer. There was no *you don't have to make it quick* or *you don't have to leave* or *I just had to go the bathroom* or *put on some lip glo*ss. There was none of that; there was nothing, just silence.

Unbelievable. This was simply unbelievable! He waited all week for *this*? Now he got a bit mad, and a bit short. He was as ready to go as she was to see him leave.

"Anyway, what I was gonna say was, that Earl would love to watch your cats with Ji- Sue, so I assume you were serious about letting him do that, it was just...."

She cut him off again, speaking in a scold.

"I already told him I would; I would never tell Earl something like that and take it back, just as some juvenile code word to you. I respect Earl much too much to ever do that. Just like you respect Earl, right Cord?"

Fucking bitch; he couldn't believe this.

"Yeah, I do; he's my best friend."

"Really? The best friend who doesn't know you're sitting on the porch, solo, with the girl he's *stone in love with,* even though his big sister disapproves."

Although he never said that last part, it was certainly true. And Cord wasn't falling into that trap. So he didn't answer.

"And asking the girl he's stone in love with, while you flirt with her, if she's wearing any underwear? Do me a favor, please don't ever be *my* best friend."

That was it, final straw.

"Have a good one; thanks for the cheese."

Cord barked, as he stood briskly; his legs were actually tingly, a combination of anger, embarrassment and humiliation. She sat perfectly still, sans reaction, watching him get up, push the ottoman aside and head for the steps.

"See you and Earl tomorrow for our usual breakfast date, I assume you'll invite Earl along to that one, right? Should I wear any underwear?"

She called to him sarcastically as he quickly skipped down the porch steps, to which he responded.

"Go fuck yourself."

'I plan to.'

She whispered to herself; like she usually did, more nights a week than not.

She was surprised by her own reaction, overreaction really, to C's mostly benign comments about Earl and Lilly. But it really wasn't about that, it was about feeling bad sneaking around, meeting with Cord for some mysterious reason that he never coughed up, not that she really let him have the chance….and flirting. And as much as she accused him of it, she was just as guilty, if not more so. She was a big girl, she knew how

Earl felt, yet she chose to dress the way she did to meet Cord – he set the erotic stage, but she chose to play – all the way. And she was only kidding herself if she didn't think she was hoping something would happen with Cord tonight – and if it did, she had made up her mind to let it happen, and keep it a secret from Earl, for his own good.

And now, pretty suddenly, snapped into focus by Cord's *Lilly's little brother* and *nice move* comments, his inference that she was somehow using Earl as a pawn to chalk a win against her nemesis no-doubt, she had a queer, uneasy feeling about the whole episode, and Cord took the brunt of her bitter taste. No offense, but C was her casualty, a pill to feel better.

Cord no sooner took a dozen strides down her bluestone walk when a car crawled up Hardwick Street toward him; it was the only car that had come by since he arrived at Carol's; otherwise, the Park and the roads surrounding it were silent, cloaked in darkness.

He looked to his right annoyed, waiting for the sole car to pass till he crossed the street, to bisect the Park and make his way home, to go to bed….and end this God-awful night.

But this car was rolling slow; he cursed aloud.

"Come on already, for Christ sake!"

Carol just watched him from the porch.

Then C realized what was happening; the metallic-blue *Mini Cooper* convertible rolled slow beside him; the windows was partly cracked, but the cab was dark. It didn't matter, he knew who was inside. He dropped his head and shook it, leaning down toward the driver's door.

"Fuck, I'm sorry Mae, I know I was suppose to call; I was gonna…."

But before he could finish the lie, all he heard was:

"Get lost, asshole!"

As she gunned the engine and sped off, driving right through the stop sign twenty feet in front of her, jerking the wheel to the left and speeding down Third, till the two red taillights disappeared in the dark.

"Jesus fucking Christ!"

He yelled out loud, as he started to jog up Hardwick Street, away from home, in the direction of the long-gone *Mini Cooper*.

Great!   Great fucking night! he mouthed aloud to himself, but Carol heard that too.

It couldn't get much worse; he lied to Earl, blew a chance with Lilly, embarrassed himself in front of Carol, after making nice with her earlier – all for naught, felt ashamed of his flirting with Carol, even though he went there with good intentions for Earl, didn't he? And now this, with Mae, after he already had to mend relationships with her yesterday.

What a complete, bumbling fuck-up.

And now he was hoofing it up to Mae's place, for what? For another shot at redemption?

Truth was, he didn't feel like going home, not now. Maybe he would just wander around Town and feel sorry for himself; maybe he would go and yell at Carol, since she was no doubt laughing at him out in the Cemetery, the ringleader in this whole mess, for sure.

And in few moments, Cord, and all his problems, disappeared into the ink down Third Street.

Gone.

Carol sat on the porch in silence. She felt bad for C, but not too bad. More importantly, she felt a whole lot better about herself; she kept her dignity, and didn't betray Earl. And soon enough, her thoughts left the topic of Cord Brin.

Carol got up and switched seats, reposing in her favorite chair. She propped her feet up on the ottoman and spread her legs apart, sliding her already short skirt further up her shapely smooth thighs.

She grabbed her glass of port, barely touched and took a long taste – it was smooth – no doubt. 1963 was a good year indeed. And she welled good thoughts; she thought about Earl.

She slid her hand up her leg, right to her crotch, and pushed aside her panties, lightly brushing the tight-trimmed, thin strip of hair on her pussy with her middle and pointer fingers. And she began to slowly rub her clit, alone, in the dark, on the porch, thinking of having sex with Earl in a variety of ways, like she usually did when she wanted to come quickly, and often. Thoughts of Earl were her best sex toy by far. She loved imagining how big his horse-cock must be, and how she would ride it, long and slow at first, then fast and hard to finish.

It didn't take long for her to arch and moan to herself gently; as usual, it felt better than good.

Thank you, Earl she mouthed.

It wasn't just Earl's attractive looks, or how big she dreamed his cock must be; it was the fact that she was having sex with Earl that made it so enjoyable, that he was such a good person. She had never been with someone good; they always had an agenda, always a play.

Not Earl.

She fixed her panties and grabbed her port again, holding it aloft, tilting it toward the stars in the sky, over the darkened trees rustling gently in the Park. And she toasted him.

Have a nice night, Earl; I wish you could only know that I'm thinking about you, and that you make me feel so good, in so many ways.

Earl had no idea what she was doing or saying.

He was just sitting on his mom's bench, in the middle of the Park, looking at Carol sitting on the porch at *L'antre du Lion,* all alone.

And he was crying.

CHAPTER 80 – FROZEN BEFORE THE SPECTACLE, SCREAMING GUTTURAL

It was one and four-tenths of a mile, door to door, and Cord ran angry the entire way, sockless in his tassel loafers, light tan dress shorts and untucked, white button-down Oxford.

His mind raced in ten directions, fuming about Carol, fuming about Mae, worrying about Earl, thinking about Lilly, and wondering why in hell he was even in New Jersey, in this bum-fuck corner of nowhere, and what he was running to, and from, and how any of it made *any* sense.

He ran up Oxford Street, past the Cemetery, never even giving Carol a glance; he was pissed at her too. He ran right up the steep hill toward Brookfield, his gait unchanged.

He did think, not too seriously, about running right past Kensington Circle, bypassing *Brookfield*, right out to Route 46, to sit by the road, under the shadow of *Luigi's Rancho,* to wait for tomorrow's bus. That had to be another two to three miles, but what-the-fuck, he had all night to get there.

It was a fleeting thought, but the ability to do that, to really consider it an option, should have soothed his racing brain. But it didn't. Plus, he couldn't leave on his own anyway, as much as he might have wanted. He made a lot of bad decisions in the last twenty-four hours, but breaking the rules was not going to be one of them. *Those* consequences were a whole different ballgame.

He looked up and realized he was standing along the arc curbline at the far end of the Derby Lane cul-de-sac, his chest heaving, feeling the burn of raw, bloody blisters on his bare feet.

A single bulb glowed amber in the kitchen; the car was resting in the dark garage. He thought about Carol, and about Mae, and he got mad all over again.

He half-ran to the side door into the kitchen, and saw her diminutive frame sitting at the small table, hunched forward, her head in her hands. He tried the knob; it was locked. With the heel of his right hand, he pounded on the door in three loud raps, which brought her to a startled attention.

"Open the door Mae!"

She slowly stood up, pushing the chair back with her legs. But she made no advance, nor retreat. He could only see her silhouette through the opaque sheer; she was staring at the door, motionless.

"Open the fucking door, Mae! Now!"

He pounded again three times, harder still, rattling the glass violent. Nothing moved inside.

He immediately felt heat burning his ears vermilion; his hands slowly clenched into tight balls of rage, his forearms cramped as he squeezed his fingers shut on themselves. He closed his eyes as he turned and walked away from the door, back toward the cul-de-sac.

She saw Cord turn and retreat into the darkness; she leaned toward the door as if pulled by a magnet. But she never made it more than a half-step, before she heard a low rumble, followed by a sonic boom – a percussion chased by an explosion of hardware as the door disintegrated around him. He landed projectile on his side in a rain of wood splinters and shards of glass, cascading tidal across the kitchen floor.

She stood frozen before the spectacle, screaming guttural.

CHAPTER 81 – SHE LOVED HIM, SHE HATED HIM - JOIN THE CLUB

Cord rolled slow onto his back and laid still for a bit, the wind knocked from him. He sat up in slow-motion, slivered glass and needle splinters stuck to, and from, his back. Tiny blood blots emerged on his white shirt, slowly growing large as he sat still, the red spreading like a ripple in a pond, absorbing into the cotton fabric.

He planted his hand on the floor; she could hear the glass crack under his palm. He never flinched, as a long, thin shard pierced his skin, imbedding deep into his palm as he pushed himself vertical.

He stood up and quietly pulled on the back of his shirt, dislodging bits of glass and wood, then grabbed the filiform glass in his palm and wiggled it a bit, before slowly pulling out the sliver of silica, a good half-inch backed out of his hand, followed by a healthy stream of fresh blood, running past his wrist, down his forearm.

He gave it no notice.

Her hands, which had been over her mouth, slowly fell to her side, as she watched the bloody ritual in silence.

Cord walked to the back door and slowly closed what was left of it, and held it for a moment, to see if it would stay in place. It didn't; in defiance, it swung open a few inches. He dragged over a chair and pushed it against the door frame, pinning it shut. He shuffled over to the sink, and turned on the tap, unbuttoning and removing his Oxford to the sound of water splashing in the sink, his back to her.

Neither one spoke for awhile. It was Mae that broke the ice, tentatively, quietly.

"Are you okay?"

"You should have just opened the door, Mae."

He turned to look at her, standing in his white tee, soaked red in the back, with the bloody Oxford draped over the back of the nearest chair, a paper towel stuffed into his bleeding palm. Her eyes were puffy red; she had been crying.

"I said I was sorry, and I meant it; why can't that be good enough?"

"Because I'm not going to stand at the back of the line, behind black girls on the sidewalk, and rude girls on the deli floor, and rich girls on the porch, and whoever else there is running around inside your head. I'm not going to do it anymore; I've never had to, and I won't do it now."

"You won't do what now Mae? *Do what?* Are we dating? We're friends, friends who may end up fucking each other, but that's it! You wanna fuck? Let's go fuck, but that's it."

"That's not good enough."

"What fucking street am I on? Sunset Boulevard? Are they gonna find me face down in the pool Norma? Do you even know what I'm talking about?"

"Yeah I do; I guess you figure since I'm so old, I have to know who Norma is. Well I am, and I do know who she is, and what you mean by it, so thanks for that – thanks for making me feel even older and shittier than I already do, so thanks. You know, I've done a *lot* for you; from the moment we met I've been helping you, without strings, and you always seem to take it. And I've never asked for anything in return; well, now I'm asking. I'm tired of being the one you pay attention to when there's no one else around to pay attention to."

"There have always been strings, on both sides, Mae, on *both* sides; there always are….don't pretend not to know that."

She looked at the towel in his hand, dyed crimson, and the blood soaked deep into his tee-shirt. She walked over to him and put her head on his chest; he kept his hands by his side.

"Why does it have to be just that? You know, you're not so young yourself. Why can't it be okay for me to just take care of you, and you can take care of me? Why is that so impossible? Why can't that happen? Why can't we even talk about the possibility of that happening?"

"Mae, you don't know *anything* about me, not a *fucking* thing, not really; you don't want this package, trust me."

She jerked her head off his chest and stared at him intently.

"Oh, that's a bullshit line! If one of the other ones would have you, would smile and spread their legs, you'd be all over it in a minute, don't think I don't know it. But you're here, which means, for whatever reason, those cards are folded. Bad for them, good for me. Why were you walking angry off that porch anyway? It was clearly before you knew it was me coming down the road."

Cord just looked at her, but didn't answer; what could he say?

"I know I'm getting a mixed bag, and don't think I haven't tried to fill in the blanks with you – even with my resources, no luck….yet. You are either very good at hiding, or Cord Brin doesn't really exist, and God knows who you *really* are. Bottom line is, I don't really care. And if you think I can't find a boy-toy to fuck, you're crazy; I can go online and get a fucking string of twenty-somethings to ball me, in much better shape than you, trust me - my neighbors do it all the time, and they're fat and ugly, with saggy tits, fat asses and stretch marks. So don't think I'm hard-up for sex - I'm not. I choose not to sleep with young boys and old men. I care about you, the package, since the minute you stood behind me in the deli line. Why? I have no fucking clue; I wish I didn't, but I just do."

She wanted to tell him that she loved him, because she knew she did. But she wouldn't dare say it, she had already said enough. Her speech was done; now she waited for the reaction.

"Say it doesn't mean anything, Mae, and I'll pull your little panties off right here, right now, and do whatever it is you want me to do, but you have to say it's for fun, nothing more."

She shook her head slowly, knowing she wouldn't hear what she wanted to hear. The tears welled up in her eyes as she tried to squeeze them in, to stop them from running down her cheek. She didn't want to look weak, but it was a losing battle.

"I won't do it."

She said, her voice quivering.

"Say it, Mae!"

She closed her eyes and shook her head hard left to right, in defiance. The tears wet her eyes.

She wanted to tell him to get out, but she knew she never would; she was afraid when she told him to get lost in front of Carol's house that he would never speak to her again. Her whole body tingled when he showed up at the door, like it did now; she wasn't sure if it was affection or derision.

She loved him, she hated him - join the club.

CHAPTER 82 – AND WHAT A SURPRISE IT WAS

Cord hadn't noticed the small, glass cookie jar, set to the right of the back door. Despite the violence of his entry, the glass jar survived, sitting pretty, just inches from the melee, chock full of light orange *Circus Peanuts*.

He smiled; he grew up devouring those nasty cavity-forming confections - it was one his father's favorite vices.

He liked them soft; his father favored a slightly stale outer crust. But Cord ate most of the peanuts before they achieved the state of stale his dad enjoyed; so his father would endlessly horde and hide them in odd places around the house, waiting for them to harden, hoping Cord wouldn't pick them off, predator and prey. Cord usually got the best of him.

C closed his eyes and gently pulled Mae toward him, being careful to keep his bloody palm from her clothes. He looked down at his chest; no blood on his front - with that, he pulled her so she was resting against him….she was warm.

Detente settled in.

"Circus Peanuts?"

"Joe likes them; I dole them out, like a dog biscuit, after he does chores around the house. I keep them by the back door so I can hand him one or two while I swish him out the door; pretty mean, huh?"

Cord didn't answer. He kissed her gently on her forehead, at her hairline; he felt her try to crawl into him.

"They were my dad's favorite candy; he and I used to fight over them. Actually, I didn't even really like them, made my teeth hurt - pure sugar - but it was fun eating them before he got to them. Kind of a never-ending game."

Cord looked down over her shoulder at her outfit.

"This for me?"

He said as he pushed her a bit away from him, to get a better look at the get-up, which he hadn't focused on till now. She just frowned, embarrassed at the attempt.

But he liked it.

"Let me see, a set of black suede pumps, skintight light gray wool skirt, summer-weight, showing the lower half of a very shapely thigh. Matching gray short-waisted jacket, overlying a white, spaghetti string cotton top, sans bra, with stiff nipples pushing on the fabric, slight V-cut to reveal some of that lovely breastbone, tucked in….very nice."

"Maybe we can talk about it later? Can we at least talk about it?"

He kissed her again on the forehead, this time a bit longer.

"I give pretty good sex, I've been told, but the rest of the package, tends to disappoint. Trust me Mae, take the sex and leave the rest at the curb, it's safer that way."

"I'll take the sex, but I want to taste the rest - can I at least have a little taste?"

"What's a taste?"

She slowly slid her hand down to his crotch and slid it up inside his shorts cupping his cock in his briefs, which was now in kind of a ball. It didn't take long to react, as she slowly slid her open hand up and down his shaft through the black cotton.

He dropped his hands by her thighs, and slowly slid them up the outside of her legs, pulling up her skirt with them. He purposely went slow, watching as he revealed more and more of her shapely bronzed legs, waiting for them to join at the gift-wrapped surprise waiting at the top.

And what a surprise it was.

CHAPTER 83 – A LONG QUIET MOAN, REPEATED OFTEN

He figured her panties would be black; never did he expect white.

He got neither.

As the last vestige of gray wool cleared the bottom of her cunt, all he saw was a beautiful light brown muff of slightly wavy hair, perfectly manicured, every square inch of skin tanned to the same tone….not a hint of a line, not a stray hair to be found. Her skin was tight, not a wrinkle. Perfect. How could it be so tight? Mae had some have-to wrinkles on her face and neck – it came with sixty-six, for sure. But the rest of her body was smooth and supple, almost too perfect. How could that be?

He could honestly say that was one of the best looking pussies he had ever seen, just the way C liked it; a poster child for No. 8 on his woman wish list.

She could tell he was genuinely pleased.

"I told you it got better the further you went up."

She whispered sly as she slid her hand under the elastic of his briefs, cupping his cock for the first time.

"Oh God, how long I've been waiting to feel this."

She said, slowly running her hand up and down his shaft in a slow, deliberate massage, squeezing his cock every now and then. He was rock hard when she asked, in a faint whisper, once again.

"So, can we talk….later?"

"Shh."

Was all he said, as he slid his finger, in one slow thrust, deep into her cunt, to the last knuckle, making a wide, clockwise circle inside her, over and over. She reacted immediately; God, she had been waiting for that finger forever. And she wanted more, much more. But for now, she closed her eyes tilted her head back, and enjoyed the beginning of the ride.

C liked how Mae came; a long, quiet moan, repeated often.

CHAPTER 84 – CHRIST, TROUBLE COMES QUICK

Sunday, June 25, 2006; day sixty-seven, at a dead-end on Derby Lane.

Cord slowly opened his eyes and focused on the ceiling; the early dawn cast a veiled light across half the room. Features were visible, in opaque.

He was flat on his back; legs slightly spread in a vee, cocooned in a blanket. He was usually hot, but the air conditioning was cranked low and he felt the diffuser over the corner of the bed wash him in a cold downdraft, just the way he liked it.

The comforter felt good and he was relaxed, a general sense of lassitude.

Between his legs, a linear lump moved under the covers. She rested her thin arms on his upper thighs, and without using her hands, she slowly rose and fell on his cock, sliding it in and out of her mouth, taking it out to lick the shaft while his cock rested against her face, down to his balls, then back up, to swallow him again in a slow, wet stroke, tonguing him all the while.

She didn't make a noise; she was like a machine. If he lay still pretending to still be asleep, he wondered how long she would keep it going. He wondered how long she had already been at it.

If she was any younger, he swore she would have ridden him to death last night; where does she get the energy? And how could his cock possibly be hard again?

He was good for two hard-ons on a long night, at most, with a long recovery period between. Even when he was young, he wasn't one of those guys who could come and stay hard, or get hard again quick; he truly had limited shots. So he always worked to make them last.

But not with Mae.

She somehow suspended that reality last night; he didn't remember how many times she woke him and actually got him hard again, but it was more than two. A least a couple more….at least. God, he loved that little pussy of hers, no doubt about that.

But that adoration was quickly tempered with the fear that this little soiree was tied up in long, thick strings, and he already knew he was in trouble, just by the way she was working him now.

He lifted the covers.

"Need some fresh air?"

With that, she never looked up, but slowly descended on him, taking his cock all the way in, to the balls, without a gag, a whimper, a sound. And she kept it there, just sucking and working her tongue.

Good God, he thought.

"You know, you could make a little bit of a gag, like it might be a bit too big or something; that looks a little too easy."

She slowly extracted his dick, effortlessly, licked the top in a tight circle and gave a tiny mock cough; then she smiled.

"How was that?"

"Pathetic."

"Well, you do have small hands."

Mae said, smiling some more.

"But you're obviously the right size for me; I came enough times – lost count. It's been a long time since a night like that."

She said, as she slid from between his legs and saddled up next to him, sharing his pillow.

"Besides, it's not the length, it's the girth that matters."

She said, like the team mascot.

"Thanks, Mae; next time I'll be sure to brag about the girth with the boys, that should impress 'em."

"It's true!"

She exclaimed, as if the declaration, if stated in an emphatic manner, somehow made the findings official.

Then she settled back down and placed her head in the crook between his shoulder and head, like it was meant to set there, and slowly ran her hand across the hair on his chest, and down to rub his belly, and back up again. Since his belly had become flat, or relatively so, he didn't mind her touching it. When C was fat, there was no touching of the belly, that was the rule.

Her fingers ringed a light trace around the first of the many raised scars scattered across his front and sides; it was the first time she really focused on them, the first time he realized they were about to become the topic.

He beat her to the punch.

"Don't ask, it's not up for discussion".

She tilted her head, feigning surprise, when in fact the words were just about to leave her lips.

"What?"

"Not now okay; not now."

She resettled her head on his chest in quasi-frustration and began to retrace his skin with the tip of her pointer finger, without saying a word. She wrapped her legs around his thigh, like a body pillow, and pushed against him, to create friction on her pubic bone. He was sure she was going to start humping his leg like a dog, but she didn't, she just laid still, her cheek on his chest. He could feel the heat from her crotch.

Soon enough, as he suspected, she focused on the four linear skewer scars, they always did. They were the flattest, faintest of them all, but the peculiar linear layout caught one's eye, it appeared astrological – a straightaway of stars.

He didn't say anything at first; he let her fester, focusing her finger-line up and down the four circular marks, equally spaced. Then he spilled, but just a bit.

"I was twelve; I got stuck on a fence."

She didn't respond, she just tilted her head and lightly kissed the closest circle.

"You know, after that happened, it was like my life bent a bit off-course. Like running your hand up a smooth, straight branch, then coming to a kink, a node, and veering off in a skew. I don't know how to describe it any better; my life, whatever my life was for the first twelve years, felt decidedly different prior to that day. Since then, its always felt a bit off, not bad, per se, just....*off*."

Cord stared blankly at the ceiling.

"What happened on the fence?"

"I got introduced to a puppet, crickets and flies."

She raised her head in confusion.

"I had a *terrible* nightmare that night – never forgot it, like it left an imprint that you can't wash, or wish, away. Strange, I don't know if that fence, hole-punching me open like it did, let them in, or let them out....but they introduced themselves that night, and they've been with me, in me, ever since. Always just offstage, to the side, behind the curtain, perhaps, but always there – and always sure to remind me they're watching. I've never been able to shake 'em."

"I don't understand."

"Me neither, never have."

C said, deadpan.

"How's your hand? Your back?"

"Hand is fine."

He said, looking at the bandage she put on last night, before the assault in bed.

"The back is a little rough from friction."

She smiled and he could feel her start to grind her crotch on his leg; good God, she was ready for another round.

To his utter surprise, so was he.

"I don't know how Mae, but whatever you do, bottle it; guys my age would pay big bucks for eight hours of stiff cock."

As he looked at himself. She looked as well, and smiled at her good fortune.

"Well, this is the last one; I gotta take a shower and get home....can't be your boy-toy all day, you know. At some point today, I have to show up for work, customers to take care of."

"Isn't that what this is, customer service? Although, I don't want you passing it out to just anybody."

She ground on him a little more deliberately.

"And why not stay? Whatever Sam pays, I'll top it."

"What? And lose my self-respect? You forget I'm sensitive, and not for sale."

"One thing I *have* learned hanging around you is that you have no self-respect, and very little feelings, and everyone is for sale, the price just varies. And I think I could get you....*cheap*."

"That hurts Mae."

"No it doesn't."

She snarked back; C smiled in agreement.

Then Cord sat up in bed, ready for the final play.

"Okay, in your mouth, your pussy, or your ass – you've had all three; where are we gonna end this?"

"You know, I'd never had it in my ass before – guys tried, but that's the first I've unclenched those cheeks. Can you believe that? Sixty-six years and a coolie-virgin. I liked it, I really did, but more than a bit sore down there right about now; can't go there."

She said as she climbed atop, grabbed his cock and slowly slid it into her pussy. Sitting upright, cowgirl, he had a perfect view of her little tits, stiff nipples with tiny areola.

"You know, I'm proud of these."

She said, cupping under her tiny tits, showing off the minimum of sag.

"Sorry, not a tit-guy, strictly below the waist interests me; I mean I like small tits, but really just to look at."

"I know, no action at all for them last night."

She said, as she jiggled them a bit.

Mae's cell phone rang on the nightstand; it was a familiar jingle, but at first, C couldn't place the tune. She closed her eyes, smiled, planted her hands firm on his chest and started to hump him fast, leaving the phone untouched.

"Isn't....that....*pop....goes....the....weasel*?"

He said staccato, between violent pelvic thrusts, as she ground him hard into the mattress.

But she paid no attention; pumping fast and furious, trying to finish quickly; a woman on a mission.

The phone kept ringing and she kept pumping, breathing hard, like a sprinter. It stopped, and a moment later, she came hard. In all the distraction and movement, he lost his focus, and slowly went limp inside her.

That happened more often than not at forty-three.

"Nice....thanks; at least you enjoyed it."

He said deadpan.

She rolled off, just as the phone beeped, indicating a message.

"Sorry."

Was all she said, as she dismounted and laid beside him, breathing heavy.

"And?"

"It was *Toolbox*; I wanted to come with your cock in me when he was on the phone calling me."

He just looked at her.

"I know, childish, but now every time he calls, and I hear that tune I programmed just for him, *Romper Room*, it'll remind me of having sex with you....kind of our signature."

She said, giving him a peck on the tip of the nose.

"*Romper Room*! I knew I knew that tune! God I used to watch that as a kid; having sex to *pop-goes-the-weasel* and *Romper Room*....that's just not right."

He sat up a bit and just stared at her.

"But I'm sure Joe will appreciate the gesture."

She smiled a wide grin and gave him a long, affectionate kiss on the lips, and snuggled up next to him.

"Don't go just yet C, lay here a bit longer. Hey, how bout dinner tonight? Anything you want, just name it, I have an *in* with the fresh produce manager at the market in Town - got him the job....can get us a good deal on exotic vegetables."

She whispered in his ear; she was positively giddy.

It was the first time she called him C; that was what Lilly and Earl called him.

Christ, trouble comes quick.

826

CHAPTER 85 –KNEES TREMBLING AND AN IMMEDIATE NEED TO URINATE

It was 6:48 am when he first heard the footsteps; Cord was sitting at the kitchen table, reading the local rag and nursing a mug of coffee; some public relations firm logo wrapping the white ceramic. He was in his black boxer briefs and white tee-shirt, with a three-day shadow on his face.

He turned to see a State Police cruiser parked at the cul-de-sac curb, an officer, a State Trooper, hand on his gun, slowly approached the door, another trailed him and a third figure lagged far behind.

Fuck, this had better not be....

He didn't finish the thought.

"Mae, you better come out here!"

No luck, the water in the shower was running, and she didn't hear a thing.

No time for him to get her, the Troopers were nearly at the kitchen door; any sudden move and he would likely be in trouble he didn't need; so he just sat, and waited for what he knew was coming, hoping it wasn't what he thought it might be.

"Mrs. Batests? You okay in there? Hello?"

The first Trooper spied Cord at the table through the cracked back door.

"YOU! ON THE FLOOR! NOW!"

"She's in the shower officer; she's taking a shower - I'm her friend."

"ARMS OUT TO YOUR SIDES! NOW!"

The officer kicked open the broken door; the chair went flying. He drew his gun and directed it at Cord, who now was prone, face down, on the cold ceramic tile. It felt good.

"Did you hear…."

"SHUT UP! MRS. BASTES, ARE YOU OKAY?"

Cord lay still, careful not to provoke the yokels. Rural White Township had no police force of its own, so State Troopers came to the rescue, regardless of the nature, or severity, of the infraction. But these guys, even though they were Staties, were clearly Mayberry, so he breathed easy and waited for the men in blue to solve the crime.

"Billy, water running, *watch him!*"

Cord had his head to the side, looking out the back door; surprisingly, no senior rubber-neckers had yet gathered, but it was still pretty early on a sleepy Sunday.

A lone individual stood on Mae's lawn, arms flared a bit out to the side, a rat ready to run for safety at the slightest hint of trouble. Their eyes met at the same time.

"I knew it!"

Toolbox yelled in a high-pitch to the Trooper standing just inside the door.

"I knew that guy was trouble; he's the one I described to you officer - he's the one!"

Toolbox Joe to the rescue.

"CALM DOWN SIR; PLEASE GO BACK HOME, WE GOT IT UNDER CONTROL."

But Joe wasn't going anywhere; saving Mae and hardcore State Trooper interaction on dead-end Derby Lane, all before 7 am on a Sunday morning; this was going to be a jackpot weekend for Mr. Fishel. Joe planted his hands on his hips in utter self-satisfaction, a shit-eating grin plastered his face.

A few moments later, the water stopped, and out strode the officer, followed closely by Mae, quickly dried and sporting an oversized white terry robe.

"Yes, that's my friend, Cord Brin; doesn't he have a cute little butt?"

The officer wasn't amused, nor was Cord.

"Sorry sir, you can get up; we had a report of a possible break-in, with a description of a potential suspect that looks a lot like you."

"Not a problem."

Cord said, as he got up slowly, and assumed his position back at his paper and cup of coffee, like a routine lay on the floor at gunpoint was part of the breakfast program. It looked as if Cord had run that routine before.

"Ma'am, we had a call from a concerned neighbor, who stated he was on a morning walk and saw your kitchen door broken and ajar; he also said you had a visit from a stranger yesterday, fitting the description of your friend here. He said he tried to call you, but he got no answer....sorry again."

"Not a problem officer, my phone did ring this morning, but I was too busy to answer it. Cord, dear, why didn't I answer that phone?"

Mae was all about innuendo, and having fun with it, as she did at Sam's yesterday with Anne and the *pisang susa* bananas. At this point, Cord was not interested in innuendo.

"Because you were too busy riding my cock."

Cord said, as he took a sip of coffee, never moving his eyes off the paper.

"Oh, right."

Mae smiled sheepishly.

The officer didn't know quite what to say to that; so he said nothing, flipped shut his notebook, turned and headed for the door.

"Sorry to bother you, ma'am….better safe."

"I agree officer, thank you for your prompt attention."

"You should get that door fixed."

"Oh, the lock jammed, and we had to force it open; Cord will get right on it, thank you again."

Cord looked at her sideways.

"Get *Tool-Boy* to fix it."

Both officers started down the walk, leaving Joe flabbergasted that Cord was not somehow in wrist cuffs, on his way to the back of the police cruiser for booking and a long stint in the slammer.

"Hey, Officer, aren't you going to do something about *him*?"

Joe turned frantically to Mae.

"Mae, are you okay? What happened to the door? Why didn't you answer the phone? I called first, but you didn't answer. What is *he* doing here?"

Mae glared at Joe, then turned to the Troopers.

"Oh, Officer, I forgot one thing."

Mae shouted, stopping both men, who turned and slowly made their way back to greet her.

"I did have something stolen yesterday, you know, of a personal nature, I would like to report it."

She said, softly, but loud enough.

Oh, Joe didn't like the sound of that; this whole thing might be going south, in a hurry.

He slowly started to back up, retreating toward his house as quickly as inconspicuous could get him there.

"Yes ma'am, what is it?"

Mae spoke a few hushed words to the officers, and before he could turn his back, Joe Fishel heard the words that a man whose criminal past amounted to parking meter violations, had never heard before.

"Sir, stop right there."

And Joe did, with knees trembling and an immediate need to urinate.

CHAPTER 86 – THE LACE FELT GOOD, BAD-BOY GOOD

Shaking like a leaf, Joe stood as still as he could, trying to hold his bladder, while the trio approached. By this time, Cord stood, shirtless in his black boxers, in the kitchen door, coffee mug in hand, drinking in the scene. This had the makings of something good.

"Mr. Fishel, Ms. Bastet has stated she believes you have taken an item of a personal nature from her, an article of clothing, yesterday, when you were in her home; is this true sir?"

"Uh, I was only trying to be helpful; I thought I would wash them for her and bring them back, you know, I was just trying to be helpful, uh, I'm always helpful, aren't I Mae? Tell them Mae."

No rescue line from Ms. Bastet.

"Give me my underwear back, Joe."

"But they're in the wash! I can't give them to her until the wash is done Officer, then I'll bring them right over, right away; *sorry* for trying to be nice."

Joe got a little indignant with that last fragment, which surprised him, considering the predicament he was in. But he figured he needed to go on the offensive.

He was quickly shot down.

"Joe doesn't do laundry on Saturday Officer; he does laundry once every two weeks, one load, on Thursday, in the afternoon."

A direct hit by Mae. The Trooper looked at Fishel sternly, realizing he was being played by the diminutive Jew.

"Last time I ask, sir; return the undergarment right now, or we have to make this matter more public than it needs to be. Trust me, you don't want that Mr. Fishel, not for this; now cough up the panties, sir."

Joe stood frozen, unsure what to do. The Officer's patience ended.

"NOW! If they're in the wash, go get 'em; in the hamper, go get 'em, in the dishwasher, go get 'em. Wherever they are, cough 'em up, *right now*!

And upon that bark, Joe fumbled with the button on his trousers, hurriedly downed the zipper and was in the process of pulling down his pants toward his knobby knees. Which quickly revealed the frilly fabric of a pair of petite black panties, which fit him amazingly well. The three let out a collective sigh of disgust and turned their eyes from the horror.

"Oh my God! Keep 'em!"

Mae was unfortunately closest to the wreckage, and spun fast, hoping to miss any glimpse of Joe's package, veiled in lace.

"Pull your pants up! Jesus!"

The lead Trooper yelled, while his partner simply laughed and shook his head. Cord just chuckled and sipped his coffee; God he loved this place. The two Officers regrouped and made their way into the squad car in silence. Joe ran in the opposite direction, buckling his trousers on the way, and quickly disappeared into his house.

"That was *fucking strange*."

The first said, turning the ignition, while the other just shook his head and spoke.

"White Township, senior citizens, way too much free time; you couldn't make this shit up."

They both chuckled as they rolled down Derby Lane, another crime solved.

Joe sat down gently on the living room couch, staring at the chowder-heads droning on the television. He sat up and leaned back quickly to peak through the sheer, and let out a sigh of relief when he saw the police cruiser had left, Mae had gone inside and, once again, all was quiet on Derby Lane.

That bastard grocery boy he thought to himself, moving in on his girl. But he did dodge a legal bullet, and smiled at his good fortune. He felt a little reckless, like a bad boy; maybe Mae would be impressed.

And he got the keep her panties; bonus!

He wore them the rest of the day; the lace felt good, bad-boy good.

CHAPTER 87 – THE SORDID STORY SLOWLY SPUN

Mae sat across from him, smiling to herself, at the back of his newspaper – he was engrossed in the *Week In Review.* She savored her cup of Earl Grey; she liked the feel of him in the kitchen.

She sat in silence, thinking about that jackass Joe and her underwear, and she smiled about all that happened. She thought about last night; funny how sometimes, when you least expect it, things turned out all right. She would have to work on Cord, but in the end, she knew she could convince him to put his chips in with her. She was pretty sure anyway; worth the effort, at least.

He dropped the paper in front of him and looked at her.

"I really gotta go…."

"Do you want anything to eat? Eggs, an English muffin? Something to go?"

"Nah, I don't eat breakfast, never really have."

Conveniently forgetting the banquet buffet he ate nearly every weekend with Carol, frequently followed by a second, courtesy of Lilly. Cord looked over at the coffee machine.

"I will take a cup to go, if that's okay?"

She looked at him cocked, mocking that he felt the need to ask permission.

He opened the pantry door, looking for a travel mug, and noticed the neatly handwritten menu spreadsheet, hanging on a hook, on the inside door face.

"*John Marzetti,* and pumpkin pie tonight?"

"Does that mean *yes* for dinner?"

She looked hopeful.

"You got the whole week set out, no....*two weeks*! Dinner and accoutrements every night:

- Stewed chicken, mashed potatoes and banana cake on Monday;
- Chop-suey, with pineapple upside-down cake on Thursday;
- Swiss steak with potatoes and carrots, pineapple/pear salad and cherry pie next Saturday;
- More chicken, this time with baked potatoes, peas, carrots, Waldorf salad, tomato juice, coffee, and chocolate cake – that's next Sunday.

What's up with that, Mae, expecting company, lots of company, the next two weeks? Or maybe *way* too much time on your hands."

She took another sip of tea.

"Old habit from being a good wife and mother. I'm very organized; why do you think I'm down at Sam's all the time, buying food?"

"Because you're looking for an excuse to see me."

"Well, that too. Unfortunately for me, that's true, and it's unfortunate you know it. Although I also do actually shop you know, and I eat the food; rather, I cook the food, and have friends over, play canasta, trade flower bulbs, whatever, or just give it away, even to our pantie-friend next door. Can you *believe* he did that?"

Cord laughed along with Mae.

"Classic. But not to throw *Tool-Box* too far under the bus, I have to admit, when I was a little kid, not a senior citizen, mind you, but a kid, under ten for sure, I used to sneak into my mom's dresser and finger her bras and underwear. I used to put them on too, just for a minute or so; I remember them feeling pretty damn good."

Mae looked at him and smirked, trying to picture Cord in a bra and panties.

"Come on, it was only once or twice."

Mae looked at him with raised eyebrows.

"Okay, maybe more than twice, but no more than ten, maybe. Hey, guys do all sorts of goofy sex things as kids they never admit to; actually they do lots of things as adults too. I just happen to admit it more than others. But I have to say, there are only a select few who know about that one; actually, come to think of it, *no one* knows about that but you, not even my mother, so keep it under your hat, young lady."

She smiled, then seemed to look past him, through him, at the far wall. Contemplating.

"I don't like that look; that's not a good look."

Cord said, fearing what was about to come.

Now Mae never told a soul this particular story; most everyone has one of these stories, some more than one. The one thing, the *big one*, that you've done in your life you truly regret, a real head-shaker. You can't even rationalize why you did it, or how you did it, but you did it nonetheless, and have to live with the consequences for life. Mae had one of *those* stories; she was ashamed the minute it was over. And the guilt had haunted her for the past thirty years. It was *that* bad.

Yet she wanted to share it with Cord; she wasn't ashamed to tell him; probably because she could see him doing the same thing. There was a bond in sharing such stories with a special soul, someone you could trust with your darkest secrets. Mae wanted that bond with Cord. So she spilled for the first time since 1976.

"If I tell you something, something I've lived with for a long time, something I'm not particularly proud of, will you promise it doesn't leave this kitchen? Promise?"

"Mae, don't front-load like that; do yourself a favor, don't even tell me. There's plenty I don't tell you – trust me, so we're even. You can still hold my mother's bra and panties thing over me, though, I'll give you that; put it in your pocket….it's yours."

He took a long sip of coffee, hoping she would change the subject.

She ignored him. She had kept this albatross to herself far too long; she still thought about it more often than you would think, with the passing of so many years. She certainly was reminded every time she saw her daughter, which was less and less, almost never, in fact.

She was thirty-six at the time - by no means a kid - she couldn't blame it on youth. And to this day, only one other person knew.

And so the sordid story slowly spun.

CHAPTER 88 – SMACK ON THE LIPS – IT WAS LONG AND DRY

"I was thirty-six and in killer-shape; most guys noticed me, especially the ones I wanted to notice – a pretty hot and frustrated mom, with a boring, sexless husband and a sixteen year old daughter, almost seventeen, but not quite."

"I don't really want to hear this Mae. If it's something illegal, you realize I'll have to call back our friends in blue."

Cord interrupted, pointing to the cul-de-sac. She half-mockingly yelled at him, more of a plea than anything else.

"Stop interrupting! This is important, really. I need to say this."

"Do you really need to say this? *Really?* It's been thirty fucking years; I don't think you *really* need to say anything. I'll be fine, you'll be fine, if you don't....trust me."

She shook her head in defiance and continued.

"I made a mistake, got pregnant young, nineteen; at least it was young for a girl like me, who had plans beyond cooking casseroles. He wasn't the first guy I was with either.

Anyway, this guy is a year younger than me; he was still in high school, for Christ's sake, a senior, but he looked older than he was. He was also a top-notch wrestler – big muscular guy, a heavyweight – must have weighed about two-hundred twenty pounds – big.   Anyway, he was someone I barely even knew; I never dated him or anything like that - it was literally a one-shot deal. He was out of the picture before he even pulled his pants up, so to speak.

He was wrong on so many levels; getting together with him wasn't close to being an option. His family was a half-step above trailer-trash, and I didn't even like him. But he was hot-looking, for sure, with a ripped body, hard as a rock. I still remember that part.

Anyway, it was a stupid, stupid mistake; one night, and your life changes forever. Wrong place at the wrong time, and lots of hormones. I wasn't even drunk, I can't even blame it on alcohol; sometimes you just don't have any rational explanation for the mistakes you make.

[Mae frowned to herself and shook her head]

Anyway, after awhile, can't hide it any longer, and I have to tell my parents, who go ballistic, even though I'm an adult. They were pretty protective, and I was still living at home – I was only nineteen. The wrestler never even knew; no point in telling him – he was never going to be part of the picture, in any way, shape or form. In fact, I never spoke to him, or saw him again. Never. Just carried around his genes. I wonder what ever happened to him?

Anyway, there would be no abortion, that was out of the question, and my parents had a thing about *giving up their genes* to some stranger; why that was so God-damn important I have no idea. So they wanted the baby kept in the family – no adoption. I never understood that; it would have made everything so much cleaner, so much easier; I should have stood up to them about that, but, at nineteen, in 1959, I didn't. My dad was a pretty tough guy, my mom too; standing up to them wasn't something you did, you just didn't. At least I didn't; I should have, but I didn't. It really wasn't an option.

They talked to some of their closest friends about it, in secrecy of course, and next thing I know along comes this guy, a good guy, goofy but good, someone waiting in the wings, someone who always liked me, and was willing to marry me, even though my child wouldn't be his.

This guy would *never* have had a chance with me - average looks, average body….not a *Joe-bag-of-donuts*, but close, kind of blah - just about average in every way; the kind of guy you look right past, the kind you never even notice. We lived in the same town, but he went to some other school, a Catholic school the next town over, and I didn't know him. But he knew all about me; if there was one thing he was, it was relentless when he wanted something.

And he wanted me.

He was smart, polite, respectable, and he got me at a weak, scary time, so I said yes – actually my parents said yes and I didn't object - it was a way out. Actually, it was the beginning of many, many, unhappy years, but I didn't know it at the time. It just looked like an easy ticket out of a jam."

"You know Mae, hate to tell ya, but that's not so fantastic; that kind of shit happens all the time, every day of the week, even in 1959. By the way, I wasn't even *born* yet, just fyi."

"*That's* not the story! It's just the set-up. And thanks for that tidbit, jerk."

[Mae stuck her middle finger up at Cord; he thought it was funny, seeing her do that to him, and smiled]

"Now that I like! In the gutter."

He said.

"You have no idea what a segue way that comment is; now, would you please let me finish?"

He put up his hand to give her the floor.

"You know, I've always had a difficult relationship with her, my daughter; even today, probably more so today, it's a deteriorated mess. She's pretty quiet, but rebellious in a reserved, even dignified way, especially to me – we're oil and water. I hate it; she's just too polite, but in a veiled, vicious kind of way, if that makes any sense. A *vicious polite* is the only way to describe it; anyway, those aren't my genes, for sure.

Funny, whenever we argue, which is pretty much anytime we talk to each other, she would tell me she *got dad's genes;* he was always quiet, and never raised his voice. And I would shake my head, knowing she's a wrestler's daughter. To this day, she doesn't know her father isn't her real father, biologically, anyway.

[Mae shook her head]

Everyone thought we were the model mother/daughter duo, and with the faces you keep in a jar by the front door, we were. But quietly, privately, there was a seething rivalry and resentment between us. She was super pretty, athletic and a smart kid, but so was I at her age, and she always felt I judged her by who I was and what I had done at her age, whatever that age may be.

It was unfair, I guess, but I was trying to help her avoid some of the mistakes I made, the biggest being getting pregnant and having her at such a young age. In a sense I guess I've always been punishing her for robbing me of my life right at a time when a baby was the last thing I wanted….Mrs. Robinson syndrome, I guess.

Anyway, that was a long-winded introduction, still want to hear the rest? The not-so-proud parts?"

"Mae, I didn't want to hear *any* of it to begin with; we all have baggage, everyone, no big deal, that's life. Life's messy, it just is, end of story. My suggestion - drop the bag of bricks."

He looked at her and noticed the age spots on her forearm and the back of her hand; he never really noticed them before. If you focused, you could see a lot of them, camouflaged by a golden tan.

"Okay, if you don't want to hear it, forget it; forget I ever mentioned it."

Mae started to sulk, ever so subtly sticking out her lower lip; she was a pretty good sulker.

Cord looked, really looked, at the women with which he spent the night. She had attractive blonde, shoulder-length hair; not many sixty-plus year-olds could get away with that, but she did. She had high cheekbones and intense, blue eyes; her collar bone was pronounced and her neck muscles revealed whenever she spoke. Her lips were thin and aristocratic; a pale red, sans makeup.

He liked her, C thought to himself, he really did. He wondered how long this one would last; probably not very.

"Okay, okay, if you want to tell your story, tell it, but it better have good sex in it."

Cord smiled at her and settled back in his seat.

She continued.

"Anyway, she's sixteen, a junior in high school, no real steady or serious boyfriend to speak of yet, double-dates here and there. She's beautiful for sure, and has loads of guy-friends, but she's more into her dancing and schoolwork than boys.

Then she meets a guy. And you can tell this one is different. And, just like my mistake, go figure, he's a senior wrestler at school. Some sort of cruel joke. This time, though, she's the youngster, not him.

Now this young man is handsome, with a great body; a catch for any girl in the looks department. And he's a stellar athlete; a national-caliber wrestler, with serious scholarship potential, at a decent school. But he's dumb as a stump, with dead-end parents; sound familiar? I swear, not making this up.

[Mae held up her hand]

In all honesty, he actually seemed like a nice kid; he was always polite to me and my husband, courteous, the whole package, sans brains, of course.

Anyway, I see this starting to get pretty serious in a hurry. She's caught up in the whole first serious boyfriend act and he's a catch that all the girls want; he's all about lassoing one of the best-looking girls in the school, who everyone knows has been on the sidelines, untouched, so to speak; a coup for both of them. Plus, honestly, in his defense, I think he really liked her; he wasn't just a player – he liked my daughter, and treated her super-nice, as far as I could see. But sleeping with her, her being a virgin, was a *big* bonus for him – and I knew, I could see in how they acted, that sex was quickly becoming front and center, and he was ready to take.

It was clearly time to have a talk with her.

So I sit her down, and remind her about how I had her at nineteen, unplanned, and though she is the love of our life, nineteen was too young to have a child, and at sixteen she's just a kid herself, and certainly has to put those kind of things out of her head - period. If he's a good boy, a truly good boy, he'll understand, and wait. If not, you don't need him.

You know the speech; I actually thought I did a good job. And it seemed, for once, I got through to her. She smiled, listened, nodded to everything I said; but you know, in hindsight, she never actually said she agreed….she never said the words. That was the kind of thing she would do - agree, or seem to agree, but not really....verisimilitude. She was good, *very good,* as such things.

Anyway, this boy, his name was Loe, Loe Bryson; he ultimately joined the Navy and made a career out of it. I always liked that name, Loe.

Anyway, Loe starts coming around less, and she doesn't talk about him as much, and I figure my talk did the trick. She got the message, listened to her mother, for once, a miracle in and of itself, but anyway, end of story.   Maybe this was the turn in our relationship, where things might get better. Success on all fronts.

And so the issue goes back-burner; I always had too many other fires to deal with, and this one is out.

About two weeks later, I happened to come home early in the afternoon, unexpectedly – I can't even remember why. But I'm never home at that time, for sure. And see Loe's bike by the back door, leaning against the house, in the driveway. She never said anything about Loe coming over after school; her home alone with an eighteen-year old boy was not something she could do without permission. Especially *that* boy.

[Mae closed her eye for a few moments and let out a long sigh. Thinking about a story is one thing, speaking the acts aloud are another]

So I go inside, not quietly, but not extra noisily either, in the back door. The house is silent; no television or stereo playing - no one to be seen. I take off my shoes, and I walk through the downstairs, toward the staircase to the second floor.

No one downstairs.

I stop at the bottom of the steps and strain to listen; I don't hear anything. That's good, I think. Maybe they aren't even home. I'm a bit hopeful, and embarrassed at thinking the worst.

So I start up the steps; these steps are carpeted and quiet; the kind kids coming home late would love - no creaks, no noise. Not a one. I get to the top of the steps, and to the right is the master suite, down the hall to the left is her room.

So I start left, to see if they are holed up in her room, when I hear talking to my right, coming from *my* bedroom. Now, almost immediately, my blood starts to boil; she *knows* my bedroom is off limits, *especially* when I'm not home. She knew that all the way back to being a little kid. It was just a rule I had – stay out of my bedroom – it is not for play, and not for exploring. And my bed, it was always made neat and crisp, for me to sleep in, not for kids to play on. So this blood-boil erupts, knowing she is in my room, along with what I sensed was coming.

So I sneak into my dressing room, which has a door directly into my bedroom; the view is of the back of the headboard; the bed, which is a huge full-tester, a real show-stopper, sits freestanding in the middle of the room; so you can walk right up to the back of the headboard.

And you can pretty much figure what I see. There are my daughter's bare legs, white socks still on her feet, sticking up in the air like flagpoles, on his shoulders, just from the knees down to her feet, and I see Loe, facing the dressing room, fucking my daughter, *on my bed!*

[Cord could see Mae getting upset, thirty years later]

And they're on *my* side of the bed to boot, which wasn't an accident on her part, trust me. She was fucking him and mocking me and my speech at the same time….multi-tasking. *[Mae shook her head at the indignity]*

Now the mother in me wants to run in there screaming, throwing him off of her, my innocent, impressionable child, call his parents, call the police – he's eighteen and she's a minor - press charges, banish her to her room for life, you know, the whole nine yards. All that ran through my head in less than ten seconds.

Now, do you think that's the big secret story Cord? A mother walking in on her sixteen-year old having sex? Hardly.

It's that I *didn't* run in, like I should have, and create a scene. That's what I should have done, what someone normal in that situation would have done, right? What any good mother would have done for her daughter.

But I didn't. Not even close.

Instead, I did something that to this day I don't have an explanation for, I'm mortified and disgusted and embarrassed to even say it out loud. I just don't know why I did it – I don't. Maybe I saw myself, all those years ago, maybe not. Maybe I felt threatened, because here was this gorgeous sixteen-year old young girl, lying in my bed, coming into maturity, not needing my wing anymore. Not that she ever wanted my wing; she was her father's daughter – I was always an afterthought. She resented me because I resented her, having her so young. And since my pregnancy had profoundly affected my early years, not in a good way, and I told her so, her mocking of my advice hurt; it made me angry and spiteful. I felt….dismissed.

For one of those reasons, or all of those reasons, maybe none of those reasons, which all flashed by in a couple seconds, I didn't run in [*Mae squeezed her eyes shut, and told the next part without looking at Cord*].

Instead, and this just kind of happened, I didn't think it through, or plan it in any way, I just kinda slowly stepped out from behind the door, and stood still looking down the hall, from the dressing room, with my finger over my lips, in a shush sign, waiting for poor Loe to look up from all his hard work, having his way with my daughter, to see me. As I stand there, quietly, all I can hear is the bed groan, him breathing hard and her head lightly hitting the headboard, *my headboard*, as he's fucking her. Surreal.

You would have thought I would be nervous, or my blood would have been boiling – my face beet-red - or I would have been crying, or something, *anything*! But I felt *nothing;* just watching him voyeur, having sex with my daughter, like some perverted observer.

And then, and I remember like it was still yesterday, I felt a pulse of energy in my crotch; the kind of debilitating adrenaline rush you get when you crack open a test and don't know the answer to the first question, or the second, or the third, and you feel helpless...and the helplessness spreads until your extremities tingle, and you go numb.

So I just watched him, like he was in slow motion, having his way with my virgin daughter, my only child. Until, after a few moments, but it felt like forever, he looks up, and sees me.

Then he stops pumping; just like that, he's frozen, and stares at me.

He doesn't instinctively jump off her, like most guys would, right? Wouldn't you have done that – jump and run? But he doesn't do that, not at all; he just stops and stares at me. I thought that was the strangest thing; why didn't that kid just jump up and run? Or at least make a noise, an *Uh-Oh!* Something, anything, to tip off my daughter that big trouble was coming. But he didn't; it was surreal, it really was. I can't believe I'm even saying this out loud. And then I hear my naïve, pure, virginal daughter speak.

'What? What's the matter?'

She whines; she sounded positively irritated that he stopped ramming her head into the headboard.

[Mae stopped herself and just sat silent, eyes still squeezed shut – she wasn't sure she could say the rest – how did this ever happen?]

With my finger still over my lips, telling him to keep my presence silent, I clenched my fist and thrust it horizontally, slowly punching the air back and forth, like a piston, telling Loe it's okay, just keep fucking my underage, virgin daughter, just keep doing her.

[Mae's face contorted, disgusted by her own words; she covered her face and spoke through her hands]

The poor kid doesn't know what to do.

So he slowly starts up again, kind of erratic, looking at me intently, scared, waiting for the next set of instructions, and wondering if I had a butcher's knife behind my back, or something. I'm sure he's wondering how quick he can get up and run when I pull out my gun.

I only wish that was what I did.

But instead, I watch him go back to the business at hand, and he must be good, because all I hear is my daughter moaning in pleasure, talking in gasps about how much she loves his cock and how good he makes her feel whenever they fuck, which is apparently often. I can't believe I'm hearing these words from my daughter's lips, a girl I thought was still a virgin. I had no clue, none.....*none*.

So I slowly take my finger from my mouth, stop the hand-pumping gesture, and nod my head in the affirmative, telling him to continue as-is. Keep violating my daughter, while I watch.

[Mae dropped her hands, opened her eyes, clearly upset. Cord is simply looking at her, he isn't laughing or making jokes, just quietly listening, mouth slightly open]

It gets worse; should I stop?"

Cord whispered to her.

"Mae, you're telling this story for *you*, not me. If you want me to listen, I will, if you want to stop, just stop, and we'll never talk about it again, okay? Life is what it is, and does what it does, and regret doesn't do any good – it doesn't fix a fucking thing. I heard that line in a movie once, something like that, and never forgot it, because it's true. Everybody does shitty things at one time or another, including your daughter, even to people they love."

[Mae reached across the table and reached for Cord's hand, which he gave her; she squeezed it, forced a small smile and closed her eyes tight again]

"I just stared at Loe as I slowly started to unbutton my blouse, one button at a time. And he's watching me, intently. It seems like it takes me forever to finish; I can't imagine how she doesn't know I'm there.

850

My white silk top falls apart, now fully open, so he can see my whole front above my skirt. I unsnap my bra, and slowly drop it into my hand, which I then drop to the floor, letting him eye my breasts, the ones you didn't care too much about last night.

But I could tell he liked them; I could tell by how he was starting to pump her harder, more wild, like an animal.

And right then, I knew he wasn't having sex with her anymore, he was having sex with me, and me with him. My daughter was a bystander.

[Mae studied Cord for the look of disgust she expected, but he didn't give it to her....he just stared and listened to her confess]

And that's when the adrenaline, that debilitating helpless throb between my legs, the inability to help my daughter, changed to anger, and to lust. It was then I knew I wasn't done, not by a long shot. He wasn't going to just see my tits, he was going to get the whole package.

So I slowly ran both my hands up the outside of my thighs, up under my skirt, grabbed my panties and slid them down my legs, letting them drop to my ankles. I stepped out of them, then shimmied up the front of my skirt, giving him a full view of my pussy. I could tell he liked what he saw.

I extended the tip of my tongue out and licked my upper lip, running my hand down through the hair between my legs, while he continued to fuck her.

I sat back on my *bergere*, picked my legs up and spread them in the air, just like my daughter was spread, pulled my lips apart and buried my middle finger, till it couldn't go in any further, while he watched.

And I was wet, *very* wet. I don't think I was ever more sexually charged than I was right then, ever.

And I couldn't believe that kid didn't finish right then and there, but he didn't. He had staying power, for sure; pretty impressive for a young kid.

I knew for sure I was going to come quick, fingering myself, and I actually thought about the idea of coming at the same time she did, or he did, or both, that was what was actually going through my head *[Mae shook her head in disbelief]*.

Can you believe I did any of this?

Thankfully that never happened. I only got a couple strokes in; once he saw me playing with my pussy, he was pretty much finished. And in his excitement at seeing me, and pumping her wild, he forgot to pull out; that was the only birth control they apparently employed, the *pull-out* method.

Well it didn't work that time; he came inside her, most of it anyway, the last of it ended up on my sheets. He didn't know what to do; he didn't know what I was going to do.

Neither did I.

She knew he came inside her, even though he tried to deny it, saying he held it and came on the sheets, pointing to the evidence. While they argued, and she was yelling at him, both still in my bed, what did I do?

[Mae smirked in disgust]

I picked up my bra, kicked my panties under the chair and hustled downstairs like a child myself. Back on the bra went, I fixed my blouse, then made a lot of noise to let her know I was home, unexpectedly, and soon found the two of them standing by my side, looking a bit harried.

'You know the rules about boys in the house without my okay? What's going on?'

I asked her, innocently.

'Just studying, lost track of time, sorry she didn't call first, it's not like I can't trust her.'

She says. The whole thing a big set of lies.

And me, the hypocrite, listening to her while standing next to her boyfriend in the kitchen without my underwear on, lying to her at the same time about my whole role in this charade. And turned on by the whole thing to boot, pretty pathetic *[Mae just shook her head]*. Poor Loe, never even made eye contact; he just stared at the floor, waiting for the hammer to drop.

But I didn't drop it.

Instead, I asked if they were hungry; maybe I'd treat them to a pizza. I told Loe to get in the car; he and I would go get it, to give me a chance to get to know him a little better. He looked at me in horror, but she was actually okay with it; it would give her time to go upstairs and check to see if all was okay on the bed, you know, stains and things on my side of the sheets, pull them tight and crisp, like I always left them *[Mae had an angry inflection in her tone]*.

So Loe and I got in the car and drove to the pizza parlor. We took quite awhile to get back; I had other plans for that young man."

"Mae, what did you do? Did you threaten him?"

Mae just shook her head in regret.

"Oh no, did you bang that kid? You fucked him, didn't you?"

"What I already told you is bad enough; what I did, what we did, what I made him do....*[Mae didn't even finish the sentence]*."

I'm sure he needed counseling after that, I know I did. Turns out, years later, I found out he was only seventeen, not eighteen like he said, not that I needed anything else to make the story worse.

Anyway, after we were done doing what we did, I ended up dropping him at home; we never did get that pizza, and we came to an understanding with respect to my daughter.

We never saw him again, nor did she. I don't know what story he used to end it, I gave him some ideas. But she never found out what I did that day, none of it. And he never came back for his bike; we sold it, months later, at a garage sale, for a buck.

[Mae took her first sip of tea since the story began]

Pretty bad huh?"

Mae let out a long, low breath, staring at Cord.

"I'm trying to think of one that can top it....I'm still thinking."

C said, deadpan.

"But it didn't end there, not by a *long shot*."

"Good God, Mae, you're scaring me."

"She got pregnant of course; it always happens, and it happened because of me, getting that kid all worked up so he forgot to pull out *[Mae shook her head]*!

And when she couldn't hide it from us any longer, she cried and cried, confessing to having sex with Loe, saying it was the first time they did it, and that she didn't want to do it, and they did it in her bed while they were studying - he pressured her - and that she broke up with him because of what he did.   All lies, of course.

But I certainly couldn't correct the record and call her on it, now could I? Have Loe come over for *his* version of events?   That would hardly do, now would it? Thank goodness my husband, ever pragmatic, did not insist on involving the boy or his parents.

She wanted to keep the baby, like I kept her, I guess. She said *she* could handle it, implying that I couldn't, and didn't, with her *[Mae snorted in disgust]*.

Obviously, I wouldn't let her keep it, nor would I let her abort; we were raised Catholic you know, so that was out of the question."

[Cord stared at her, incredulous]

"You had sex with a minor, with your sixteen-year old daughter's *boyfriend* no less – and God knows what depraved acts you performed, right after you watched him having sex with *her*, in some kind of weird threesome that even I couldn't think up, and doesn't have a name as far as I know, maybe we can call it a *Mae-some*, and yet you couldn't let her get an abortion because you're a *good Catholic*? Are you kidding me?"

C chuckled in disbelief.

"It made sense at the time. You don't have to make fun of me, you know."

['Sorry' Cord mouthed to her, shaking his head]

"Anyway, she carried to term; the baby was tiny, and it didn't really show till late, at which time she went away for awhile, and came back and resumed the life of a now seventeen-year old.   No one knew, not even Loe, just the two of us, and my husband, of course, and the aunt she went to stay with."

"What ever happened to the baby, any idea?"

C asked.

"No I don't.   It went up for adoption and we forbade anyone from contacting us, ever. I try not to think about it, about the fact that I have, or had, a granddaughter, somewhere. And it's a topic that's never discussed in our family, ever. This is the first time I've even spoken about it in years....many, many years. You know, she's forty-seven now, and never had any kids, any other kids, anyway.   She did that on purpose, I know she did. Never married either. So I have no grandkids, well, none that I know.

[Mae shook her head]

You know, one of the worst parts, and I know I already said it, is knowing she got pregnant in the first place because of me, standing there; I don't know how I've ever lived with that, with any of it, really. How did that ever happen? Aren't mothers and daughters supposed to be best friends? Aren't they supposed to have some kind of special bond? Aren't they?

[Mae just frowned, dejected....sad]

So that's the story; do you believe me?"

[She was kind of hoping he wouldn't]

"Oh, trust me, I believe you. I don't think *anyone* could make that one up."

C said sarcastic.

"Am I really that bad a person? What kind of mother does that?"

Cord just looked at her sympathetically, as he stood up.

"Mae, I'm the wrong person to judge anyone, trust me. And I'm sure your daughter turned out fine. Funny, in that whole long, detailed story, you never *once* said her name; in fact, until today, I never even knew you *had* a daughter. What *is* her name, by the way?"

"It doesn't matter, not central to the story."

Mae said, looking down at the table.

"Uh huh, afraid I might be the next Loe? She sounds hot? Where's she live? I'd like to meet her, Mrs. Robinson."

No answer; then one came, quietly.

"She's not your type."

"Uh huh. Yeah, I can see all is well with Mae and the mystery daughter; glad you got all those old issues worked out."

Mae ignored him, as she got up to get her keys, to drive him home. C thought for a moment, shook his head while looking at the floor and laughed to himself, waiting for her by the back door.

"What?"

She said to his snicker.

"Just so you know, not to make you feel worse, but if you think that little story stayed between you and your boyfriend for the last thirty years, you're delusional; Loe told that story a thousand times, and every guy told it to ten more. I'm surprised *I* never heard it before. And he was in the Navy? Forget it! You're a sex legend, Mae, and you don't even know it. The absolute, ultimate MILF. And although it would be hard to top that story, you can be sure the version floating around thirty years later beats it, by a long shot, and they *all* know what happened in that car on the way for pizza, by the way, even if I don't. Guys have been jerking off to that one for the three decades; you were probably in the *Penthouse Forum* for years. And now with the Internet, good God!"

Mae looked at C incredulous; never once in thirty years did it ever, even remotely, occur to her that Loe might have told that story to anyone; she figured it was a secret between just two. *She* certainly never told anyone. And now, for the first time, she realized how right Cord probably was, and how naïve she had been. She was probably all over the Internet, and she didn't even tell Cord what they did in the car, and elsewhere; she couldn't bring herself to relive all those details out loud, even with him. *Oh my God*, she thought.

C laughed out loud, seeing the look of utter, horrible enlightenment on her face.

Then Mae simply shrugged; unable to do anything about it, it was best to just put it out of her mind. That was a classic Lilly move. Cord saw the horror had passed, resignation set in.

"Well, not for nothing, but suffice to say *you win*, Mae, you certainly win. That one beats my story, hands down - my mom's underwear, you know."

"You think so? And are you the prize I win?"

And just before they went out the door, she smiled and kissed him, smack on the lips – it was long and dry.

CHAPTER 89 – THIS COULD BE GOOD....OR THIS COULD BE REAL, REAL BAD

The same Sunday morning.

The window to the right of the bedroom fireplace was open; the southern yard, landscaped with large beds of dark-green liriope, violet rhododendron, red and white azaleas, peonies and an expanse of green lawn edged by a bluestone sidewalk along Third Street, lay below. Edamame occupied a good portion of the sill; as usual, her back was pressed against the window screen, intently watching a pair of nuthatches work their way, headfirst, down the *Cryptomeria,* the prehistoric conifer set against the south side of the front porch. She gave a big stretch, lost interest in the birds, and closed her eyes, napping on the sill.

Life was good being Carol's cats.

Carol laid in bed, staring at the ceiling, listening to a cacophony of morning birds, gray catbirds, blue jays, cardinals, others, all largely drowned by the loud cackles and calls of a murder of crows who congregated, like clockwork, at the very top of a large sugar maple in the Park, directly across from the Episcopal Church, every morning at 7 am. Twenty to thirty of them, every morning, same time, year in and out. It was the crows who woke Carol up this morning, which wasn't unusual; they were a reliable alarm.

She slowly spread her legs open, making the lower half of a snow-angel in bed; she loved to feel the cool sheets across her skin as she moved her legs open and shut, like a kid. It was a Sunday morning, the sun was shining, the start of a beautiful lazy day.

She really loved being in Belvidere on the weekends, especially these days.

She got up, still in her mid-thigh nightie, and slipped into a navy silk bathrobe, shuffled down the steps in bare feet, and pulled out the coffee machine. She opened the inner front door, it softly moaned like old doors do, and grabbed the knob of the large, black outer door, swung it open, and let the morning sun in, filling the foyer with summer.

Wow, she thought, much different look than the cloak of last night. She was a bit ashamed of the whole fiasco with Cord, but was at least glad nothing really happened and Earl was none the wiser. Ay would get over it, eventually. In the end, no harm, no foul.

It was the first time since last night that she wondered what happened to Cord after he turned the corner of Third Street and disappeared into the night. She wondered if Earl would come up to the Park and run today solo, since she was pretty sure Cord wouldn't show his face, not for awhile anyway. Not that she would blame him.

She stepped through the porch and down onto the front walk to retrieve four scattered papers, the *New York Times*, the *Wall Street Journal*, the *Newark Star-Ledger* and the *Express-Times*, the latter being the local daily rag, which was somewhat of a dim bulb, but if you wanted information on local-local goings-on, you had to read it. To her, it was part of the fun that was the sticks; she actually enjoyed reading it, an easy, calorie-free *aperitif*, before more serious newspaper reading to follow.

She already had the gloriously lazy day planned; she would curl up in her favorite chair on the porch, dissect and spread the papers, reshuffle the sections and stack them in the order she wanted to tackle, and then spend countless hours reading all three, broken by trips inside for coffee, light snacks and an early evening cigar, with a glass of red wine. No checking emails, no cell phone gabbing, no work.   Not today - she woke with the lazy-hat on. And she was so happy last night was over; it was a fresh day, with no problems and no mistakes - not yet anyway.

She couldn't wait to see Earl. She missed seeing him all week; she found herself more often looking forward to his visits, greeting his smiling face, knowing Earl had no agenda other than the joy he seemed to have in simply seeing her. That was nice, simple and sincere. They do grow guys like that….a pleasant discovery.

She gathered the papers, tucked them under her arm and looked about the Park. Already a couple sets of walkers were taking their daily spin around the Square, including the Episcopalian priest, Ryan, and his longtime partner, Tommy. They were twenty yards down the sidewalk across the street, heading her way.

That was another thing she loved about this place; an openly gay priest and his boyfriend walking around the Park, and it was no big deal, nor had it been for years. Two great guys and good neighbors, nothing more, nothing less.

"Hey guys, morning."

Carol called out and waved, standing in her bathrobe and bare feet.

"Morning Carol; how're the cats?"

"Fat and happy."

They smiled.

"That's the best way to be; we always look for them up on the porch roof."

Tommy said, as they power-walked by; they would put in a mile or so every morning; the standard routine.

Carol heard the bang and rattle of metal from an old military-looking truck as it passed in front of the Courthouse down on Second Street, a block away. It was a short-bed truck, painted black, with an all-white cab section, sporting big, black letters on the driver's door. It simply said:

COAL

Belvidere still had a coal business, run by the local hardware store, delivering anthracite down basement chutes for about thirty long-standing accounts scattered around Town. Someone was getting a summer delivery of coal; one of the old-timers trying to save a few cents per pound on the spot coal market; she smiled at the thought of the pennies saved.

A coal truck, she just saw a *coal truck* rumble by, how cool was that. That was one of the small stitches that held the allure of this Town together for her. It was a non-event; a passing-by of some relic of a earlier time, in her mind anyway, that made her feel nostalgic, and good, about this place. Tell someone you saw an old coal jalopy rattle by on Sunday morning as you picked up the newspaper and waved to the gay priest across the street as the crows jawed overhead and she doubted anyone would wax poetic about it, but here, to her, it was what weekends were all about.

She smiled at her good fortune.

Carol two-skipped up the porch steps and was about to disappear inside to grab that first cup of coffee, when she noticed something out of place on the porch, something she missed on her way out the door, set off to the left, lying quietly on the sofa.

Oh boy, this could be good….or this could be real, real bad.

864

CHAPTER 90 – SHE WAS *REAL*

It was his favorite one, by far.

No matter how fast Earl could run, she could keep up, effortlessly, laughing and smiling the whole way, holding his hand, always holding his hand, and squeezing it tight.

He swore he could feel it.

From the Park bench to the boat ramp chairs measured four and a half blocks, and it was always a sprint. Out came the chairs from their hiding place in the brush, out came the bags of bread, off came the shoes and into the water his feet went, laughing and splashing away. No matter, the ducks didn't mind the laughing and splashing one bit, to them, it meant bread, lots of bread, was on its way. They weren't afraid of his big feet, not one bit.

Earl looked at Carol and smiled; she was still holding his hand, sitting next to him. Her feet were pulled up on the chair, knees to her chest, like she always did when she was happy.

'How was school Sweetie?'

'Good.'

'Just good?'

'Yeah, just good.'

'Do you want to talk, or just sit and feed the ducks?'

'You talk, I like to listen.'

And so she did.

She talked about the ducks, and she talked about Lilly, and Uncle Frank, and Uncle Sam, about Farmer Gill's farm, and the cows, and how they'd run across the field when they saw Earl, because he always had something special to feed them, and they loved when he scratched their heads and necks, licking his hands and arms with their thick, rough pink tongues. And she talked about rainbows and the River, with all the big fat channel cats lazily swimming along the bottom, ready to suck on your toes if you waded too far out. She talked about Mrs. Gregson, his favorite teacher, and how much she liked him - how she'd always tell her that Earl was her favorite student, ever, and that he was such a good boy, even when he was bad. She talked about the sun, and the moon and how the cars slowly crossed the narrow bridge just upstream, and all the racket the tires made on the open metal grating, and how that sound always reminded her of the boat ramp. And baby beef ravioli and Brussels sprouts and flank steak and yellow rice and ice cream, all his favorites; she talked about it all, and he listened while a swarm of hungry mallards pulled the bread from between his fourteen-year old toes. He laughed as they tickled him, and she smiled at the show, like she always did.

And all the while, as Earl leaned forward, his mom ran her hand gently over his scalp, running her fingers through his black hair, down his neck, where she would draw little circles and shapes on his neck; that was his favorite part. He would scrunch his shoulders when she did it, because it tickled, just a bit….but he never tired of the show, nor did he want her to stop, ever.

Carol leaned over and whispered in his ear, as she placed her hand on his shoulder and gently squeezed it, then she rubbed it, and squeezed it some more.

"Earl, Earl."

She breathed lightly, but he didn't answer. Then his mother whispered gently in his ear.

'You know what? A little bird tells me you have a girlfriend.'

'What! I don't have a girlfriend!'

Earl looked surprised and horrified, all in one scrunched face.

'She's sweet, Earl, good for you Sweetie, good for you. I like her; I like her a lot.'

'Hey! Stop teasing, I don't have a girlfriend! I'm only fourteen!"

She gently rocked his shoulder, a little harder this time.

But he didn't want to wake up; these were the best ones, the dreams he never wanted to end. He never ran out of bread, the ducks never left, his mother never ran out of stories, and she was happy.

Earl turned to look at her, and she smiled at him with the face of a mother who couldn't be prouder of a son she loved more than anything….a love that hurt. She didn't want to go, but she had to, for now…for awhile.

'Earl, Sweetie, wake up, it's time to wake up….come on."

He slowly, reluctantly, opened his eyes, and the boat ramp faded, the River disappeared into a sea of white and he found himself staring at a porch ceiling, and to his surprise, to his utter delight, Carol was looking down at him, smiling, her hand still resting gently on his shoulder.

And she was *real*.

Carol's cheeks blushed; she felt flush, like you do when you say something unexpected, without thinking, that just comes out, like a blurt. Not that she didn't feel it was the right thing to say, it just wasn't something she thought she was ready to say, out loud anyway, to him.

"Did you hear what I just called you?"

Carol asked him tentatively.

Earl slowly shook his head in the affirmative, in slow motion.

"I'm sorry Earl, it just kind of came out."

"That's okay, my mom always calls me *Sweetie*; that was her favorite thing to call me."

Carol stuttered a bit.

"Earl, I didn't mean to say anything that would remind you of your mom; I'm sorry."

"It's okay, I talk to her all the time, she doesn't mind."

Earl conveniently failed to mention his mom's comment about the *girlfriend* part; he would rather die.

"Uh, okay."

Was all Carol came up with.

The subject changed, and she asked Earl the question she didn't necessarily want the answer to.

"Earl, why are you sleeping on my porch?"

And suddenly all the goodness in his dream, and all the happiness in seeing Carol, faded with the memory of why he was there to begin with, sitting in the Park last night, watching her and Cord, together.

"Is C your boyfriend?"

That's exactly what she was hoping *not* to hear.

She sighed, her shoulders drooped, and she proceeded to sit on the tiniest edge of the cushion, by his head. Normally Earl would move, being so close to her made him nervous, but this time, he just laid there, last night's sadness returned.

"Why do you ask that?"

Carol whispered.

"I saw him on your porch last night; I was sitting in the Park. He was supposed to watch *The Blob* with me, but he said he was tired and was going to bed after he read. But maybe he'd come down. But he never did. So I went to look for him, to see if he was okay, because he's my best friend. C said he might go for a walk, so I went to the boat ramp, but he wasn't there, and then I went to Park, that's where we both go together all the time. Anyway, I heard him on your porch. Is he your boyfriend? I hope so, because C is *really* nice, and he would be a good boyfriend to you. He's my best friend you know."

Carol smiled; only Earl would say such a selfless thing, no guy in the world but Earl.

"Cord's not my boyfriend, Earl, he's just a friend, that's all. And I probably shouldn't tell you this, but I will. Cord came here last night to talk to me about *you [Carol lightly placed the tip of her pointer on Earl's forehead, and held it there for a long moment]*. It was some secret thing he wanted to tell me, some kind of neat surprise for *you,* but we got into a little argument about something else and he never told me what it was. That's why he didn't watch *The Blob* with you; he had been planning all week to come see me to talk about you and your surprise. He told me you were his *best friend* too."

Earl sat up like a bolt.

"Really, a surprise? What kind of surprise? Will I be surprised? *Oh boy, I can't wait*!"

And just like that, the issue was resolved. Carol smiled; the truth, it's a pretty cool thing, when you tell it.

"I can't tell you because even I don't know! He never told me; maybe he'll tell me this morning when you two come back to run."

Carol knew that was unlikely.

"Oh no! What time is it? I'm in big trouble if Lilly wakes up – I never left a note last night, telling her where I was going, and she'll be worried!"

Earl got up to run home, looking for the shoes he kicked off last night.

"Earl, you find your shoes, I'll pick you up out front; we'll get you home in two minutes or less, promise!"

Earl just stared at her.

"In your car?"

"We'll I'm not bringing you piggy-back; find your shoes!"

With that Carol dashed inside, still in her bathrobe, grabbed her keys and ran out to start the *Spider.* She slid behind the seat, and Earl was already inside, a sardine squeezed in the passenger seat, his head even with the top of the roll bar.

"I couldn't sit in the back seat; you don't have one."

Earl said apologizing for sitting next to her.

She just laughed and put her hand on the side of his face; to his surprise, he didn't pull away. Her hand felt smooth and warm on his skin, just like his mom's used to feel, and he liked it, he liked it a lot. He didn't even want to think about her being in her bathrobe, right next to him; he didn't want to think about that at all.

"I don't think it's such a good idea for you to drop me off in front of the house....sorry."

Earl whispered, his head down.

"No worries, I understand, I'll drop you in front of the old Firehouse, and you can run the last half-block."

"Okay! Wow, I always wanted to drive in this car! It's red; I like red!"

Earl ran his hand across the tawny leather on the dashboard and the sculpted seat.

Carol opened the floor console and pulled out her mirrored shades and handed them to Earl.

"Not sure if they'll fit; but you can't drive in this car without the shades."

Earl looked at her with a little-boy smile and slipped them on; they were a bit tight....actually more than a bit tight, but doable. He checked his look in the mirror, placed his elbow on the open window and struck the pose of a seasoned co-pilot.

And with that they were off – their very first date.

872

CHAPTER 92 – IS SHE YOUR GIRLFRIEND?

"Do you want to go past your friend's house, on the Park?"

Mae asked in mock innocence, wanting to show-and-tell her prize.

"Just drive down Oxford."

C snapped dismissive.

"What? Embarrassed to be seen with me? I'd like her to know where you ended up."

"She doesn't care; neither do I. She's just a friend."

"You mean like I'm just a *friend*?"

Cord tilted his head toward her in annoyance.

"Mae, please; let's just get across Town, okay?"

She clammed up, mad at his tone.

He was pissed, reliving the whole porch incident as he drove within two blocks of Carol's place. There would be no run today, that's for sure. He had to figure out how to get out of it with Earl, without spilling the beans about his run-in with Carol last night.

As they came to the stop sign at Oxford and Hardwick, across from the Belvidere Hotel, a red blur went jackrabbit on Hardwick, the cross-street in front of them, racing the intersection. To his utter surprise, he saw Earl's body stuffed inside the blur; two pounds of bologna in a one pound sack, wearing designer shades.

"What the fuck?!"

He not-so-whispered aloud.

"What?"

Mae said, missing the whole incident.

"Nothing, just talking to myself; come on, take a right, let's go!"

"Stop being so bossy! And it would be nice if you talked to me."

"Come down and see me at work, if I ever get there; I'll be happy to talk to you."

C said dismissively, distracted by the blur that just went by.

"Hey, don't be such a jerk!"

Mae snapped. But C ignored the comment, lost in thought. Mae clammed up a second time.

The *Mini-Cooper* took a right on Hardwick and a quick left on Water Street; the *Spider* was up ahead, letting Earl out on the side of the road.

"That little fucking bitch!"

Cord said aloud again, to himself.

"What? What is it?"

Mae said again; but C didn't answer, he just leaned forward in his seat, glaring out the windshield.

She must've got a hold of Earl this morning and told him everything about last night! Telling him about the whole fiasco, and putting her own innocent spin on it, of

course. Holy shit, now what is he going to tell Earl?
Exactly *what* made-up story did she fucking spill?

"Let me out by the Firehouse Mae. Stop, *right here;*
stop!"

Mae slammed on the brakes and pulled up behind the
Spider; Earl was just shutting the door.

"What are you doing? Why are you getting out here?"

Then she saw Earl.

"Thanks Mae, I'll see you later at the shop."

C said, de facto, already out of the car and shutting the
door behind him. She expected a goodbye kiss; she
didn't come close to one.

Carol saw the car pull up behind her, and she saw Cord
get out, as did Earl.

"Hey C, I got to ride in the *Spider*! I got to wear these
cool shades too! Carol said I could keep 'em! I like red
cars!"

"That's great Earl. What are you doing with Carol,
alone, so early on a Sunday morning?"

"He slept over; he's *amazing*....and such a gentleman
too."

Carol called out to Cord, but he didn't even look her
way; he wouldn't give her the satisfaction of even
acknowledging her words. Because of that, he didn't see
the bathrobe; that would have cinched it.

"I had a great time Earl, thanks; you're the best Sweetie.
I'll see you for breakfast in a little bit; I assume you're
coming alone?"

And with that, without waiting for the answer she knew she wouldn't get, she sped away, leaving the two of them in a little cloud of gritty dust. C still never looked at her, even as she drove away.

"Fucking cunt."

Cord whispered low to himself, shaking his head and eating her kicked-up dust for the second time in twenty-four hours.

"Slept over?"

C said, turning to Earl with raised eyebrows, seeing himself in the reflection of Earl's new shades.

Earl just blushed, and was about to talk, when the *Mini-Cooper* crawled up beside the two of them.

"Cord dear, thanks again for last night. I'll see you later; we're on for dinner?"

He leaned over and whispered something to her in the car, which Earl couldn't hear, then she drove away without another word. Earl looked at his friend, smiled wry, and asked the inevitable question.

"Is she your girlfriend?"

CHAPTER 93 – ESCAPADES IN A MINI-COOPER - *NO* DETAILS SPARED

"I told you Earl, I'm not going for breakfast; you're lucky I'm even running with you around this stupid fucking Park. You go solo, you seemed fine driving in the car with her; you two bonded."

"That's different! That was just because I was nervous about Lilly finding out! Thank God she was still asleep, so she never even knew I was out all night!"

"You didn't look too nervous to me, wearing those designer shades."

C snipped.

"Well I was."

"Regardless, I'm not going….have fun."

Earl looked at C in distress.

"Hey, Earl, I'm sorry about last night; sorry you had to sleep on the porch. I felt really bad lying to you, but it's because of the surprise, nothing more. Besides, as you know, she and I aren't getting along."

"What happened last night; why'd you leave?"

"What did *she* tell you happened last night?"

C said, trying to be nonchalant.

"Nothing, she didn't say anything – just that you got in an argument; she didn't tell me about what. Hey, did you really have a sleepover at Mae's?"

"Yeah, I did, but that's between you and me, Earl. Carol I'm sure figured it out, but no one else knows, and Carol doesn't talk to anybody anyway. So keep in under your hat. The person I gotta worry about blabbing the most is Mae; I'm sure she's got it half way round Brookfield by now."

They swung past Carol's house, starting the tenth and final lap. A couple moments passed, and Cord started in again.

"Let me tell you, though, she is fucking amazing; at sixty-six, she can still bang like a kid, and *good*! I'm in trouble Earl, that woman is gonna kill me, one way or another. Jesus, what a great cock-sucker too."

Earl blushed, but didn't say a single word, except.…*Wow*.

He wanted to ask Cord all the details about how he did it: what order, how long, who went first, what he said, what she said, did he do the whole book! Isn't that what you're supposed to do? The *Kama Sutra* is pretty darn long; did it take all night? But Earl was too embarrassed about all that stuff, even with Ay, so he didn't say anything more, just a single, monotone, *wow*.

Carol had been counting, so she knew this was the final lap coming round. She was reading on the porch, but except for Earl's *Hi* and histrionic wave at each pass-by, and her return wave, there was none of the usual banter. Cord never looked at her house, never even turned his head her direction, all ten laps; he didn't want to give her the satisfaction – he wanted to *punish* her, sulking like a little kid.

As they finished, Cord pulled up the front of his shirt, wiped his mouth and said to Earl.

"Have a good one buddy, I'll catch you later at Sam's, okay?"

Earl caught him by the arm, and held it firm, not letting go.

"I don't wanna go alone."

"Then you're not going, sorry. No-can-do Earl, not this time, and no amount of your usual whining is changing my mind."

Cord tried to wrest free, but that was pretty futile with Earl - he wasn't letting go.

"Earl, let go; *let go!*"

Nothing doing. The big man just stood there, with puppy-dog eyes, silently begging for Cord to cross the street with him.

Carol broke the stalemate.

"Oh, for God's sake, stop pouting like a baby! What? Never been scolded before? Come on, the eggs are waiting to be made; Earl and I will do all the work, like usual, and you can supervise and pretend you're in charge."

Carol yelled across the street. Earl smiled the biggest grin he could make, and that was pretty damn big. But Cord still wasn't ready to budge. He still had some pout left in him.

And that's when, in one swift motion, Earl scooped up C and threw him over his shoulder, like a small sack of potatoes. It was just about then that Cord realized it was inevitable that he was going back on that God-forsaken porch, the one he vowed he would *never* step on again. That vow lasted less than ten hours.

"Jesus Christ!"

He whined as Earl carried him across the street.

Breakfast was the usual routine, but there was less talk than normal. Cord was still sulking, and most of the yammering was Carol asking Earl questions, and him answering in succinct phrases, or asking Cord to answer that one. He knew it was childish, but Cord couldn't help himself, he wasn't letting her off the hook that easy.

Finally, after a little more than an hour, breakfast was done and the weekend routine was drawing to a close.

"Earl, if it's okay with you, why don't you let Cord stick around for awhile and tell me all about that big surprise he has for you, unless, of course, you want him to go with you, in which case, we will never be able to talk about it, and the surprise may never come; your choice Earl."

"I'm going! *Right now*!"

Earl yelled.

"Earl, I gotta get down to Sam's soon, I'm already running late. I can't stay here with her to talk; we'll do it some other day."

"He's right, Earl, we'll do it some other day, in a month or two, maybe longer, whatever; the surprise can wait for months, I suppose."

Earl's eyes bugged.

"No way! I'll cover for you, C, I'll talk to Sam, no problem. See ya!"

And before Cord could speak, Earl was out the door, running down the walk; in a flash, he was half way across the Park.

"Great."

Cord said aloud, so she could hear. He shook his head in disgust.

She walked over to him, and faced him, square on.

"Do you know what Earl said to me - the first thing he said when I woke him up, sleeping on the porch sofa? He said *you* were his best friend. And he thought you and I were boyfriend/girlfriend, and he said he hoped we were, because you're really nice, and you would be a good boyfriend to me. And he meant it, he really did. Can you believe that? You don't deserve him."

"Neither do you."

C said, with distaste.

She frowned and shook her head slowly in agreement.

"On that we agree."

And with that, she stuck out her hand in a truce, waiting for his to shake.

"I'm sorry about last night; what I said was wrong, and you didn't deserve it. I was feeling guilty, and took it out on you. We were both at fault, and we both hurt Earl, more than he will ever know. Friends?"

Cord looked at her hand a moment, frowned, and then slowly extended his, and shook hers gently.

"He **is** my best friend, regardless of what you think. So yeah, friends….and sorry…too."

They let their hands drop.

"Now, help me carry the dishes inside and tell me about this surprise we have planned for Earl. Oh, and of course, I want to hear all about it, escapades in a Mini-Cooper – *no* details spared."

CHAPTER 94 – DO THE FUCKING DISHES!

"There were no *escapades* in the Mini-Cooper."

C snarked.

"Uh huh, well where were they then?"

"I thought this was supposed to be all about Earl; you make a grand statement about misunderstandings, wrong-doings, you accuse me last night of being a pervert, and then you are right back into sex talk again, pumping me for gossip. Good God, maybe *you're* the pervert."

Truth be told, Carol was keenly interested in the backstory; it had been a long dry spell, sex was on her mind, and she needed new stories to get off on. And she figured he would want to brag about it anyway, so she'd give him the floor, to make him feel better about it. She was surprised he declined.

"Fine, I'm sure it was pretty quick anyway."

"Yeah, I wish."

C said poker-face, which made her smile, and jump right back in the gutter.

"You wish? Well, then I assume you got lucky last night."

She waited for him to speak, and he just stared at her, with a blank face. Nothing.

"Well? What happened? I know you want to talk about it."

She goaded.

"Maybe it would be best if I just showed you what happened? Do you want to go upstairs? I got the whole routine memorized; it'll take a couple hours."

"Okay, okay, smart-ass, back to Earl's surprise."

"Well, number one, I'm tired of hearing from him as to when you're going to finally start letting him watch the cats; so talk to Ji-Sue for God's sake, and let him start this week....he's killing me."

"Done; next."

"As you know, Earl's gonna be the big four-o this year, October 7th, so I thought it would be fun to throw him a surprise party - the key being the *surprise* part. No one knows about it yet, except you and me. I want to keep it a secret up until as close to the end as possible. I know I will probably need some help, and I need someone who no one likes or talks to in Belvidere....someone just like you."

"Thanks."

She carped.

"You're welcome."

"And what if I say no?"

"Number one, you can't - it's your chit payment, and number two, you won't, because it's for Earl, and you have a very big soft spot for the big guy."

She smiled at Cord.

"You know, I really do."

"I know you do, so do I. I'm actually wasting the chit on this, since you would do it anyway, but it's for a good cause, so I'll take one for the team. Let's lay out the plan; I got a couple of cool ideas - maybe we can decide who has to do what, and work our way back from the 7th - you know, set a timeline."

"This is so cool – what a great idea! I haven't done a surprise party in years. Okay, I'll write, you do the dishes."

C just stared at her, incredulous, with eyes that screamed audacity at the request.

"What? I make you breakfast every weekend I'm here, which is just about *every* weekend lately, and then Earl and I do the dishes while you stand around and pretend to *supervise*. You do it *every* fucking week, stand and watch us work.

Now it's your turn; do the fucking dishes!"

CHAPTER 95 – DARKEN MY DOOR, VULTURE-BOY...I LIKE THAT

Cord had been jawing for the past fifteen minutes or so, laying out the agenda for the day; it was clear he had been thinking about it for awhile – it was pretty detailed. Carol liked it, except for the fact she *might* not be able to join in for most of the day's events – she wanted to be integral, front and center, from the morning on, but realized it simply might not work out that way, not with the *Lilly* factor. But C assured her that possibility was remote, and the trio would most assuredly spend the day joined at the hip. And because of that fact, she didn't whine about it as much as she wanted to; she too was trying to be a team player, even though she knew Lillian would afford *her* no such courtesy. But this was all about Earl, and even in the remote chance that it went to shit, she was still happy with her later starring role in the surprise. And, just as important, she was happy that Cord used *this* as the chit.

Really happy in fact. It said a lot about Ay, and it made her regret even more how she treated him the night before. He really was, or could be at times - she corrected herself - a nice guy.

Cord was wiping down the counter, the finish to the dishes routine. As he stroked the green marble with the dish towel, he looked out the elliptical window over the sink, at the Methodist Church tower, the one Carol not-so-anonymously donated to the church several years earlier. She noticed the gaze.

"I love that church steeple."

"I know, I heard all about your *secret* donation. People have all sorts of opinions on that one, none of them very flattering."

"Yeah, I've heard 'em all too. But I really did it just because I like to look at it when I'm in here, and it never looked right, kind of squatty. Someone showed me an old postcard of how it originally looked, you know, horse and buggy days; someone lopped off the top third for some reason, I think it fell down in a storm, or something."

Cord didn't answer; he just stared long at the steeple, in silence. He wasn't sure why.

"What are you thinking?"

"Nothing in particular."

C said deadpan.

"Uh huh."

She answered, unconvinced.

He continued to stare at the steeple, as if deep in thought.

Looking at the back of his head, she spoke.

"You know, after the guys finished the steeple, the construction crew, the very next morning, I remember it was the first weekend in September, I came down to the kitchen to see it. I was so excited to look at the new top; like it looked almost a hundred years ago.

Anyway, I walk in the kitchen and look out the window, and you know what I see on my beautiful new steeple?

[C shrugged his shoulders, still facing away]

I'm mortified. Two huge vultures, perched side-by-side, right up against the copper finials! Big claws, *huge* claws, they almost looked too big, gripping the wood frame. And jet-black eyes....dead, black eyes.

Black vultures.

And I can't seem to take my eyes off them; they were up there for fifteen minutes or more, preening, scratching their beaks with those scary over-sized claws, like a big old dog scratches himself. And they were staring out into the distance with those dead eyes, turning their heads and staring some more, it seemed like they were looking at nothing and everything at the same time. Then they would make some noise, kind of a half hiss, half grunt, in unison, one-two....one-two. The kitchen window was open and I could hear them as clear as day, as if they were perched right beside me. I just watched them, mesmerized for fifteen minutes, maybe more – I don't know why."

"Fascinating, you really need to get out more."

C said sarcastic, as he turned to face her.

"And then one of them turned its back to me, and stretched open its wings to the sides, all the way out. It was *huge*, and it stood frozen in place. It looked like that Nazi insignia; you know what I'm talking about? It looked like a statue, fake. It was really creepy."

"That was an eagle, by the way, a Nazi eagle, not a Nazi vulture; but yeah, I know what you mean."

C snarked.

"Whatever, you know what I mean. You don't realize how big those birds are till they spread their wings; it was huge, and sitting up on top of the church, it seemed, I don't know, blasphemous. Kind of scary, like it was telling me something."

Cord chuckled.

"Afraid the Big Man really knew you just liked the look of the steeple? So he sent his vultures down to let you know he knew it wasn't providential, just some sort of selfish architectural dressing for the rich girl in Town? You know he knows these things; you can't hide from God – he's kind of like Santa, he *can* see what you're doing under the covers."

"You don't think that means something?"

Carol asked earnest.

"Yeah, I do; I think there are black vultures living around here that just found a neat new roost to spy road kill, and two of them had a meeting to check it out."

C said blunt.

"But I never saw them again, not after that first day, and that was a couple years ago."

She wasn't convinced.

"Well, apparently, it wasn't such a good lookout after all. Hey, remind me not to invest my money with you, vulture-girl; do your clients know you sit and stare at vultures on church steeples, wondering what you did wrong, and if the Big Man has got special messages for you? Not good for fund management relations; I'd keep that one under your hat."

Carol ignored his commentary.

"You know, I look up there every day I'm here; it's an anticipation thing, like going for the mailbox, or checking email – there's always the potential of getting something good....a surprise.

Well, coming into the kitchen every morning, the first thing I do is look out that window and check the steeple, to see what's up there. Over the past couple years since that thing was put up, it's usually empty. Day in, day out….empty. Every now and then, there are some crows or pigeons hanging out, mourning doves, but that's about it.

For years, no vultures, not a *single* vulture, after that first day. They never came back."

"Uh huh. And your point is?"

C said, bored with the conversation.

"Well, that's not exactly true, they did come back….once."

C looked at Carol, not so bored, waiting for the rest of the story.

"I came down in the morning, like I always do, and I looked up at the steeple, like I always do, expecting to see nothing but a steeple, which is what I always see.

But this time, staring right at me in the kitchen, like it was waiting for me, with those beady-black, lifeless eyes, was a lone black vulture. It was *huge*, much bigger than those other ones, the biggest bird I've ever seen. It was so big, it looked fake. And its wings were spread wide open, like a gargoyle, like it was going to reach out and grab me. It seemed to be looking right *through* me! I know it saw me standing by the sink, looking up at it, it *had* to. It was like it was waiting for me to come into the kitchen, to find him, to see him.

After years of seeing nothing up there, to walk in on that big bird, tip to wing tip, it took me aback. It was scary. Anyway, I ran to get my binoculars in the dining room, to get a better look. But when I got back, and it had to be less than thirty seconds, it was gone. No trace of where it went, no noise when it flew away, nothing. Just vanished.....gone, into thin air.

You know why that was so creepy?"

Carol asked Cord.

"Because you're a nut?"

He said.

"No, because that vulture was sitting up on the Methodist Church steeple looking down at me on a beautiful, sunny Friday morning in April, *this* April....April 21ˢᵗ to be exact. That's the same day, just a couple hours later, that I opened my front door and first saw *you* darken my door, vulture – boy."

Carol looked to Cord, waiting for the surprise reaction she expected to surface. But she got none.

C's eyes turned to ice, his face emotionless, a blank canvas. He stared straight through her, sans a single word. He didn't even realize he transformed; it was as if, for a bit, he was someone else.

It scared her. But just for second.

Because as quick as the shroud appeared, it faded away, as if it never happened, as if Cord blinked and missed the whole affair.

Then he simply cracked a wry smile, a friendly, familiar grin, and parroted her last words, followed by a chuckle.

*"Darken my door, vulture-boy....*I like that."

CHAPTER 96 – THREE WORDS HE DIDN'T WANT TO SAY: *LITTLE APPLE CREEK*

"That's pretty dramatic; what's it mean?"

"I was hoping you'd tell me."

Carol responded dry.

"You're scary; you really think that means something? Some harbinger of evil?"

She just stared at Cord, expecting an explanation.

He chuckled.

"Well, I'm not a nice guy, so maybe it does mean something, but I really can't help you; guess you have to ask the man upstairs, or downstairs, maybe one of them might have some answers. But I'll tell you one thing I *do* know, you better keep those fat cats off the porch roof. Black vultures don't just eat dead things, young lady, they swipe newborn pigs out of barns, that's what I've read, anyway. Your cats are just like furry piglets. And I don't expect they move too fast; easy pickings for big black birds."

"So you *do* know all about vultures! *Interesting!* How do *you* know they eat newborn pigs?"

"Oh, for God's sake, you *are* a fucking nut, you know that. Don't say I didn't warn you, about the cats, that is. And I'm a vegetarian, remember, I don't eat baby pigs, not anymore, anyway."

Cord leaned back against the counter.

"But I know what you mean by a close encounter, I had one once."

"Really, with a vulture?"

Carol said, earnest.

"No, not with a vulture; Jesus, get off the vultures already. I was running, alone, in the early morning, and I came upon this little jut of land called Brockton Point. It was a paved pathway, you know, for bikers and runners, tucked right along the bay. The path curved sharp around this little empty outpost, like a guard shack, only it was shaped like a tiny lighthouse, maybe it was a real lighthouse at one time, I don't know, but it was right on the bay, so it probably was real, a lighthouse, that is. Pretty spot.

Anyway, just as I turned this blind corner by this little lighthouse, right there in front of me, only a couple feet above my head, was a *huge* bald eagle – I mean big, suspended in air, like it was on a string, just waiting for me to come around the bend. I didn't startle it, it was already airborne when I saw it - like I said, it was like it was somehow waiting for me, hovering, knowing I was about to round the bend. It was really early in the morning, just past dawn, so no one was out on the path – not a soul in either direction, just me and the eagle.

The hair on the back of my neck and my arms tingled and I stopped dead in my tracks. I swear that eagle looked right *into* me – right through me, as if it *knew* something. It had hard yellow-white eyes, with big black pupils, I remember it….vividly.

It hovered for a second, and let out a piercing screech; it's talons, four of them on the closest leg, looked to be inches in front of my face, that's how close they felt. Those fuckers could rip your face right off, easy; it was scary.   But as quick as it happened, it was over. He flew off into a tall conifer just ahead of me, further down the trail, in plain sight.

The whole encounter lasted just a few seconds, at most, but it had a profound effect on me; it still does. And that was *years* ago.

I just stood there, numb, trying to figure out what just happened. All I could hear was myself breathing, and the sound of the water below me in the bay, lapping on the rocks. I was alone, utterly all alone. I watched it perched there in the tree, about twenty-five yards away, and it watched right back. We just stood there, looking at each other; neither one made a sound. I finally started to run again, and it watched me run by, underneath the tree, till I turned the next corner, out of sight. And that was it. I don't know if it meant anything; it did to me, I guess."

"What did it mean, to you?"

Carol asked.

"All I know was that it was an incredible feeling; it made me feel special somehow – like he found me, like he knew I was coming around that corner and was waiting for me....I don't know why it felt like that, but it did."

Did anything happen? You know, after."

"Sure, lots of things happened."

C said, matter-of-fact.

"Like what?"

"That was years ago, Carol, *lots* of things happened."

"Like what? Good or bad? I bet they were bad; tell me something, anything, good or bad - it would be more than I know now."

"You know I was running around Brockton Point, I told you that much."

"So where's that? Does that mean something? Where have you been? Why were you there?"

"This is stupid; it was just an eagle, and yours was just some vultures - it doesn't mean anything other than what you want to pretend, or hope, it means. Hey, I told you about Earl and the junk mail, right?"

"Don't change the subject! I want to know more about Brockton Point; I want to know where you're from, what's your story. I've known you for two months, and I know jack-shit about you. And it's not because of some love interest; you know all about me, and I know nothing about you. Friends should know about their friends."

"So now you're my friend? I didn't think so last night."

"I already apologized and said we were friends; **stop** changing the subject. Where are you from? Why are you here? You know why I'm here; why are *you* here?"

"Jesus, okay, we can talk all about me, but in a minute. I want to finish our discussion about Earl first. This was suppose to be about Earl. Remember, about how I told you he never gets any real mail."

Carol huffed in exasperation; he did this to her all the time.

"Yeah, I remember, so what."

"Well, as part of the chit, in addition to helping me with the party, do me a favor and send him something in the mail, a letter, something real; I don't know what, use your imagination - he would die if he got something that was real for once, especially from you."

Carol thought a bit.

"Okay, let me think about it; I'm sure I can come up with something."

"Good. So you know what you have to do for the party, and now you're on the mail thing; that should do it for the chit - congratulations, you're paid up."

Carol smiled in acknowledgment.

"So?"

"So what?"

He feigned, innocent.

"Finish the story."

Fuck, he didn't shake her; buy some more time.

"Where does the towel go?"

Cord turned to return the dish towel to the drawer.

"In the drawer."

Cord opened the nearest drawer, the one he thought she was referring to; he was sure it was the one she was referring to - the one in the island, the one he thought held the towels.

It was the wrong drawer.

As the drawer slid open, he saw the Alumni magazine, the one he least expected to see in Belvidere, in her kitchen, the one with bold, black and gold lettering that announced:

He could feel the blood flush into his face; the rush of adrenaline you get when hit unexpected. He wondered if she saw it, sensed it. He looked down, pretending nothing was awry. He felt like a cornered dog.

He was set up, he knew it.

Asking about his past, *harping* on it; she hadn't brought up that subject but once before, and it was a month ago, in passing. Why now? Why so insistent? And why would she have a *Mizzou* magazine in her kitchen drawer? Out of every place in the country, hundreds of colleges, why that one? Why would she even know what the word meant?

His mind was racing; his first instinct was to bolt, like that night. But it was stupid then, and it was stupid now. He got lucky then, he might not be lucky again.

But if she really knew anything, if she could tie anything, he would have sensed it; she would have slipped long before this. *Mizzou* was just a fluke. It had to be. It was so long ago; long enough to be forgotten by most, but maybe not long enough to be forgotten by all. But the only thing that mattered right now, was the what, if anything, the woman standing in the kitchen with him knew.

The only way to know her intentions would be to say it, to acknowledge *it* and gauge the reaction, the hint of knowledge, a look, any sign of familiarity. If so, it would demand action, fast action. Some haunts, it seems, never go away.

He continued to look down, into the drawer, his neck was hot and surely vermilion. He slowly pushed it shut; in a low voice, just above a whisper, but clearly loud

enough, he said the three words he didn't want to say;
the ones she would likely know, if she knew anything at
all; they were the three words he didn't want to say:

Little Apple Creek

CHAPTER 97 – WITHOUT HESITATION, UP IT POPPED

The drawer glided silently shut; it made no sound, nor did she. Not a word in response. He went to open a second drawer, to do something to fill the awkward silence.

"What did you say?"

'That was a delayed response; what does that mean?'

C thought.

"Nothing."

C said static.

"What's Little Apple Creek?"

It sounded innocent enough, or was she playing with him?

"I thought you didn't hear me?"

C said, innocent enough.

"I didn't, at first, before I spoke, but then it registered, what you said, after I said it, that is."

She smiled goofy at her awkward sentence.

"Don't you remember when we were kids? It was an apple juice brand; don't know why it came into my head, it just did….kind of strange."

C proffered.

"Oh, I don't think I've ever heard of it."

Of course she didn't; neither did he.

He breathed a bit easier; he didn't think she knew anything about that place, or what happened, which was good. But why was that magazine there? Just some weird fluke? Should he ask? Should he just tell her and get it over with? **No** was the obvious answer to his own stupid question. He was here specifically *not* to tell her, or anyone else, about happenings in the past, before *here*, wherever *here* happened to be at the time. Those were the rules.

He wasn't going to ask about it, or talk about it; crisis averted - let it pass and move on.

The second drawer slid open; still no towels. But this one had a neat pile of papers, atop which sat a colored newspaper article, ripped from the *New York Times,* the *Sunday Styles* Section.

Cord quickly scanned the series of photos; he stopped and bent over, squinting, trying to get a better look at the color photograph in the upper right side of the page, the one which caught his eye, the reason that paper sat in the drawer.

"Are you kidding me? You kept a picture of yourself from the *Evening Hours* Section? That's pretty gauche."

C chuckled as he said it.

She knew that stupid clipping was in the drawer; she forgot it was on top. *Shit.*

"What? What's the big deal; I just kept it for a bit, till I throw it away."

She tried to sound nonchalant. Cord looked at the header.

"It's dated September 9th; it's June 25th; how long's *a bit* [*Cord held up his hand and counted aloud the intervening months*]. Nine months seems a bit long for *a bit*, don't you think? At least you didn't frame it; good God, maybe Lilly's right."

Carol shot him a dagger with those deep-set, slate-blue eyes; that was for the Lilly reference.

"Please, frame it, how pathetic would that be?"

Truth be told, Carol had been looking for the last nine months to find a frame she liked, just the right frame, for that golden photograph. Thank God she hadn't found it yet, and had that damn frame on the kitchen counter, where she planned to put it.

Carol was standing alone in the snapshot, looking down, solemnly, at a drink in her hand. It was the *Ferndale Equestrian Classic*, a Hampton's mainstay charity event, attended by a thousand plus elite, graciously shuffling between three luncheon venues adjacent to show rings. A must-do affair for Carol's social set.

C studied the text accompanying the spread of photos sharing the page with Carol and her drink-in-hand.

"Let's see what they said about you; hmm, you are Photo Number 16….nothing! Just your name – *Carol Crowe;* no witticism, no insight into your deep thoughts….too bad. At least they spelled it right. What are you drinking?"

"A Southside; always a Southside at those events, just kind of goes with the territory."

Cord just stared at it, shook his head left to right and snickered.

"Pathetic."

Carol stiffened her spine in defense.

"Hey, it's not like I went looking for it, that's what's pathetic; girls who hunt for that kind of thing, borrowing designer dresses, *Girl About Town* thing, arm-candy to some schmuck. Or they bring their own boy-toy, there were plenty of them at that event, trust me. Paparazzi wanna-be's, looking to be the next talk show circuit-jumper. And not one got a shot in by Cunningham, *not one*. But I did.

That's part of the reason I kept it, childish, I know, but sweet, nonetheless. I paid for my dress. And I was alone at the event, like I usually am, because I refuse to bring an escort for looks, and camera fodder. And Bill apparently found me, or, actually, found my outfit – he only cares about the outfits, the clothes, not who's in them; I didn't even know he took the shot till it was done. He takes lots of shots; I didn't think it would be used.

That event is a pretty regular stop for me; a lot of clients attend – you have to make an appearance – you can't just send in a check and not show up - they check-off when you show up to get your tag, and it *is* noticed by the powers-that-be if you aren't there, trust me.   I support more charities I don't give a shit about than I can count, simply for client relations….cheap marketing."

Then Carol realized she was justifying herself to Cord, and got mad for traveling that road.

"Like I give a shit what you think anyway; and it's the *Times*, not some social rag, and there's gotta be what, fifty other people on that page?"

She added as a trailer.

"Uh huh, and what about this one?"

As she was talking, Cord flipped to the next item in the pile; it was the *On The Street* page-long photo spread, from the same day, September 9th, and there she was again. Cord just looked incredulous and held it up in front of her, without saying a word.

"I think that's pretty cool; I got shot twice in the same day, in a City of eight million, and it showed up in the same edition."

"What did all your friends say? I bet they were pretty impressed with you, Miss Celebrity."

"Are you kidding? Most didn't say a word – but they all troll those pictures with a magnifying lens, especially the professionals who pretend not to give a shit, all looking for themselves, even part of an arm or leg. I couldn't care less, and I got in two in one paper, kind of ironic."

"Yeah, couldn't care."

Cord said sarcastically.

"What, Mr. Bigshot, you get your picture in the *New York Times* so much that its all old hat?"

Cord half-smiled.

"No, not in the *Times*."

"Oh that's right, in your hometown paper, which would be? Geez, I wouldn't know, what's the name of that paper again?"

"What's up with this kooky outfit anyway? Although, I have to admit, those lace-up black pumps, halfway up your calf, pretty sexy. Small black clutch, clunky bracelet; dolled hair – bit of a wave – I like that. You've got a lot of leg showing young lady, well north of the knee, and the too-short white frilly dress, what *is* that? I bet it's a silk charmeuse, or maybe a silk chiffon/lame combo, hard to tell with all those feathers. Is that ostrich? Or is it turkey? Or maybe vulture? Any event, looks pretty cool – I like it."

Carol cocked her head.

"How did you know it was silk charmeuse? It *is*, by the way. How do you know that? How do you even know what that means? Guys don't know that stuff, guy-guys anyway. Do I have to worry about you? Actually not worry about you?"

"Of course I know all about couture, I read the *Sunday Styles*. Oh, and I look at the pictures too, do more looking than reading, especially all the society girls, not guys....girls. I'm interested in the society girls, you know, like you."

"Please! I'm not a socialista, just because I cut two newspaper pictures out."

"Is that cleavage I see?"

"Let me see that! There's no cleavage showing!"

Cord just smiled as she swiped the paper from his hand.

"Well, this has been a blast, but I gotta go, there's a big charity event happening downtown, called my job."

And in a flash, Cord was out the door, before she could remember, for the third time, to ask him about his past.

'Fuck! He does that every time.'

Enough of this, she said to herself, as she marched over to her computer and typed it in.

Without hesitation, up it popped.

CHAPTER 98 – IN WALKED THE THIRD ACT

Saturday, July 1, 2006; seventy-three days and still no word from Jenny.

The past week flew by; Cord was busy at work. New organic fruit and vegetable lines came in; obscure Asian and Central American natives, driven by customer suggestions and requests, which Cord was always hustling to get. He liked that part of the job.

Frank refused any assistance in such matters, not that Cord would have allowed him near the produce anyway. Earl was spending more time at the store, to the mild dismay of Marty's pop – who needed the big man out on the farm. Earl did the work of two men, for half the price. He would actually work for free, but Lilly wouldn't let him. Even when Marty's dad offered a hefty pay raise, and ran it by Lilly to help seal the deal, it was to no avail – the carrot that was Cord was more interesting to Earl than any amount of money – he just liked being around C, hearing his voice, eating lunch together, talking about music videos, quoting and re-quoting *Neighbors* at nauseum, sharing scenes from old movies, talking about girls – mostly about the having-sex-with-girls parts - although that was almost exclusively Cord. Earl loved it all. Earl didn't talk to nearly anyone, but he loved to talk to Cord, almost as much as he loved to listen to his best friend.

It also made him think more about his mom, not that there was any real deficiency in that department. But Earl knew his mom liked when he spent time with Cord.

'Look out for each other....'

She would tell Earl,

'....that's what best friends do.'

And Lilly came into Sam's more when Earl was there, and Earl was always sure to get Lilly to engage Cord, which didn't require nearly as much arm-twisting as it used to. And that made Earl happy. He thinks it made his mom happy too.

But the best part, the part Earl looked forward to the most, was talking with C about the girl up on the Park. And he didn't talk about her to anyone but Cord, not even his mom. Earl would pepper Cord with questions about her incessantly; ask, then re-ask, then ask once again. Earl never tired when the subject was Carol. And Cord always accommodated, albeit a bit testy, by the fourth iteration.

Things in Belvidere were settling into a pretty good routine, Cord figured, pretty good. Indeed. Except for that complication named Mae.

Mae was in Sam's as much as ever, maybe more – but her usual frontal assault on Cord had morphed. No longer loud, abrupt and attention-grabbing, it was more subdued, subtle, yet urgent….and serious. Too serious.

It was a worry for Cord, and it showed. He hadn't been back to her place in a week; no dinner, no deliveries. Yet Mae didn't blow up at him, figuring that strategy would backfire; instead, she tried indifference - friendly, but aloof. But she didn't pretend particularly well.

Mae had parallel goals. The near term was simple, get Cord back in the sack; that was strictly carnal. The true ring, however, what Mae really wanted, was him to really want her, and to convince Cord that such an idea was good for *both* of them, and not some wacky fantasy by a doyenne afraid to grow old. And the matter of Lilly, and her thaw with C, obvious to all who cared to pay attention, complicated the situation for Mae. What to do with Lilly? That was utmost on Mae's mind. How to subtly, or not-so, if necessary, get her out of Cord's mind, and out of the picture. With her gone, she felt her prospects increased significantly.

It was a lazy, sunny Saturday afternoon, five minutes to five, and Sam's was about to close.

Frank had covered the meats and seafood in the deli case, and was cleaning the last of his knives, apron donned. Untying and tossing that bloody white cloth was the last act before he exited the back door, without a word to anyone, heading home to greet and down that first of countless swill on the couch, staring blank at the tube.

Mae had not been in all day, which was unusual. Cord felt uneasy about the whole affair; he knew he shouldn't have slept with her, but he also knew it would have eventually happened, the collision was inevitable. It wasn't a bad wreck at that, and he jerked-off to it often the past week.

If only he could get the pussy without the strings; but then, that's what's called a whore. Maybe he just needed a dependable whore.

The problem was, he enjoyed the whole Mae package; the intellect, the sarcasm, the witticism, the looks *and* the sex; hookers didn't provide a package deal, simply taco.

He needed to work on Mae, to convince her he wasn't worth the trouble, a throwback, but still get her to spread her legs on demand, without the other bothersome conditions. That was the balancing act, and Cord's homework assignment. He would work on it, since it was becoming a priority.

The tinny bell broke his concentration.

"Shit!"

He whispered aloud; she beat the bell.

But to his initial surprise, it wasn't Mae who crossed the threshold, but Lillian. He smiled at his good fortune.

But before the door had a chance to swing closed, Mae's hand clenched the handle and re-swung it open; only then did Mae realize Lilly was just ahead of her. They both seemed to hiss at the sight of the other.

Now, Mae's disdain for Lilly made sense, given her obvious distraction of Cord. But Cord had largely himself to blame for the reciprocal.

Cord, because he occasionally had diarrhea of the mouth in such matters, had told Lilly of Mae's general ill feelings toward her, and her desire to push her aside. While Lilly outwardly laughed at the geriatric competition, inside she seethed. Any form of male-related competition was won by Lilly – it *had* to be won by Lilly – that was her throne, her lot, even if the competition was in the senior category – it simply didn't matter. That Lilly had started to foster the faintest of feelings for Cord was utterly beside the point; no one went head to head with Lilly on the subject of men, especially in Belvidere, *especially* some old, wrinkly hag from Brookfield. That alone was insult enough.

Plus, Lilly needed a new nemesis, someone to motivate her, to give her a purpose. Carol had been put in check and throttled for years, save the Saturday and Sunday post-run breakfast scraps with Cord and Earl she was thrown, which Lilly conveniently chose to ignore for the moment. Carol was old news. Lilly would dispose of this gammer quick enough, but not before having some fun in the process.

As the two stood by the front door, Cord assessed the battle front from a safe distance.

"This should be interesting."

He whispered to himself.

"Deli is closed, Mae."

Frank called out loudly, clearly staking his position in the drama first. No way was this situation going to result in his doing an ounce of additional work; his knifes were cleaned and his mind was already prone on the living room couch, suds in hand.

Sam had scolded Frank a hundred times; the deli closed promptly at five, not a minute earlier. Cleanup was *after* five pm, on Frank's dime; *professional time* Sam called it; Frank called it something else, and inched that time up to *ten minutes to* on most days, bolder when Sam was absent, as he was today. Considering it was five of, Frank figured he was already being generous.

Before Mae could answer Frank, or Lilly could strike, that tinny leitmotif jingled once again.

And in walked the third act.

CHAPTER 99 – I'LL LET HIM WATCH AS LONG AS HE WANTS

It had been fourteen years since she had crossed that threshold, fourteen years since she stepped foot into Sam's lair – pushed out by the lithe blonde now standing no more than ten feet from her.

And here they were, after fourteen long years, face to face in the same space, in Lilly's most sacred home turf, more so than even her own bedroom, which Carol owned.

Carol had decided not ten minutes earlier to come down; she hadn't told the boys during their post-run breakfast this morning, simply because she didn't know herself. She was on the porch, feet propped on the ottoman, buried in the *Times Book Review*, delivered on Saturday, her favorite section, when she felt a hankering for eggs, some fancy fruit and grilled vegetables. Tired of hearing the two boys yack about how great Sam's now was, she figured she'd see for herself – fourteen years seemed long enough, stranded on the Park-side *motu*. Encountering Lillian Liddell was not part of the plan, but an unexpected bonus nonetheless; she was feeling confident, and not shy for a fight.

She smirked at Lilly, who stood flabbergasted, flat-footed – rarely was she caught so unprepared, and strode confident past Lillian, toward the counter, to the drunken butcher she last saw over a decade ago. Carol's initial impression was that Frank seemed shorter, smaller now; his greasy hair had receded, his belly had grown and the years of liquor had distorted his face – he looked old, and broken.

"I'll take three filet mignon steaks, no, make that two, one *extra large*. Cord, dear, you're still vegetarian right?"

She said as she turned to C, standing behind the glass, but at the far end of the case, away from Frank.

Fuck C said to himself; *this is going to get ugly in a hurry.*

Now, Earl hadn't moved a muscle, frozen in place like a frightened cat in the middle of Aisle 2 since the front door first opened, eyes the size of plates, with a mackerel mouth. All he was thinking, was *please don't let that extra large have my name on it.*

"Deli's closed!"

But that loud declaration didn't come from Frank; it came from behind, from Lilly.

"It's two minutes before five; store closes at five – I'd like those steaks now....**please**."

That wasn't such a nice *please*.

"And I'd like a dozen clams, and Grade A rib-eye – and I was here first!"

Mae piped in, throwing her hat in the ring. Now, she only came for hamburger meat and to see Cord, but no way was she ordering hamburger after filet mignon.

"Sorry Ma'am, you were first."

Carol gestured to Mae, deferential to the senior citizen. She didn't know who she was, at first.

"I'm not a *Ma'am*, young lady!"

Mae snapped.

Carol looked at her oddly, till the light clicked.

"I think I know who you are; you drive a Mini-Cooper don't you? You must be....*Mae,* aren't you?"

Carol said it, drew it out, like she knew more than she should, as a malicious smirk creased her face, meant to convey that not-so-subtle point. But just in case, she added a condescending cherry.

"....I've heard a *great deal* about you."

Assuming, in fact, it was Mae; she seemed to fit the description. The words were dipped in treacle.

Before this was over, for sure, *someone* was going down, Cord thought; he hoped it wasn't him.

"And I about *you,* especially about....well, never mind, that's not polite."

Mae was super-quick on her feet; that on-the-fly counter-punch meant absolutely nothing, but she could see it didn't to Carol, who had a comical, puzzled look, which quickly turned to a non-smile and a quick brain scan. What did this old lady know? What did C tell her?

"The deli is fucking closed!"

Lilly said, in a near-hysterical scream.

The last patron, checking out, dropped her unpaid groceries on the conveyor belt and scurried out the front door. Cod-fish Sue, caring little about the goings-on, saw the clock strike five and yelled toward the rear of the market:

"I'm outta here!"

To no one in particular, flipped the *Open* sign on the door – she rarely expended that extra bit of energy – and disappeared onto the sidewalk. The entry bell tinkled for a second or two, then fell silent; not a soul inside the store moved, nor was a word spoken.

A Mexican standoff.

Earl was the first to break the freeze; he tried to quietly back his way down the aisle, making for the front door and daylight, but the big man bumped into the nut display, spilling the smoked almonds and drawing undue attention to himself. All three women spun their heads like a pack of hyenas, ready for the kill. Earl froze in sheer terror, his shoulders inched to his ears.

"You're not going anywhere, Earl; stay here and help Uncle Frank finish cleaning up the deli case."

Lilly barked.

Now Earl never did that, ever; he didn't even know what Uncle Frank really did to clean up the deli case, so how could he be any help?

"Earl, you don't work for her; if you want to go, go."

Carol spun to Lilly as she said the words.

Now Lilly didn't respond, but Cord knew that look all too well, and it wasn't a good one. Lilly turned ghostly-white, then quickly a splotchy red on her face and neck; her nostrils flared and she made a beeline for the deli case. That meant only one thing – she was going for the knives!

Cord stepped into her path and she screamed hysterically.

"Get out of the fucking way! **OUT!**"

But C bear-hugged her hard, keeping an eye on those tricky legs.

"Where is my fucking rib-eye!"

Mae screamed.

"Jesus!"

Cord yelled.

"Would you all just calm….*Ahhhh*!"

Cord let loose a blood-curdling scream, as Lilly dug her teeth into his chest, grabbing cloth and skin in one big bite. Cord launched Lilly into the air and sprung back into a defensive pose, waiting for a second assault.

"You **are** a fucking nut!"

Carol said, as if she was confirming a fact she heard on the street.

"And you're fucking dead! Don't you ever tell me what to do when it comes to *my* brother – **never!**"

"I'm not afraid of you, you little fucking baby….you fucking *nut*!"

"Carol, please stop tweaking her, please!"

Cord pleaded.

"Why are you defending her? Why are you always defending her? You think she's a nut too, just admit it!"

Oh boy, Cord thought, now he's definitely toast.

"Please stop."

Was all Earl said, quietly, from the aisle behind the fracas. He looked like he was about to cry, his hands covering his ears, eyes closed.

And just like that, they did, all of them.

Cord sighed.

He turned to Frank and said quietly, so no one could hear.

"Go on, leave; I'll take care of this."

But Frank couldn't make it easy.

"I don't work for you, and I don't…."

Cord cut him off, and made it clear he wasn't debating.

"Get the fuck out of here, now! Or I'll beat the piss out of you, right here and now, and I won't stop; I won't fucking stop."

Cord was spraying saliva onto Frank's fat jowels as he spoke; his face was turning beet red.

This was a stand Frank wasn't ready to make on his own – he was afraid of Cord. He looked over at Lilly for help, but she knew she was trumped and kept quiet, letting Frank swing in the wind. Frank frowned, knowing he was flying solo; he threw his knife, hard, in disgust, against the counter and disappeared into the back room, apron on. The rear door slammed shut seconds later.

Cord turned his attention to Mae, who had inched closest to the glass, as if proximity cemented her place in line.

"Mae, go home; I'll bring the steak and clams over in a bit."

She shook her head violently in disagreement.

"That's not good enough, it's not nearly good enough!"

"Yes it is; make something I can eat, we'll have a drink and relax. Just let it go, please….let me take care of this mess, please."

She just looked at him, head static, knowing she was going to lose again.

"Please…."

C said a second time, more urgent.

"What makes you think I want you to come over? I just want some groceries delivered."

"Oh, for Christ's sake grandma, we all know what kind of *delivery* you want."

Lilly bristled.

And with that, Earl screamed ***STOP!*** at the top of his lungs and ran out the door.

"Great, nice job, Lilly….nice."

C snapped.

"Shut the fuck up, asshole!"

Lilly snapped right back at Cord, as she turned to go after Earl. As she reached the front door, she shouted back at Cord.

"You better not give her that steak – I swear Cord!"

Now Lilly didn't identify who she meant, Mae or Carol, but Carol took the bait – the obvious target.

"Hey, how's your boyfriend? Did you like that disk?"

Carol had been waiting three long years to say that line; somehow she had hoped it would come out a bit wittier.

But it did the trick – it stopped Lilly dead in her tracks.

"You'll pay bitch, trust me."

The venom oozed from Lilly's words as she turned and left the shop.

"Still waiting."

Carol said in a sarcastically chipper tone.

Now just the three of them remained at the deli case.

The two women stood, uncomfortably, next to one another, waiting for something to happen.

"Mae, I'm about to have a fucking heart attack; please, let me walk you out. I'll be up in a bit, promise."

"When? Who's trimming the meat? You're not checked out on the slicer."

"I'm checked out on the *knife*, you know it's trimmed with a knife, not the slicer, Mae."

That was her little dig at him, in front of Carol, trying not to appear too much of a pushover. He walked her to the front door, hand gently on her shoulder, and opened it for her.

"I better not have to drive over to *her* house to get you!"

Mae flung her head in a short gesture toward Carol. Cord ignored the inference.

"I'll see you in a bit."

He whispered.

"I'll pick you up."

Mae countered.

"I'll ride my bike; I need the exercise."

He squeezed her shoulder, and gently escorted her out the door. And with that she frowned, and slipped out onto the sidewalk.

Two down.

As he walked back to the deli counter, he stared down Carol with a face full of annoyance.

"Nice, nice timing; fourteen fucking years and you have to pick *now* to come in? Fucking Sam, that lucky bastard….AWOL."

"What did you tell her about me?"

"What? Who?"

"Don't *what-who* me; the old lady, she started to say something that she knew about me, but then stopped, and didn't finish her sentence. What is it? What I say to you is *private*! I can trust Earl, but I guess I can't trust you."

Cord looked down at the dirty counter in disgust.

"Why the fuck do I have to clean up this mess? I'm the produce manager, not the fucking deli."

"You told him to go, not so nicely."

"He's a fucking waste….and a liability."

Cord started to wipe down the counter, ignoring Carol in the process.

"Well, I'm waiting! Don't ignore me; what did you tell her?"

"Jesus, I didn't say anything to Mae about you….about *what*? What the fuck do I know about you worth talking about? She's a fucking politician, and a lobbyist; she fucks with people for a living. She *played* you with that nonsense line; you're a sucker."

Carol frowned.

"Really?"

"Yeah, really."

C snorted, pissed that he was doing Frank's job.

"Well, when do I get my meat?"

"You don't. And for what? You won't eat it alone, and you sure as hell aren't making Earl come over and eat it with you. You aren't putting him in that jam with his sister, that's for sure, so just forget it. No meat for you."

"No way! I said I wanted…."

"Yeah, it sucks to want….drop it!"

C snarled.

"Did I win?"

Carol snarked back.

"What?"

"You heard me; did I win?"

"I think you know the answer; did you see her face when she left?"

"Say it! I want to hear you say it!"

Carol barked; Cord sighed no response.

"I swear you both, all *three* of you, are little fucking kids. Okay, you won; congratulations, Carol, you won."

Carol cracked a wide winner's grin, savoring the sweet victory over Lilly.

"I didn't even want the meat anyway, I came in for vegetables to grill and for some organic eggs, for omelets for tomorrow morning, and also, just to look around. You have no idea how liberating this is!"

And she meant it. Carol flitted around like a kid in a candy store, eyes wide, trying to drink it all in - picking up stuff, sniffing it, putting it back down and moving onto the next basket of goodies.

"This place is great!   Nothing like it used to be; this place could be Downtown!"

"It is downtown."

He said flat. She spun and flashed him a cocked smile. He answered her facial.

"I know, I get it - *Downtown* downtown, as if Manhattan is the only city in the world. Now stop fingering everything, take a basket and load up, it's on me. Go figure, the grocery boy subsidizing the billionaire."

"Not yet, but getting close...."

She said in a flippant tone. Then she caught herself:

"Sorry C, that was stupid to say."

She got red; she never bragged about her money, especially to people who didn't have it."

"No worries, you never know about people."

She wasn't sure what he meant by that, but she let it pass without comment.

"I used to have an account at this place, maybe it's still open."

"I'm sure I can reopen it for you, but you need some character references; have any?"

"Just two, Earl Liddell and Cord Brin, two friends; one a very close friend indeed, and one who secretly wants to be....something more."

She smiled at him, impressed with her own impromptu riddle, more witty than she planned.

"Willem Buytewech – *Dignified Couples Courting.*"

Cord said, as he continued to wipe the deli counter in broad, arching strokes. He knew she had no idea what he was talking about, so he continued.

"Circa-1618, if I recall; two couples sit in a courtyard, or some such place. One is an established couple, but the other is in limbo, and the girl in limbo, seated next to the man she desires, has her arms crossed in front of her, each holds a single rosebud. She asks her hopeful lover to turn his head, and select a hand, which will determine which women he selects, her or her rival. Either way she wins, she gets the man she wants."

"How's that?"

Cord demonstrates, by crossing his arms in front of him, pretending to hold a rosebud in each.

"So, choose."

Carol pondered for a moment.

"Oh, I get it; she can make either one the one he picks; either one can be the *left* hand, or the *right* one, so to speak."

Cord smiled and shook his head in acknowledgment.

"So what; what's your point?"

"My point is, young lady, you're the girl in limbo and you *think* you hold the rosebuds, and win, no matter what."

"What!"

She yelped in mock protest. Cord just smiled.

"I'm no girl in limbo."

She thought some more.

"But I *do* hold the rosebuds; I do, I hold 'em….I do."

"Uh huh."

Cord said as he folded the rags and finished Frank's janitorial duties.

"And what do *you* think, that you're the *hopeful lover*?"

Carol queried.

"I was only commenting on the girl, that's all; you're the one who started it with your talk of *unnamed friends, with secret desires.*"

She just looked at him, mildly amused, mildly annoyed.

"So where did you pick that one up? And how often do you use *that* line on the girls?"

"I never used it, you're the first; it was in the *Rijksmuseum*, in Amsterdam….Willem was Dutch."

"And should I even ask how you know or remember such nonsense, and why you were there to begin with, instead of, say….Vancouver."

Cord smiled at her.

"Ah, Brockton Point, so you looked it up; how long after I left?"

She was going to lie, but didn't.

"About five minutes. That was easy; I searched for it right after I looked up *Little Apple Creek*. An apple juice brand when we were kids *[Carol smirked]*. Nice try, there's no such thing."

"It was the first thing that came into my head."

Cord said, in defense of the lie. Then he waited to hear the shoe drop, to hear what she knew about the Creek.

"I have to admit, I wasn't sure at first where you were going with *Little Apple Creek*; there's one in Ohio, one in Illinois, it's got something to do with plants in Canada, but then, on the third search page, was *the* Little Apple Creek….am I right?"

Cord just looked at her; his heart raced a bit, waiting to hear more.

"I assume it's the one in Cape Girardeau, since you said it after you saw my *Mizzou* alumni magazine. I went there, you know, big shot on Wall Street is just a Lady-Tiger from the Midwest - main campus, in Columbia, smack in the middle of nowhere in the middle of the country. Went there following a guy, believe it or not. One of my many man mistakes. But I ended up liking the school, so I stayed, long after he was history. It was big enough that I never saw him anyway; think he transferred, or dropped out, or something - whatever. But how did *you* know what *Mizzou* was? It's not like that's a household word; nothing on the cover says Missouri - I checked - and you only saw it for a glance. So are you from the Midwest? From Missouri? You gotta be, to know *Mizzou*. Did you think I went to the Southeast campus, *SEMO*, in the Cape? But even if you did, no one down there would know *Little Apple Creek*, it's a piss-ant stream crossing under Route 55, like a drainage ditch or something, in the middle of nowhere, between exits; I looked it up on Google maps, it means nothing. Why'd you bring it up? What's it mean? And what's it have to do with Vancouver?"

And with that, it was clear - he knew she had no idea about *Little Apple Creek*; that was good news, real good. It meant he could stay, for now, and stay on the right side of Jenny and the rest. What happened there happened a *long* time ago, true, but he was surprised nothing came up on Google – Google knows all, and never forgets. But this time, it seemed it had, or never knew to begin with; either answer was good enough for him, for now.

"I never said it had anything to do with Missouri; maybe it did have to do with plants in Canada – last time I checked Vancouver's still in Canada, you know."

"No way, it's Missouri, isn't it?"

"No more hints; you know more than anyone else, including Lilly and Earl."

"Know what? I don't know *shit*! Unless maybe you knew me back in the day, when I was in Columbia; did you know me? But then why would you talk about some stupid little creek, drainage ditch, in the Cape? If I knew you in Columbia, the Cape is way too far away, like three hours away, probably longer, hundreds of miles from Columbia; it makes no sense. Did you go to *Mizzou* too, at *SEMO*? Do you have a degree? Maybe you do, but then, no. Did you know me or not? I don't get...."

Carol racked her brain, sorting our scenarios, none of which added up. C smiled at her fumbling, trying to figure how she fit into his equation.

"You know, just maybe, it isn't all about you, as hard as that is for your big ego to fathom."

C whispered.

"Well what is it then, *friend*?"

Was her retort.

"Close friend, or something more?"

"You answer first."

She said, schoolgirl.

"Jesus, Carol."

Cord laughed.

"I'm not telling you any more, except this - I'm not really sure why I'm here, in Belvidere, but I do know this, I don't want to answer questions as to why I'm here, where I was, or where the next stop is....where I'm going next."

"What do you mean *Where the next stop is;* where are you going?"

Cord didn't answer.

"Are you leaving?!"

Carol surprised herself at how anxious that sounded.

"Not yet."

"But when? Soon? Does Earl know you're leaving?"

"Everyone's on their way somewhere else; that's not good, or bad, it just *is*."

"Earl's not on his way somewhere else."

"Earl's different."

Cord said, looking down at the counter, then he continued.

"But you never know, maybe Earl's on his way too, and just doesn't know it yet. It happens that way, sometimes."

Carol wasn't satisfied, not at all.

"But wait, I don't get it, I don't know if I...."

Cord cut her off.

"Listen, fill your basket with lots of good stuff, stuff you're going to end up feeding to me and Earl, your only friends in Belvidere, and make Sam happy about the revenue and the new *old* account, and the fact that he missed the fireworks, and tell me all about the disk."

"The disk! You never heard the disk story?!"

Carol acted surprised, but wasn't really; it wasn't the kind of story Lilly would go around telling, and she doubted anyone else knew about it, besides Button, that is.

"That, my friend, was the *coup de grace*, the silver bullet that shut that little bitch up three years ago. A little story about her boyfriend, ex-boyfriend, thanks to me, Mr. Button Pierce."

Cord leaned forward; this, he had to hear.

"Oh, so you're interested? You want to hear all about Lillian's Achilles heel? She was, still is, I guess, crazy about that guy. He is a real cutie; actually not cute, handsome is more like it, chiseled – celebrity look - drop-dead gorgeous, and what a body! I'll give him all that. But nasty, and not too swift."

That wasn't the kind of thing Cord wanted to hear. He didn't want to hear about how crazy Lilly was for this jerk-off, and that Carol thought he was so cut and good-looking. He wanted to hear that he wasn't so great, and that Lilly thought he was a jerk-off too.

"So, what do I get? One disk story for an Amsterdam, a Brockton Point and an Apple Creek?"

"Forget it, not that interested."

Oh yes he was.

"Okay then, we'll see who cracks first. But my story, it's pretty naughty, beyond naughty – doubt yours even come close – that's why its worth three."

Carol waved three upright fingers at him, taunting him.

"Is that jerk-off gone because of *you*? Did you bang him? Oh my God, how are you not dead?"

C said, astonished, and pissed that Carol and Lilly both seemed to drink the same Button Kool-Aid.

"She's not so tough."

"Says the girl who hasn't been downtown for the last fourteen years."

"That was my decision."

Carol thought of Sam's betrayal, like it was yesterday. And she got sad, and angry, all over again. She started going down the aisle silently, socking produce into the basket, throwing it hard, in disgust.

"Doesn't sound like it."

Said Cord, from the deli counter. Carol made her way toward the front door.

"See you in the morning, with Earl; you can collect the basket at the house."

"Sure, we'll be there....*both* your friends."

She didn't look at him, but stopped short of the door and just stood there, her back to him.

"Hey, hey, look at me."

Cord said, in a sympathetic tone.

She turned to look at him, with a half-frown.

"I thought Sam was my friend back then - I believed him, I really did. He treated me, for awhile anyway, like his daughter. After all these years, it still…."

She just shrugged her shoulders, and didn't finish her sentence.

"Whatever happened, happened, you can't undo it; trust me on that one. This is *my* store, Sam just happens to own it. You're welcome here any time. And both your good friends will see you tomorrow morning for breakfast, on the porch, but I'm not doing any more fucking dishes - that's for you and Earl; I'm the supervisor, remember that."

Carol smiled at him, a real smile, a thankful smile.

"Make sure she doesn't keep you up all night; pretty pathetic Cord, that you can't keep up with a senior citizen."

"She's relentless! I don't know where she gets the energy; it's like she stores it up and turns the switch when I show up….brutal.   I'll give you one of the stories if you stand in for me, and let me watch, of course."

Carol laughed at him. And the last thing C heard, as the front door shut, and the tinny bell faded to silence, was Carol saying sexy.

"Maybe for Earl; I'll let him watch as long as he wants."

CHAPTER 100 – IT CAN'T BE HER; IT MUST BE HER....IT'S *HER*

Sunday, July 2, 2006. Seventy-four long days and still no sign, no message, no nothing.

The six o'clock sun, dangling low in the sky, wouldn't let go. The day had been a scorcher; high nineties and humid; the ripple of heat waves from the baked sand was still visible at the water's edge.

"It's still fucking hot; I can't believe it hasn't cooled off. It's gotta be after six."

Cord said aloud, mainly to himself, the river swallowing all but the top crown of his feet.

"Man, that was really scary."

Earl said, for the eighth time since yesterday, as he tossed a rock far into the placid river, standing in his favorite shorts, his bumblebees, with surf shoes on, sinking slowly into the dark brown silty sand, where the river kissed the beach.   The stubborn sun cooked his broad shoulders.

This time, Cord answered.

"No shit; thanks for having my back in there buddy. Oh, that's right, you ran away like a little girl and left me to the fucking wolves."

"Sorry Cord, but everybody was yelling; I got really scared."

"Yeah, me too; I thought someone was gonna get stabbed for sure, most likely me, by one of those wing-nuts. But I bought myself another marathon sex session with Mae. Not that I'm complaining about that part, beats the pants off jerking-off."

Cord said as he mimicked Earl and tossed a stone into the Delaware, not nearly as far as Earl. He rubbed his shoulder like an old man, and witnessed the futile effort to match Earl's toss.

"But it's the noose she keeps tightening around my neck; I feel like an ant slipping in the sand. Ever see a picture of those ant lions? I see it coming Earl, I've falling in the pit, and I can't get out, waiting for my head to be crunched."

Earl looked at him with a scrunched face; that didn't sound good.

"What happened with Lilly? Did she bite your head off? She's going to have my head, I know it."

"I didn't see her."

"What do you mean? She ran out the door right after you; you never saw her?"

"No, I ran straight up to the Cemetery to see my mom; Lilly never goes there….*ever*."

"I wonder where she went?"

Cord said aloud.

"What did your mom have to say? Did you tell her what happened?"

"Nothing. She doesn't always talk to me; sometimes it's like she's not home. So I sang to her."

Earl grabbed a much larger rock, and tossed it just as far as the first, without much effort.

"You sang? What?"

"Her favorite song."

As if Cord was suppose to know.

"Which is?"

But rather than answering, Earl just started singing, in a lilting voice, effortless, really. It was beautiful. And even though Cord would have thought it would feel a bit strange, having a grown man sing at him, it didn't. Because Cord knew Earl wasn't singing to him, he was simply an observer; Earl was singing to his mother.

And oddly enough, at forty-three, the song was well known to Cord, but just the first six words….the very first line.

Until Earl sang it aloud at the boat ramp, out across the water, to the mallards and geese on the far shore, to the fish trawling below the glassy surface of the summer river, Cord never knew how hauntingly beautiful the lyrics really were.

He closed his eyes, and simply listened:

> *Amazing Grace, how sweet the sound,*
> *that saved a wretch like me;*
> *I once was lost, but now am found,*
> *was blind, but now, I see.*
>
> *Twas Grace that taught my heart to fear,*
> *and Grace, my fears relieved.*
> *How precious did that Grace appear,*
> *the hour I first believed.*

Earl sang the first two stanzas and stopped. His face was positively aglow. He turned to Cord.

"Sometimes I sing that and I start crying; sometimes I just smile – I never know which till it happens; somebody else figures those things out, I guess. But anyway, it always reminds me of my mom holding my hand and smiling at me – and that's a good thing, isn't it C?"

"You bet; nothing better."

Earl smiled at his best friend, closed his eyes and looked skyward:

Through many dangers, toils and snares,
I have already come;
'Tis Grace that brought me safe thus far,
and Grace will lead me home.

The Lord has promised good to me,
his word my hope secures;
He will my shield and portion be,
As long as life endures.

Cord found himself, looked out over the calm waters before him, but his eyes were closed. He heard nothing but his friend's voice. Then Earl stopped again.

"Man, you have an amazing voice; I can't believe it….that's incredible."

"I don't sing that good; my mom was *way* better….and Lilly, she's the best of all. We would sing together when we were kids, especially *Amazing Grace* – the three of us would start, but my mom and I would always stop along the way and just listen to Lilly finish. She was so good; I could listen to Bibby sing all day long, especially *Amazing Grace*."

"I'd love to hear her sing it."

Cord said, then continued.

"But I can't imagine Lilly ever being happy enough to sing anything."

"Oh, she won't sing that song….*never*. Once my mom left, Lilly never sang anything again; and she would never sing *Grace, never*….no way. She won't even let me sing it around her; she gets *super mad* if she hears me sing it….**really mad**."

"Earl, what *doesn't* get your sister really mad?"

And with that, they both chuckled.

"Hey, why don't you try and sing it – it's easy. I bet you'd be good at it."

"Trust me Earl, you don't want to hear me sing, it's very scary. Nobody in my family can sing."

"Come on, maybe if you sing, my mom will talk to you too."

Cord looked at Earl skeptically, but Earl just kept smiling at him.

"You'll be good; I can feel it."

And with that, Cord shrugged his shoulders, cleared his throat and asked Earl to repeat the first stanza again, since he already forgot it, past the first line.

Cord shifted his feet in the sand, took a deep breath, closed his eyes and gave it his best shot, in a low, guarded voice:

> *Amazing Grace, how sweet the sound,*
> *that saved a wretch like me;*

Earl was right!

The words flowed from his lips like they never had before; it didn't even sound like his own voice, but rather as if someone, something, had taken hold of his vocal cords and was singing for him - divine intervention. Eyes still closed, and feeling confident, uplifted, he raised the decibels for the final two lines, belting out the words:

I once was lost, but now am found,
was blind, but now, I see.

He finished the word *see* on an extended, raised note, longer than typical, feeling good....better than good. He opened his eyes, smiled at his performance and looked to Earl for approval.

Earl had a *look* alright; abject horror. His eyes were squinted and mouth distorted, hands over both ears, as if someone took long fingernails to a chalkboard.

"Oh my God, that was awful! Please, don't ever, *ever* sing that song again, or any song….ever! My mother will *never* come back. It sounds like you have an old cat living in your mouth."

Cord got angry.

"I told you I couldn't sing!"

"You're right!"

Earl chirped.

"Okay, enough already; I'm going learn that fucking song some day, just because…."

"Don't practice around me."

Earl said in distress.

Cord sulked in silence, till Earl gently spoke.

"You know, sometimes my mom would ask me, usually at breakfast, but not always at breakfast, sometimes it was at lunch, or sometimes it was some other time, she would say: *What are you going to do today to be useful?* And I always tried to think of something useful; you know, since I'm not very smart, I always tried to be useful. It was important to my mom, so it was important to me. And I think it would be useful to tell you not to sing anymore, *ever*, you know, to be useful to everyone else who might be close enough to hear you….just saying C."

"Really Earl? That's the best you can do?"

Cord continued his sulk.

"Sorry C; you want to hear me sing it again? Maybe my mom will forget you tried to sing and won't be afraid to come by and visit us at the boat ramp."

"No!"

Cord snapped, but then felt bad.

"Go 'head, sing the fucking song….stupid song."

And Earl did.

> *Amazing Grace, how sweet the sound,*
> *that saved a wretch like me;*

And then Earl stopped cold.

Cord was looking out over the river, his back to Earl. He casually turned to see what happened, and caught

Earl staring blankly at the top of the boat launch. It was just the two of them, no boats on the river, no cars crossing the upstream bridge, utterly quiet, now that Earl fell silent.

The two of them were all alone, except for the silhouette of a silent, regal woman standing alone in the distance, atop the ramp, arms gently crossed at the wrists in front of her, looking forlorn. The summer heat waves shimmered in a sheet, the thermals rippling his view. Cord blinked his eyes, then blinked them again, trying to focus the blur, staring intently at the silent figure….an apparition at the top of the launch. He couldn't see the details of her face, but it looked as if she gazed past the two of them, out over the river. It wasn't clear if she even saw them.

But Cord couldn't take his eyes off her; she was beautiful, orphic. Earl and Cord stood silent, staring at the figure; it was clear they both saw her.

Then C whispered to himself, barely believing what he saw, and what he was about to say.

It can't be her; it must be her….it's *her*.

CHAPTER 101 – MOUTH WIDE OPEN, GUMS EXPOSED

The figure stood silent, at the crest of the ramp.

"Sorry, Lilly."

Earl called out meekly, head down, ready to be scolded.

*Lilly? That wasn't Lilly! No fucking way, **no way!*** Cord screamed silent to himself, shaking his head negative. He rubbed his eyes and moved a few steps closer to the ramp, and Lillian came into focus, like she stepped from behind a smoky glass.

Cord kept shaking his head slowly in denial. He felt it; he just knew it.

That wasn't Lilly; it was her - it was really her. It was you wasn't it? he mouthed to Carol, looking skyward, a gesture mixed with disappointment and a sense of self-conviction.

But Lilly it was, in the flesh, standing atop the boat ramp mount. She was far enough away that the two of them couldn't see her red, watered eyes. She had just happened upon Earl singing as she got to the crest of the ramp, looking for the two of them, and couldn't help but stop and listen, as much as she wanted to cover her ears and run. And with the song, came memories of her mom, of times when she felt happy, and safe....and loved. The bittersweet, followed by the hate and the hurt ripped her apart; she wanted to scream, and she wanted to fall down and cry.

Most of all she just wanted her mom back.

She wanted to know the why, yet she didn't.

She would never read her mother's note....*never*; out of fear for what it might say, and for fear of what it might not say. Not knowing, a life in purgatory, was far better than seeing those words and regretting ever laying eyes upon them. It would be the last time her mother would ever speak to her, and Lilly never wanted the finality. So she saved those last words for a day that would never come.

She took a deep breath and felt the swell of her eyes disappear. The tears had dried, and the redness had faded; it was safe, so she moved slowly toward them.

She never responded to Earl's apology. She wasn't going to ask him where he went; she knew the answer and didn't want to hear him say it....she hated the Cemetery.

Cord looked over at his friend as Lilly walked down the ramp. Earl's head was bowed and his whole body was trembling; he was so scared he simply couldn't stop shaking.

Lilly walked over to him, but he never looked up; he had gone limp. She saw him trembling. Earl looked at his shoes, waiting for the screaming to start. Lilly grabbed him loosely around the waist, didn't say a word, and just hugged him hard, her head resting gently on his chest. Cord could see she had been crying; her eyes betrayed her.

C was happy she was being kind to Earl. He knew, not so deep inside, Lilly was scared and lonely, more so than Earl ever was. But at times like this, she could be so kind; despite the bristles, somewhere deep inside, hidden, was a good sister, a good person....a best friend. Cord smiled at the two of them.

"So asshole, you go around telling people I'm a fucking nut?!"

She spun to Cord with vicious venom. So much for sympathy.

"I never said you were a nut, *never*. But Lilly, you **are** a nut."

"Why am I a nut?"

"Says the woman going for the butcher knives, the woman who fucking **bit me** in the chest, leaving teeth marks and drawing blood!"

Cord ripped off his shirt, showing the still-red oval jaw print on his chest from yesterday's attack.

"Wow, that looks like a really big hickie!"

Earl said, as he snickered at Cord.

"Oh, grow up, it's not like you don't have any scars; you won't even see it after awhile."

"*Grow up*? You're telling *me* to grow up? I'm the bitee; you're the bitor!"

Lilly turned to Earl.

"He wishes it was a hickie, Earl. Hey! *[yelling at Cord]*, that's as close to a kiss as you'll ever get from me, mister."

Lilly laughed at her own joke.

"Gee, thanks; I didn't know I was holding out for one. I might have to get a tetanus shot, you know."

Cord fingered the oval, looking for signs of swelling.

"You know you want one; if I tried to kiss you, right now, tell me you'd turn away? No way, you'd be all over it!"

"I can't believe you are so full of yourself; it's unbelievable! Please, don't flatter yourself."

"Oh, you're telling me you wouldn't want it? Seriously? Oh, that's right, I hear grandma's a real good kisser! You know that's disgusting, right?   She's really, *really* old and wrinkly, for God's sake; does she even have real teeth, or *any* teeth? Yuck."

Lilly stood with her hands on her hips, in a defiant pose.

Cord didn't answer.

"I thought so."

Lilly answered herself, satisfied she made her point. Then she moved on to a more pressing topic.

"Did you sell her that meat? **Did you?!**"

Cord didn't answer directly, he just looked at her.

"Who? Which one?"

He finally said.

"Don't *who-which-one* me! You know which one, the ugly one."

"No, I didn't sell her the meat."

Cord said, after a too-long pause, as if he had to think about the answer.

"You *gave* it to her?! You fucking gave her the meat, didn't you? **Don't lie!**"

Lilly screamed.

"No, she didn't get any meat okay. No meat, no God-damn meat, so calm down.   You won, okay? Congratulations, Lilly, you won; she didn't get the meat."

That was all Lillian had to hear; after that she was fine, just like that.

Lilly sported a big grin, Earl wasn't afraid anymore, and Cord avoided another frontal attack – all was right with the world, at the boat ramp anyway.

"Hey Lilly, we're thinking of going swimming, like we did as kids. I told C, before the Town pool, everyone used to swim down here!"

"It's too dangerous Earl, you know that, the current is tricky, even now. And you can't swim, or did you forget?"

"I didn't forget!"

Earl said, annoyed, scrunching his face at her.

"I only go in to my knees, you know that, and Cord can swim."

"Wow! You're pretty talented; you can swim too?"

Lillian snarked.

Cord smiled and shook his head in exasperation.

"Can you say anything nice, ever, without sarcasm."

"You have nice knees."

Lillian snapped back.

“What?”

“You heard me, I said you have nice knees.”

“What’s that supposed to mean?”

“Nothing, it’s just a nice thing to say.”

“So, you like my knees?”

“No, they're ugly; I was just trying to be nice.”

“Stop talking to me, please!”

“Fine, now who’s not being nice?”

Cord turned away from Lilly, in an attempt to ignore her.

“Earl, what song are we on? Whose turn is it?”

“It’s yours, and were going on Number Four.”

“What’s Number Four? What’s going on?”

Lilly immediately jumped in the pool.

“Must you stick your nose in everything?”

“When it come to my brother? Yes, I do.”

Now if Cord wanted to start another war, he could have easily retorted with a quip about Carol and Earl, but he didn’t. No need to poke the hornet's nest.

“Fine; we’re putting together the best fifty music videos we remember from the 1980’s, mainly the 80’s, anyway.”

Now, this was actually subterfuge; Cord was trying to compile a surprise birthday jukebox song list for Earl, on the sly. This was a way to find out what Earl liked; plus, it was fun.

"What are the first four?"

"We're **on** Number Four! We only picked three so far; pay attention if you're gonna butt in."

C said.

"Sorry, Geez. I wanna pick Number Four."

"Well, since it's my pick, I'm gonna have to say….*no!*"

C snapped.

"What do you mean *no*?"

"Just what I said….no! No means no."

Cord said emphatically, and continued.

"For once, you're not getting your way, no matter how much you whine, or complain to your brother. Unless, of course, you have something to offer in exchange; a chit perhaps."

"Forget it pal, you're dreaming."

"Why do you assume everything about you has to do with someone trying to get into your pants? It was a simple question is all….no sex connotations."

"Yeah, right."

Lilly said, as if it was completely unbelievable to her that any guy wouldn't want to jump her at the slightest chance.

"Here, I'll make it easy for you; if you promise to stop talking to me for the next half-hour, unless I *specifically* ask you a question, which you answer with a simple *Yes* or *No*, and nothing more, then you can pick song Number Four, agreed? And if you break the rules, if you talk to me without permission, I get a chit – one per breach. Fair enough?"

Lilly hesitated, not sure if she should answer; she felt it was some sort of trick.

"It's okay, you can answer, it was a question."

Cord assured her, like she was a little girl.

"Shut up asshole; how's *that* for an answer?"

"Now that's one chit."

"I'm not playing your stupid game; pick your own stupid songs."

Lilly huffed as she folded her arms across her chest, just below those perky little breasts, sans bra, that Cord couldn't keep his eyes off, through the celadon tee, along with her extra-short twill khakis. Whenever Lilly got angry, her nipples would get hard; sometimes C would tweak her just for the thrill of seeing the involuntary reflex - a fringe benefit, albeit a dangerous one, at times."

"Okay, we will."

Cord said sarcastically, staring not-so-subtly at her tits. Then he smiled mischievously and looked over at Earl.

"What are you fucking smiling at?"

She snapped.

Earl snickered and blushed; he knew exactly what Cord was up to; Cord told him all about the Lilly biology lesson.

Then Lilly looked down, and figured it out.

"No sex huh? But you can't stop looking, can you? Giggling like little horny kids; you're pathetic, Cord."

"What?!"

But C knew he was nipple-busted. Earl put his head down. Then Lilly got down to business.

"I know Number One has to be Joan Jett. If Earl picked first, it had to be *I Love Rock-N-Roll,* 1981; am I right?"

Lilly said smug.

"Yeah! You're right Bibby! Good guess!"

Earl yelled.

She spied Cord and gave him her famous know-it-all look. Cord frowned; he hated when she was right.

"And you want to know why Earl likes that song so much? Because he wants Joan Jett to walk into a bar, pull off her left glove in the doorway, and walk over and pick him up, in her tight, little red leather jumpsuit and black Cons, with her little perky tits, and flat stomach, while he's standing at the jukebox, and take him home for an all-night romp. Isn't that right, Earl?"

Earl blushed, but Lilly wasn't quite right. Earl loved Joan Jett, for sure, but not for sex; he really didn't even think about the sex part - that was Lilly's department. He just liked her; he really didn't know why, he just did.

"I think she's pretty, and I bet she's nice, and she has really pretty eyes….and I like when she wears sneakers."

Of course his sister never bought it; to Lilly, it, and everything, was always about the sex.

"Yeah right, Earl, it must be the sneakers."

Lilly said deadpan.

"I don't think she goes for the guys, Earl, but the jury's out, so maybe you got a shot. Tell her you like her eyes; girls like that."

C said.

"How do you know what girls like? Is that what you tell all the girls? I thought you liked boys anyway."

Lilly asked, and C ignored.

"I like that song too Earl, but I thought she wore black in that video?"

Cord said, to which Lilly snapped back.

"Of course it was black; it was in black and white, moron. But there's an identical video in color, it actually came first, and she's wearing all red, but the story goes that Joan didn't like how she looked in red, so they switched the video to black and white. But no matter, the color one is the one Earl loves, the *red leather*. Joan Jett in a red leather jumpsuit and black Cons….right Earl?"

He shook his head an emphatic yes, with a big smile; he *loved* those black Cons.

"And all the people in that bar scene pumping their fists and clapping to the song were locals, bar patrons; Earl wishes he was there that day in the bar, right Earl?"

"How do you know all this stupid stuff?"

Cord said to Lilly, annoyed.

"Because I live with an 80's video junkie, who watches the same videos over and over, and researches every detail, and then tells me all the stupid details a thousand fucking times, that's how."

Now Cord always had a half hard-on for Joan Jett too; C thought that was kind of cool – Earl and him growing up worlds apart, both liking her. C always liked that *dirty girl* look; the kind you could take outside and do on her knees in a gravel parking lot. It would have been the perfect opportunity to inject that little anecdote, to share the story, a snippet of his former life outside this place, but for some reason, he chose not to; he didn't say a word.

"Okay, what's Number Two C, since it was your pick?"

"*The Boys Of Summer.*"

Lilly nodded slowly in agreement.

"What, no wisecrack?"

"No, that one's okay."

Cord was surprised.

"Why that one?"

Lilly asked.

"I don't know, I really like the song, and the video was good too, but the song, the lyrics, stand on their own. But I do like when the little kid drumming looks back at the screen, you know, the man and woman running on the beach, and the older version of the kid, at least what I think it's suppose to be, he does the same thing from his desk at the office, breaking a pencil….I like that. I don't know why. But you can't go back, you can *never* go back….a one-way street."

Now that's what Cord said aloud to Lilly, but it was a sidestep, a half-answer, partly true....partly.

What really happened every time that song came on, every time, was C driving her forest green Jaguar on that sunny mid-summer Saturday afternoon, with her by his side, that song spilling from the radio. Her eyes were closed, and he just studied the side of her gorgeous face, her button nose, framed in sunshine, wispy blonde hair dancing in the wind as they barreled down Swamp Road, on their way somewhere he long since forgot. At one time, that time, he thought she might be a keeper; the thought of that now was a bit funny. He long-since concluded such a thing could never really happen. But then, when he was young, things like that seemed possible. Christ, that was so many years ago; he hadn't seen her since and would never see her again. That was a given. He wondered how long it would be till he finally forgot her name, like all the rest. That snippet of memory, barreling down Swamp Road on that beautiful, long-gone day, was why *The Boys Of Summer* was on the list. But that conte didn't leave C's lips either.

Lilly snapped him back to Belvidere.

"I like when they kiss on the beach, and the sun is setting on the water behind them, or shining on the water. I want to see that. I've never seen that; I've never seen the ocean for real….can you believe that?

Living in Jersey and never seeing the ocean, for real; how pathetic is that?"

Lilly said, going from a high to low.

"Why don't you go Lilly? Nothing's stopping you; why don't we all go tomorrow? I'll take you and Earl tomorrow, we'll drive right to the shore, first thing."

"I'll go, I will, but not tomorrow. But I'll go, someday....I will."

Cord noticed she said *I*, not *we,* not *us*. He frowned to himself and let it drop.

"Okay, Number Three, Earl's second pick. Hmm, let's see, this is a tough one; it would have to be, just a wild guess here, Joan Jett and *Bad Reputation*."

"Right! You're so smart Bibby!"

Earl yelled again, hoisting his hands over his head, celebrating Lilly's clairvoyance.

Cord frowned, and then smiled at her; she *was* good.

"Okay, so now were on Number Four; my pick."

Lilly butted in.

"No you don't! You didn't agree to the terms of our deal."

As usual, she ignored him.

"Number Four is *You Might Think,* from the Cars."

Lilly smiled at the thought, which were far from the ramp.

"Okay, even though you cheated, I do like that video, that was a good one. What do you think Earl; should we let her include it?"

Earl looked at Lilly hard, shook his head slow in the negative, more of a scold, and frowned; he wasn't happy.

"No."

Was all he said, through a scowl.

"Why not?"

Cord pressed.

"She knows why; that was *their* favorite song - stupid song."

"What Earl? You like the girl in that video."

Lilly tried to rationalize, but it was weak.

Then Cord realized he just got played for a Button/Lilly song; why is this fucking guy, this loser that left her years ago, still in her head? Cord wasn't smiling either.

Lilly realized that was a pretty mean thing to do, and wholly uncalled for. So she did something rare.

"Sorry, your pick Cord."

Ay accepted the de facto apology, surprised she gave up so easily. He, nor she, commented any further.

"Okay, hey Earl, how about *Oh Yeah;* remember Ferris Bueller? You want to add that one? Who sang that anyway; that was kind of a weird video."

"Yeah, that was good! *Yello* sang that; let's make that Number Four, just because of the movie, not the video; that video was pretty creepy."

Lilly walked over to the plastic cooler they kept in the woods, next to the folding chairs, and pulled out a radio; it looked like a retro mini-boombox, and walked back over to the boys.

"Where'd you get that? That looks like it's *from* the `80's, good God."

"It actually is. It's always with the chairs; we keep it down here to listen to music. It's got fresh batteries, Earl always checks the batteries, right Earl?"

"Right!"

Lilly clicked it on, spun the volume and stuck it in the sand, just up from the water.

"I'm sure they're playing a bunch of old 80's junk, they usually do on Sunday afternoon."

And for the next hour or so, the three of them talked, joked and laughed, listening to the radio, reminiscing about music videos, arguing about good-looking guys and good-looking girls, bad outfits, big hair, cheesy sets and just enjoying each other's company on a sunny summer afternoon.

Even though it was the beginning of July, the river was still running cold. Cord took his time wading out, wearing surf shoes, carefully checking his unstable footing against rocks and submerged twigs, sinking to his ankles in silty river mud. This was definitely not a barefoot type of walk-out; in fact, the muddy sand was kinda gross. But with surf shoes, it was doable.

He made his way out mid-thigh, about fifteen feet from shore. After awhile, the cold water felt good; he would splash it on himself now and again to cool off. He had taken his shirt off; he wasn't as conscious about his scars, and his tan hid some of them. Lilly and Earl didn't notice them as much anymore. And his belly had shrunk and flattened considerably.

Earl was in up to just below his knees, but that wasn't far from Cord, since Earl was about a foot taller. Lilly scolded him from going further into the river; she was in her bare feet, standing at the water's edge.

A couple john-boats came down the ramp and embarked up and down stream, lazy summer fishing. Otherwise, the ramp was theirs. The geese and ducks, masters at knowing if food was in the offing, were nowhere to be found, realizing the trio was not there for them.

And unbeknownst to Earl, the surprise birthday party jukebox slowly filled with video songs from the late 70's, 80's and even some from the 90's; the two of them let Lilly elbow into the queue – not that they really had a choice.

The next two choices:

Video Killed The Radio Star - The Buggles; and
If It Makes You Happy - Sheryl Crow.

Cord couldn't believe Lilly would add a Sheryl Crow song, just because of her last name, but she did. He didn't ask her why. Earl was happy; anything named Crow, even without the *e* at the end, made him happy.

Followed by:

954

They both knew Cord liked the skinny, barefoot girl; Earl and Cord watched the video at least a dozen times in the apartment. Lilly thought that would have been number one for Cord, although she didn't think the girl was good-looking. Typical Lilly - no woman was good-looking but her. Of course, Earl remembered all the verses, and cured Cord's earworm.

Next:

Mickey - Tony Basil.

Earl had a thing for cheerleaders, always had. But when C and Lilly asked him why he picked the song, he answered simple.

"I think she's pretty, and she jumps good and she looks happy….I like that."

And that was that.

Next came:

Wicked Games - Chris Isaak.

Lilly couldn't believe there were really beaches with black sand. She always wanted the couple on that beach to be her and Button; for better or worse, the song reminded her of him, for what he could sometimes be, during the good times. Button never knew about that, or this song; neither did Earl, so that song made it onto the jukebox, even though Lilly didn't know there was a jukebox in play, or even a surprise party for her brother.

She just thought this exercise was a stupid best-of list the boys were fooling around with in their heads at the ramp. But even so, even though she didn't think it really meant anything, she felt a bit shitty about the Button subterfuge. But she did it anyway, her own little secret. She looked down at her toes, sunk in the sand at the boat ramp. Was Button ever coming back? Did she really want him to? It wasn't always an automatic *yes* anymore; to Lilly's surprise, some days it was a *maybe*, some days it was a *probably no*.

Was that change because of Cord? Not necessarily; sometimes maybe, sometimes not.

But it was also because of Earl; Button *hated* Earl, always had. In Button's eyes, Earl was the source of their trouble, more than just about anything else.

Lilly thought she was maybe, just maybe, growing out of the Button habit. But deep down, she knew - if he walked through the door tomorrow, in spite of herself, despite any sense of restraint or good judgment, she was his, she would run to him, she just knew it. She frowned at her weakness.

Song selection continued; next in the queue:

Don't You Forget About Me – Simple Minds;

then came:

Rain - Blind Melon.

"Why that one Earl?"

Cord asked.

"Don't you remember the video C?"

Earl asked, incredulous that Cord didn't remember.

"No, I don't."

"It's a chubby little girl, wearing big funny-looking glasses, and dressed all up in a bumblebee dance dress. She's dancing and happy but everybody makes fun or her, or ignores her, so then she's sad, until she wanders into a field full of other people wearing bumblebee suits too. Then she runs to them and is accepted in just like she is, no changes, and she is dancing and happy. That makes me happy, because I want that little bumblebee girl to be happy, with all the other bumblebee people."

Lilly smiled at Earl.

"Earl, you're the best brother ever, you know that?"

"Yeah, I do."

He smiled mischievously.

"Plus, I have bumblebee shorts; the best bumblebee shorts ever!"

Earl added.

Both Cord and Lilly smiled.

"I'll get you some funny-looking glasses, Earl."

Cord said.

"He's got 'em, his stupid fake mail-reading glasses."

"Hey! Those are my *Gregson-glasses*! That's not nice Lilly."

Earl yelled in mock protest, then he smiled and whispered to Cord.

"They're not *real* glasses, and I only wear them to read the mail, and to annoy her."

"I know."

Cord whispered back.

And the queue continued:

On The Dark Side - John Cafferty and the Beaver Brown Band;
Bakers Street - Gerry Rafferty; and
Fat Bottom Girls - Queen.

The last was obviously Earl's choice, from the race with C around the Park. The song didn't have a video, and with the smirks between the two of them, Lilly knew it had to have something to do with Carol. Not wanting to hear the details, she let it slide, but quietly fumed.

Next:

I Melt With You - Modern English; and
Got My Mind Set On You - George Harrison.

"Okay, why that one?"

Lilly asked C.

"The girl in the video arcade, I've always liked her, the blonde."

She stared at him and she could see it in his face.

"Come on, it's more than that, what is it? Who does she remind you of?"

He exhaled long.

"You ever want to take a piece of your past and just freeze-frame it, to hold onto it forever, without change?"

Lilly frowned and nodded her head yes. Cord knew what she was nodding to; he shouldn't have asked the question.

"Well, that song reminds me of a time when I thought I wanted to do that, with a person I once knew."

"But you don't anymore? And who's the person?"

"Time moves on, people come and go; that's just the way it is."

That's all she got out of him.

Windy - The Association;

Earl asked if he could include this one, even though it didn't have a real video.

"Can I C?"

"Sure, no problem, we make the rules; why do you like it Earl?"

"Because it reminds me of Bibby. Ever since I was a kid, I always think of Lilly when I hear this song, and it

959

just makes me happy, happy that she's my sister….the best sister ever."

Earl turned to Lilly.

"I love you Lilly."

"I love you too Earl."

She whispered sweet.

Next up:

Run Runaway - Slade; and
Thunder Island - Jay Ferguson.

"Thunder Island! That's pretty queer, C."

Lilly taunted him.

"I know, I know, kind of a goofy 70's song; no guy, no real guy's guy would ever admit to really liking that song, but I do. I don't know, I always kinda wanted to find that girl. Anyway, Earl doesn't care that the song is a bit queer, right Earl *[Earl shrugged his shoulders]*? And we all know you can keep your mouth shut about me liking that song, right Lilly?"

Cord said sarcastically.

"Sure, your secret's safe with me."

Lilly said matter-of-fact.

"Gee, thanks; why don't I feel too good about that?"

Just then the radio shouted out:

960

It didn't have to get past the first line when Lilly knew Cord was in big trouble; she only knew she was safe, because Cord was closer. C was oblivious, looking down the river, away from Earl.

"Hey, I love this song! Who sings thi…."

C never finished his sentence.

Earl had launched into a full sprint through the water and was on Cord in about three steps, swallowing him in his shadow. Before he knew it, the big man had tackled him into the water in a tidal wave of commotion.

Cord thought he was dead, drowned in the Delaware.

But as quick as the big man smothered him in the water, he was off him, had picked him clear out of the water and held him over his head, like a rag doll. Cord was gasping for air, water running off his bald head.

"What the **fuck!** *What the hell are you doing Earl?"*

Earl had turned Cord so he could see Lilly on the shore; she was doubled over, laughing. Cord was dangling in the air, eight feet up, at the end of Earl's touchdown arms.

"I love this song!"

Earl shouted over the music.

"Throw Danny-Boy Earl! *Throw him!*"

Lilly yelled, while she was still laughing.

"NO! Don't throw Danny-Boy!"

Cord pleaded, but it was too late; the song returned to the fateful stanza:

> *I get knocked down;*
> *But I get up again....*

And Earl let Cord rip, a two-hundred-pound shot-put called C; but Earl was sure to launch him into a deeper pool of water, just to be safe. Cord was a screaming projectile, till he hit the water in a half-cannonball, disappearing under the surface.

He came up for air, fully expecting another assault. But there was none.

"I can't come get you C, the water's too deep; it's dangerous, and I can't swim."

Earl said, calmly.

"I know you can't swim, but you can throw pretty fucking good now, can't you?"

Cord paddled his way toward shore, till he knew he could stand. Lilly was still laughing, barely able to catch her breath.

"Sorry C, that song always gets me excited."

"Yeah, I see that."

Cord said as he walked with a purpose past Earl, out of the water, right up to Lilly. She watched him come in, a dripping mess, still laughing.

She should have run.

When she realized what was going on, it was too late. Cord quickly grabbed her, and hoisted her in a fireman's carry; she tried to squirm and kick her way out of it, but Cord locked her up firm and walked into the water.

"Hey, Hey! Hey!! *Hey!! Earl!!*"

Was all she shouted as he marched her into deeper water. Cord tried to hoist her overhead, like Earl did him. But he had to loosen and shift his grip, which gave her the opening to squirm like an angry snake, writhing in his arms.

He started to lose control of her, and saw her mouth open, ready to hit him with a death-bite, so he yelled in anticipation of being bit and simply clamped onto whatever limb he could reach, rolled his shoulders clockwise in a curl and fell into the deep pool of water, with her kicking and screaming, like Ahab and Moby Dick, till she disappeared under the water with him.

Earl was too busy laughing to help.

They both surfaced together, with entirely different expressions.

"**You** are a fucking *asshole*!"

She screamed, wet hair flopped over her face.

"Uh huh; who's laughing now? Harder to bite me underwater, isn't it?"

Cord said, smiling at Earl, who was still laughing.

"Man, Earl that water is cold! How you doing over there Lilly?"

She was still thrashing, trying not to touch the slimy river bottom with her bare feet.

"Nice cheap feel! You're a pervert; asshole!"

While they were underwater, somehow, Cord's hand mistakenly slid up under Lilly's shorts, clear up to her ass. It was a fluke; he's not even sure how it happened, but it did.

"Like I planned that, with my eyes closed, under water, with you trying to bite me; come on, Lilly."

Cord said incredulously.

"But you *do* have a very soft ass cheek, I have to say; I didn't feel any underwear, either."

"That's because I'm not wearing any, shithead!"

They both got to shallow water, and Lilly stood up; her celadon shirt stuck to her front-side, nipples clearly visible; as much as C wanted those khaki shorts to be transparent too, they weren't.

He tried to look away, to be a bit less obvious.

"That's right, keep your perv eyes to yourself."

She said, shivering in the summer heat.

Apparently he was a little too obvious.

"How can you possibly be shivering?"

"Maybe because I'm not *fat* like you."

Lilly crossed her arms across her breasts, to hide her nipples.

I can't believe you did that!"

She barked.

"It certainly was funny when Earl did it to me, though, wasn't it?"

"Yeah it was."

She said.

And with that, the three of them smiled.

In all the excitement, none of them noticed what had slipped through the woods, what was standing at the edge of the clearing, less than fifteen feet from Lilly….mouth wide open, gums exposed.

CHAPTER 102 – KISSING HIS HEAD GENTLY TILL HE STOPPED TREMBLING

A low, deep rumble.

The kind that gets your attention but quick, stiffens your spine and forces you to act; the kind that means certain trouble.

A single, thick stria of white mucous swung from its mouth, inching toward the ground. It set its quads low to the sand, ass-end slightly raised, wild eyes in an oversized head, fixated squarely on Lilly.

Two-hundred twenty pounds of unpredictable anger, muscle and blackness, demanding immediate attention. His chest was broad, his head immense, like a block of stone.

Lilly froze, too afraid to utter either of their names. She knew who it was, but she was never this close, only muffled noises behind closed doors and tall fences. Newcomers in Town; white trash on Depue.

He was bigger than she imagined, and she imagined him big.

He somehow found a way to bull through the metal gate, snapping the latch, making a beeline down Depue, trying to quickly get as far away as he could from where he'd been. Then he heard the thrashing in the River; the noise drove him right for the ramp, right for the three of them….alpha instinct.

And the first he found was Lilly.

Cord froze. Only his eyes darted, searching for something, anything, to use, to attack - but he found nothing. Head to head he would be a goner.

He was impotent.

Loki was now no more than ten feet from Lilly, slowly closing the gap, his growl deeper and more menacing as he inched. Earl was a good fifteen feet to the west; Cord ten feet further still.

Loki glared at Lilly with black, dead eyes; Cord looked at Lilly, who looked helplessly at Earl, who lasered on Loki. All were now set like stone; no one moved a muscle.

Then Earl saw it; it was almost imperceptible, but he eyed it - it lasted for less than a second. Loki tensed his legs and rocked slightly, ready to explode – he would go for Lillian's neck.

In a flash, just as Loki was about to down his prey, an explosion of river water and a primordial bellow startled the dog, who took his eye off Lilly just long enough to brace for the impact. It didn't really even see it happen, he just heard the noise of the water and knew it was trouble.

In an instant, two-hundred twenty pounds of vicious intent vanished under the immensity that was Earl. The only noise was a muffled yelp as Earl's three-hundred sixty-five pounds pile-drove it hard into the wet sand; the cry of a helpless dog.

"Kill it Earl, **kill it!**"

Lilly screamed in a guttural cry, fear mastitis to venom, her eyes wild with fury.

But Earl did no such thing.

His enormous mitt engulfed the dog's massive square snout and clamped it shut. With a single hand he pinned its powerful jaw like a vice. The dog winced, then went limp in his grasp. Out of his yard, his prison, he became what he was meant to be; the ultimate alpha, who didn't know something bigger existed out there. But now, it was terrified; Earl could see it in Loki's eyes. And he felt bad. So Earl loosened his grip, just a bit.

The dog sensed its chance. It thrashed violently against Earl's chest, dug its claws into Earl's thigh, trying to get wrest free and attack its attacker.

But it was futile.

Earl simply clenched tight his hands and arms, bear-hugging the dog against the wet sand until the air was slowly squeezed from the two-hundred twenty pounder, till the fight left him, quietly deflated. Earl cradled him in silence; a massive dog, handled like a sack of potatoes. The dog lay still, breathing quietly, afraid to move.

"I'm gonna bring him back. If they would just let him out to play, pay attention to him and not hit him, he wouldn't be so mean. I feel bad for him."

There was no common sympathy from either Lilly or Cord.

"Just walk into the water and drown him Earl; he's a mean, fucking dog, and he's gonna hurt someone, like he was gonna hurt me. **Mother-fucker** *[Lilly yelled at the dog]*! No one will know; just do it, Earl."

"I'll know….mom will know.   It's not his fault Bibby, they don't treat him right; he doesn't know what it's like to be happy."

Earl put his head down and looked in its eyes; the dog couldn't move in Earl's iron grip, but he could feel it trembling. In one quick motion, Earl scooped the dog off the sand and held him, like a child, across his chest.

The dog was trembling fiercely, unsure of its fate. Earl was sopping wet; so neither Lilly nor Cord noticed the warm stream of Loki's urine that ran down Earl's leg, into his surf shoe. But Earl didn't care one lick.

He gently kissed Loki on the side of his neck, burying his nose in the folds of wrinkled fur, and walked up the ramp, toward Depue Street, to bring him back to the hell hole that was home.

And for that, he was sad. But he knew that's what he had to do.

"I'll see you guys later; Loki's gonna be all right. Sorry he frightened you Lilly."

Earl hoisted the massive English Mastiff up a bit, across his chest, and whispered kind words in Loki's ear, kissing his head gently till he stopped trembling.

CHAPTER 103 - FOR YOUR EYES ONLY - PLEASE SAY YES

Earl quietly opened the apartment door. Lilly was in the kitchen, back to him, cooking; he could smell the flank steak, his favorite.

Earl had air-dried during his walk; the blood on his leg from Loki's claws had congealed in a long jagged line across his dark skin, but it still throbbed. The smell of urine had faded to a whiff.

"I'm gonna take a shower, okay?"

No answer from the kitchen. Oh boy, mad again. Earl put his head down and made his way to the bathroom in silence.

The water upstairs was running.

C had been standing in the shower for a good half hour, barely moving, save the occasional light tap of his head against the wall, which he did without notice. His skin splotchy pink from the water, which was near scalding. His mind was racing, and he was anxious, a loop of visions in his head, which he couldn't turn off.

'You're better than you think.'

That's what Selena told him that last day together, those last minutes together, a whirlwind encounter, which seemed more than a lifetime ago.

'You're better than you think.'

She said it again on the sidewalk last week.

He still didn't believe it.

He couldn't get the thought of the tortoise out of his
head.

A huge land tortoise crossing the road, monstrous, in the
middle of the day. It must have been a hundred pounds,
and a hundred years old. He had never seen anything
like it in the wild. He was driving, and it was just about
straddling the double yellow, about fifty yards ahead.
He enjoyed it, for just a moment.

Just then, a tractor trailer emerged from around the bend.

Before he could swerve, flash his lights, lean on his
horn, before he could do anything but watch, the huge
trucker came upon the tortoise. For a split second, he
thought it was going to be safe, to make it.

But the front left wheel just caught the tail and the back
tip of the shell; it almost made it.

The wheel tipped the turtle vertical, and pushed it along
the road for ten feet or so, till the whole animal
involuntarily spun clockwise under the truck tire; in slow
motion, the shell exploded, like a grenade, spraying the
animal across the road.

The truck never slowed, never stopped. Cord stopped
his car, in shock at what he'd just seen, the thick smear
and broken shell, blood and flesh ten feet before him.

But he didn't turn the car and go after the truck, he
didn't pull the driver out and beat him to a pulp, like he
thought he would, like he thought he should. Like he
should have done.

Instead, he did nothing but drive on, and to this day, he
wasn't sure why.

And he was ashamed; to this day, he was still ashamed.
And he regretted seeing what he saw, and not being able

to prevent it, to save that old turtle from a horrible, senseless death. That was fifteen years ago, but it felt like yesterday; that clip had played in his head a thousand times….there was no delete button. He couldn't stop the vision of that helpless, harmless animal, one that had seen more days than he ever would, exploding in front of his eyes….over and over. And endless reel, him endlessly impotent. It sickened him.

And like the turtle, he endlessly looped the image of Earl smothering that dog in the sand before he could even think, while he stood there. That dog was about to leap, to hurt Lillian, and Earl acted, and he didn't.

His head hit the shower wall harder. Why didn't he move? Why?

At least Lilly was safe, no thanks to him, but she was safe.

Impotent rang his head, as he rapped the shower wall, eyes closed, blood boiling.

Earl was dressed and headed out to the front room; dinner was on the table, along with the day's mail, neatly stacked to the side of his plate, like it always was when Lilly beat him to the mailbox. He wasn't allowed to rummage through the stack till he finished eating, not even a peek; he knew the rules. Lilly would never sort it, that was Earl's job; she got the bills – he got the junk.

"Did you invite C down?"

"He doesn't eat meat, you know that."

Lillian stated monotone.

"He usually still comes down and sits with us, and he could eat the string beans – I'll give him mine; is he coming?"

972

Earl said in a bit of a plead.

"He didn't seem in too good a mood after you left. I *can't* believe he just stood there when that dog came!"

Lillian couldn't get the thought of C's inaction out of her mind. She didn't want to call it aloud what she thought it really was….cowardice.

"He would've jumped at him, but I was closer."

"Earl, he didn't move a muscle! Button would have killed that dog, broke its neck, right then and there – done. *He* would have protected me."

"Don't say that Lilly, Cord would have stopped Loki, and Cord wouldn't hurt him, either."

"That dog is way bigger than Cord; what was he gonna do? *Nothing!* Just like he did….nothing."

"What would jerk-head do? He's way smaller than Cord!"

Earl said snide.

"That doesn't matter – he knows how to handle animals."

"You mean **hurt** animals!"

Earl yelled. Lillian ignored him.

"Plus, he's in way better shape. And you know Button would have killed that dog on the spot, no problem, no problem at all. And that fucking dog *needs* to be killed!"

Earl knew she was right about one thing - Button was crazy, and if he saw something was going to hurt Lilly, he would have surely killed it, and enjoyed doing it.

Hurting Lilly was Button's job, and his job alone. But Lillian was wrong about Loki; he didn't need to be hurt, he needed someone to care about him, to love him. He needed Earl.

Earl sat silent, not answering his sister; he just pushed his string beans around the plate in an endless circle, his fork scratching the plate like nails on a chalkboard. He was waiting for her to talk and tell him to stop scraping; when it came to the silent treatment and being annoying, Earl was way better at the game than Lillian; she almost always gave in first.

First came the long huff, then the snark.

"*What*? What now?"

Earl didn't even try to convince Lillian that Loki was a good dog that got hurt all the time – he didn't even know how it felt to be happy. She would never agree. So he just stuck to his friend.

"Don't be mad at C, *please* Lilly."

Earl said, head down, still scratching the plate with his fork.

"I'm not mad."

But she was. Worse yet, she was disappointed; it made her compare Cord to Button, and in her mind, there was still no comparison, and that made her miss Button all the more. She'd forgave him, long ago, for everything….what she knew, and what she didn't….*all* of it. Why wouldn't he just come home?

"….and stop scraping your plate; Christ, you're driving me crazy!"

Earl silenced his fork, and that was that; minutes passed in silence, with just the sound of Earl eating, and Lilly longing.

Earl cleaned his plate, dropped his fork on the empty platter and watched Lilly intently as she stared numb at the wall, her own fork stuck upright, frozen in her food. She barely touched her dinner.

She finally felt his stare.

"What?!"

She said, annoyed.

"Are you done yet?"

"Does it *look* like I'm done?"

Earl didn't answer; he just continued to stare, like a hungry dog waiting for scraps. She knew what he was up to, but she wasn't budging. She prevented it all day yesterday, as punishment, for *yesterday's* Earl-fiasco, and was going to hold it some more; she wasn't ready to give in. But they both knew Earl had much more patience in these games than Lilly, and he let her off easy yesterday, because he felt bad. But *not* today; today he was on mail-mission. After about another dog-stare minute, she gave in; it wasn't worth the fight.

"Oh okay, open the God-damn mail, but don't talk to me about the stupid letters. I want to eat in silence, without your fucking commentary; you start talking, and I'm throwing it all away – every last piece of paper - I *mean* it!"

He just shook his head vigorously *yes* and pulled the pile in front of him, like the best dessert ever. His wooden letter opener, and the Gregson glasses she hated so much, were set neatly beside the pile of mail, like Lilly always did for him. Every night there was mail.

He was in heaven. It was a bigger pile than usual, a good six to eight pieces. He carefully placed the glasses on his head, in a slow, methodical way, grabbed the opener, and went to work.

The first two were standard junk fare, which Earl relished, reading every line under his breath. He was ready to explode wanting to share the gritty, inane details with Lilly; she was ready to pounce on him and throw the whole lot of it away if he did.

The next two were bills – he could tell; he was good at that. By rule, he opened them, but set them in a separate pile for Lilly to pay. Earl never read the bills….boring.

Lilly got tired of looking at her food, pushed the plate toward Earl; he always ate her leftovers. Now he was truly in hog heaven; more food and lots of mail to devour.

Lillian made her way over to the computer, to check up on what was happening in the news, and eventually find her way to porn; it always ended in porn of some sort.

Earl made his way to the last article of mail, bottom of the pile; this one was felt decidedly different. It was a thick envelope, on heavy cream-colored linen stock. A neatly handwritten address, in perfect bold cursive - it was *Spencerian Script*, although Earl certainly didn't know that - all he knew was that it was the fanciest writing he had ever seen, like it was written a hundred years ago, maybe even *more*. The liquid ink was *Maya Blue*, deposited on the cellulose through the flexible nib of an heirloom fountain pen, a gift from a grateful client, used only for special occasions, and special recipients.

It had been written with purpose and great care.

That careful mix of solvents, blue pigment and water - a regal ink - set upon the linen in a perfect mix of surface tension, viscosity and saturation, pulled together by the expressive hand of his suitor, dressed a correspondence like none Earl had laid eyes upon in all his thirty-nine years. He stared at it in silence, unable to speak, believing this was surely the most important mail he had ever received in his *entire* life.

And so it read:

Mr. Earl Liddell
249 Water Street; Suite 2
Belvidere, New Jersey 07823

Personal and Confidential - For Your Eyes Only -
Please Say Yes

CHAPTER 104 – *NO. 6 - I LOVE YOU*

Earl looked over at Lilly, nervous; she wasn't paying attention, engrossed in whatever occupied the computer screen, the volume was turned low.

He slowly, gently rubbed his fingers across the dried ink, trying to feel the words:

Suite 2

Wow, Earl never even knew he lived in a real suite!

Please Say Yes

Yes to what?! How could he say yes when he didn't even know what the question was? Oh my God, this was already a big mystery! Where were Ken and Sandy when you needed them?! They could solve this mystery fast, but Earl wasn't as smart as them, and they weren't around to ask; he was in this one alone, so he would have to figure it out all by himself!

His palms started to sweat, then he felt himself getting sweaty all over. He was never good in a crisis! He took a deep breath, his eyes darting over at Bibby. She was staring intently at the screen, her hand buried in her lap, trying to be sneaky about moving her hips. Earl knew *exactly* what she was up to, so he figured he had some time before she stopped squirming around in her seat. She always tried to squirm as little as possible when he was in the room, but in the end, Bibby could never help herself, and she would squirm and sigh a lot. But she wasn't at the real squirmy-sighy part yet, so he had some time. *Score!*

There was no return address; who was it from?! Earl wanted to open it slowly and rip it open like a Christmas present – both at the same time.

He decided on slow.

He gently lifted the red and green-handled wooden letter opener, in the shape of a Haida-style bird, and studied it. It was his mother's; her favorite knick-knack. He never knew where she got it – for as long as he could remember, it was in the house, on her desk.

She used it every day to open the mail.

He asked her once if it was from his dad; she just smiled and never answered; Earl took that as a *mostly yes*. It was the only thing he had that was his dads, whether it was or not didn't really matter. To him, it *was* his dads, then his moms, and now his. Earl didn't have many things, but it was one of the most important things he had, maybe the *most* important, and he used it every day to open the mail, just like his mom did. It was one of the most important tasks entrusted to him.

And he took the job very seriously.

Earl slowly spun the wooden bird in his hand, looking at the detail: the green body and head; the red dollop of paint on the crown, with red wings; the yellow feet that looked like shoes; and the yellow beak, or at least the base of what used to be a beak.

It had been broken off years ago; Lilly threw it across the room on Fourth Street right after their mom went away; the beak splintered to pieces when it hit the wall. She gathered it all and carried it a block and a half from the house, throwing it in one of the garbage cans in the Park.

Earl laid in bed till Lilly fell asleep. Then he quietly snuck out of bed, out the front door and, at two in the morning, ran down to the Park in bare feet. Under the amber glow of a single street lamp at each corner of the Park, he rummaged through each of the four large garbage cans set at the four Park corners, fingering through wet, stinking garbage, and open plastic baggies of stinky dog poop dumped by the dog-walkers. He spread the detritus on the ground, feeling his way in the weak amber light. Lilly took the kitchen flashlight, the only flashlight they had, into her bed, to be sure he didn't take it; she *knew* he would go rummaging.

Sure enough, he found the broken letter opener in the last can, the one furthest from the house, the only one where the street light was burned out, so he had to feel around in the can and on the ground in complete darkness.   He should have known Lilly would have gone to that furthest dark can and should have checked that one first – Ken and Sandy would have known to do that, for sure. In the end, it took him over two hours, to find it and put all the garbage back in the cans; he was wet, smelly and shivering in the April night air, with dog poop smeared between his toes. But by four-thirty in the morning, after he got home, rinsed himself with the garden hose in the yard, and crawled into bed, shivering cold, he pinned his dad's opener, his mom's opener, *his* opener, to his chest, holding it in a death-grip. It was back home....safe. But he never did find the bits of wooden beak.

Lilly never knew he found it till years later; he was home when she happened upon it by chance, hidden in his armoire. She walked up to him watching television and held it up, in his face – inches from his nose – and stood in silence. Earl started to cry, knowing she was going to break it into a thousand pieces, so he could *never* put it back together, and throw it away all over again.

But Lilly didn't say a word; she simply turned, walked back into his room and placed it in the armoire where she found it, in silence. Neither one specifically acknowledged it, nor talked about it, ever again. From then on, every night there was mail, Lilly placed the opener beside his plate, along with the Gregson glasses, and Earl was allowed to use it to open the mail.

And he was happy.

Earl spun the opener in his hand, looking at the other details: the tiny white paint dots for the eyes – there were no pupils; the green paint worn off the breastbone; and the three little grooves in the back of the wooden head, like the skin folds in the back of Earl's neck. The whole opener was so light, like a feather; the wooden blade stained a light caramel and sporting nicks and scratches on its edges, from opening thousands of letters over the past forty-plus years.

Earl smiled; he *loved* that letter opener! And it was about to open the most important piece of mail Earl ever received in his entire life, in thirty nine years.

He adjusted his Gregson glasses, and carefully, deliberately, sliced open the top of the overstuffed packet. The anticipation was thick, his heart beating hard. He splayed the envelope and emptied the contents; five pieces of expensive paper, all trimmed in gold, and what looked like a folded newspaper article.

Oh boy, like a box, within a box, within a box - all sorts of stuff to read! He didn't even know where to start!

Then he found the cover letter.

Dear Earl:

The honor of your presence is requested at:

Actaeon's Annual Fall Bacchanalia

*To thank our investors and celebrate another successful
year.*

*Kindly accept this invitation for you and a revered guest
to join me
at a private, royal reception at:*

L'antre du Lion

*Our first venture into the woods, outside the confines of
the venerable City!*

October 14, 2006

What!

Earl couldn't believe his eyes; a royal reception at
Carol's house, and he was invited! And he could bring a
guest!

What's a bacchanalia? Is it something to eat? Is it
good? No time to think about that - keep reading!

Earl quickly scanned through the rest of the cover letter,
a full page of important royal details, even though he
wasn't sure what most of it really meant:

- A black tie evening of pageantry and red-carpet
  events;
- Round trip limousine transportation to the *le
  repaire de lions*;
- Music by the *Loretto-Marigold Ensemble*;
- Live and silent auctions;
- Private commissions by on-premise *Premier
  Coup* artisans;

Followed by an agenda:

- 6:00 pm – *Aperitifs* and an artisan cheese market;
- 7:30 pm – *Haute cuisine*, epicurean delights from Europe and the Sub-Continent;
- 9:30 pm – Dessert, *digestifs* and cigar bar;
- 11:30 pm – After Party *Independent Film Festival Shorts*….to dawn; and
- ? am – After-After Party *petit dejeuner* for the rebel rock-ribs.

Wow, that sounds like a sleepover!

The letter was signed:

Carol Crowe
Managing Member

She inked over her name on his invite, crossing it out and simply scripting: *Carol.*

Earl was nearly bursting; he wanted to jump up and tell Lilly, but he knew this one *had* to be kept quiet, if he could.

Wait, there was more!

- A little gold-lined return envelope, addressed to Actaeon;
- A RSVP note on lightly textured card stock, asking for a response by August 1st ;
- Directions to Belvidere *[why'd she send him that, he wondered]*; and
- A list of properties and fund names, with all sorts of stuff Earl didn't understand.

He simply didn't know what to do; he was ready to blow.

He knew! He would run upstairs and tell Cord; maybe he could go with him as his *revered guest*. That would be the best of the best, Earl thought.

Oh boy, October 14th couldn't come fast enough! He quickly counted the days in his head: July – it was the second; how many days in July? Thirty, no thirty-one, or was it thirty? What's the rhyme again? He could never remember unless he did the rhyme! How many days does July have? Think! August – thirty-one days; September has thirty; October – another fourteen days. Wow, it was the week after his birthday! What a present! The best present ever!

He tried to do the math in his head, but he was so nervous, he kept messing it up. He got up hurriedly and ran into the kitchen to get a pencil, rousing Lilly.

"What are you doing running around?"

She said, annoyed that he interrupted her not-so-subtle porn crawl and crotch grind.

"Nothing!"

Earl said that a little too quickly, she thought. Something was up.

Earl had his tongue out like a little kid concentrating as he did the math on a scratch pad in the kitchen:

$$29 + 31 + 30 + 14 = 104.$$

One hundred and four days! That was *way* too long; he would never make it!

He would count down the days, crossing off one each morning, right when he woke up. Holy mackerel, him, Cord and Carol watching movies all night long! Maybe they could even make S'mores!

Boy he couldn't wait to tell Cord! He didn't even have to try and sneak a stamp from out of Lilly's drawer for the bills to send back the RSVP because Carol already put one on the envelope! Lilly sent all the bills and kept track of the stamps; no *way* he could risk her finding out he took one; after all, why would *he* need a stamp? Lilly was smart about these things, but Carol was even smarter! She even outsmarted Lilly about the stamp! Carol was the *smartest* ever!

He tried to nonchalantly walk back to the table to collect his secret invitation, but it wasn't easy, his heart was beating a mile a minute. He figured he would stash it in his armoire, under the *Kama Sutra*; Lilly would *never* find it there.

It was then that Earl spied the folded newspaper article, with a small sheet of white-lined paper clipped to it. It was another secret note from Carol!

He quickly sat down and read it, his back turned to Lilly.

Earl:

Please give this to your sister, she really needs it.
But don't tell her I gave it to you;
say you found it at Sam's, or something like that.

I don't think she can fill in too many of the boxes.
Maybe more people, like me, would like her….if she was
just a little nicer.
Then maybe some day she and I could be
friends….wouldn't that be nice?

Earl just stared at the note, then stared some more. His whole body was tingly. He reread the second and third paragraph six or seven times, especially the third one, fast, then slow, then slower, analyzing every word over and again; he couldn't believe what he was seeing.

He didn't think he could be more in love with Carol than he already was; but now he was.

And he knew his mom liked her, and Cord liked her….if he could only get Lilly to like her; maybe this piece of paper would help. He slowly unfolded the clipping; it was from the *Express-Times*, that pedantic local rag.

It said:

The Mini-Page - Especially For Kids And Their Families

'Oh Say, Can You Say, Polite Things All Day'

These are presents all of us can give;
polite words to others.

Oh boy, this should be fun! Earl scanned the page. What followed was a listing of one hundred phrases kids should say to be polite.

They ranged from:

- *No. 1 – You Look Great!*

to

- *No. 100 – We'll Have Fun Together!*

Earl started to giggle to himself; he could hardly imagine *any* of these coming out of Lilly's mouth. He whispered them, just loud enough so he could hear himself talk, in a squeaky girls voice, pretending to be Lilly, finishing the phrases as if Lilly was saying them:

- *No. 10 – That was fun* Earl, let's do it again!

- *No. 22 – That's a wonderful idea* Earl, you are so smart!

- *No. 29 – I'm pleased to meet you* Carol! Will you be my best friend?

- *No. 41 – You are my hero* Cord! You are so brave and strong!

- *No. 50 – Are you all right* Earl? Sorry I stabbed you with the knitting needle!

- *No 55 – I'd like to hear what you have to say* Earl, since you never repeat yourself!

987

Earl giggled some more to himself, cracking up at his own little jokes.

"No. 78 – How do you feel?"

Came the low voice, over his shoulder.

Earl turned in horror to see Lilly standing over him. She continued in a low hurt whisper, as he turned back around and sat in silence.

"Well, I don't feel very well, Earl, since my brother is laughing at me, making fun of me. Let's look some other ones; how about *No. 96 – You are very talented*….at hurting my feelings, that is….thanks, Earl.

No. 89 – You make me feel special."

Earl hung his head in shame.

Lilly quietly scooped the article and Carol's note off the table, slowly walked down the hall and into her room, gently clicking the door shut.

Earl wished she was mad; it was way better when she got mad. This was worse. His eyes were wet, and he started to softly cry.

Lilly sat on the bed, frowning to herself. She had quickly read Carol's note over Earl's shoulder, but she read it slower now. She should have been furious, but she wasn't. Deep down, on some level, she knew Carol was right, partly right anyway, although she would admit it to no one….ever. A lot of people liked Lilly, and a lot of people didn't; there was no middle ground when it came to her. She knew that; she just chose not to think about it, until now.

And she didn't know what Carol was up to, why was she being so nice to Earl, flirting with him like that; it was

kind of creepy, she thought. She *had* to have some
ulterior motive, something up her sleeve. She certainly
didn't like Earl; someone like her wouldn't *really* like
someone like Earl – why would she? She was using him
to get at her. Lilly had to protect her brother.

She unfolded the paper and scanned the list, the kid's
Mini-Page.   She shook her head in disgust, then
whispered aloud, like Earl had done earlier.

- *No. 5 – You did a good job* Cord, in saving me
  from the fucking dog;

- *No. 20 – How are you doing* Button? When are
  you coming home, to take me away from this
  place, forever;

- *No. 99 – Be careful* Carol, be **very** careful; you
  better not fuck with Earl or me or Button
  anymore.

She scanned backward, to the middle of the list.

- *No. 65 – I miss you* Lillian didn't say *mom* out
  loud, she simply whispered it to herself, in her
  brain, hoping someone was listening, someone
  would hear, and someone would answer. But all
  she heard was what she *always* heard….silence.
  Her eyes got red, and Lillian hung her head,
  sitting alone on the edge of her bed.

"No. 6! Lilly….No. 6!"

Lilly heard Earl yell from the table in the front room; she
could tell from his voice that he was frantic and he was
crying. Lilly looked at her sheet; a single tear tracked
her right cheek as she read the entry.

- *No. 6 – I love you.*

CHAPTER 105 – EVEN A LIGHT STROKE STILL HURT

It was Tuesday, the fourth of July; seventy-six days and still nary a word, nothing but silence brushing his brain. And for that, he was happy.

Cord had the day off from Sam's, but there was to be no sleeping in, as he was reminded by the rapid knocking on the door.

"C, you up?!"

Cord stretched long and wiped the sleep from his eyes. He had actually been up for a half-hour or so, jerking on and off to one of several Lilly fantasies, but he kept dozing off and never finished. He was in the middle of yet another half-hearted attempt when Earl knocked; that was the nail that made him give up for good.

"I am now."

He said, loud enough for Earl to hear down the hall. The door opened and in a flash Earl was in his bedroom doorway.

"I said I was gonna show you today!"

"Yeah, I know, but today's got a ways to go yet; do we need to go now?"

"Come on! You said you wanted to see it!"

"Okay, okay; is your sister making you breakfast? Can I snag some?"

"She's finishing it now; hurry up!"

"Hey, what did she ever do with the List?"

"I don't know; she took it in her room and I never saw it again. I'm sure she ripped it up, or burned it; it doesn't matter – I memorized Carol's letter, and you got a copy of the List too, so we still have it. Oh boy, she didn't talk to me, not a single word, for a full day and no mail again yesterday – she hid it. She can be *brutal* with the mail you know....just saying."

"Sorry buddy, but sometimes you could look at that - the no-taking part - as a good thing; if she doesn't talk to you, she can't be yelling at you. Anyway, listen, I'll be down in ten minutes – got to jump in the shower."

"Hurry up!"

"Okay! Hey, did you come up here and knock earlier?"

"No, why?"

"Did Lilly?"

"I don't think so, I was up before her, snooping for the mail - she's a good hider - and she hasn't left the house, why?"

"Somebody knocked on my door early this morning; I think it was still dark out. It was a real light knock, but it woke me up....strange. I sat up and called out, half-asleep, at least I think I did, but no one answered....and no one knocked any more. I must have fallen back to sleep. I forgot that it even happened till just now; weird, unless I dreamt the whole thing."

Earl looked positively ashen; he knew who it was, but wasn't going to say it.

Cord looked at him cocked, and annoyed.

"Jesus Earl, it wasn't the puppet okay?"

Earl wasn't buying it.

"He wouldn't knock, now would he?"

True, Earl thought, he wouldn't be so polite; he would just come in and eat you. Regardless, Earl wasn't taking chances, he was getting out of there.

"See you downstairs; and hurry up! I'll get the *Vernor*s!"

And he was gone in a flash. Cord smiled, and headed for the bathroom.

That knock *did* happen, didn't it? He thought to himself.

He woke up remembering some sort of dream; that had been happening more frequently over the past month. But he couldn't remember what it was now; it slipped away right after he awoke. He had a vague recollection that it was about his mother. He tried to remember the details, but it simply wouldn't come back, except that light knock on the door, which he thought was real.

Maybe it wasn't.

And soon enough, he forgot about it and went about getting ready.

Breakfast was uneventful; no remnant Lilly crisis nor meltdown to address. She even, for some unknown reason, put yesterday's mail on the table for Earl, without a word; C could never figure her out, never.

Lilly knew the boys were up to something today, but neither was talking, and that usually meant something to do with Carol, which Lilly would rather not know about. Don't ask, don't tell, that was her motto, at least for today, for right now.

But she did tell Cord she had a big surprise she was going to share with him that night, something to explain some *strange* things that have happened over the past several months. Earl was thinking puppet again, and looked carefully around the room.

When Cord inquired further, she shushed him and said he would find out in due time, relishing the suspense.

Lilly was going to surprise the both of them with mini-ravioli she hand-made awhile ago and stashed in Uncle Frank's freezer; at dinner, she would spring on Cord that she had been moving the stuff in his apartment for the past *three months*, starting with that soup can, fucking with him, without him being the wiser. And on top of that, she finally stumped the anal bastard; he never found that she erased some dots on his foil-wrapped packs in his closet! She finally found something that was even too minor for him to obsess about in his apartment! She had been sneaking into his place for weeks, waiting for him to find the dots, and he didn't. So the gig was up; Mr. Brin wasn't so smart, so anal, after all. She *out-analed* him! Geez, that didn't sound good, she thought.

It was also Lilly's segue into what was wrapped in that foil, and what was in the mystery box. It had been three long months of her wondering about what was so secret in that damn closet. It was going to be a big night, lots of questions answered….and a time to gloat.

Now of course Cord knew all about Lilly's repeated rendezvous into his apartment since the day they started, right from the soup can. But he played along, biding his time to rebut, but good. Given her announcement, it seemed tonight was the night to institute the counter.

But prior to her coup that night, while the boys were out doing God knows whatever she didn't want to know about, Lilly had plans of her own. She was going to relax, take a long bubble bath, followed by a manicure and pedicure; she hadn't treated herself to a real mani-pedi in awhile, always doing it half-assed on her own. She'd also have Terry, her hairdresser friend from high school, give her a quick cut – more of a trim and clean-up, just because.

After the dolling, she'd pedal a leisurely ride out to the Town Pool on her hot pink bike, where she would catch some rays in her new, all-black bikini, and allow the guys and girls to ogle her, while she read the new smutty romance novel she bought at the A&P, splurging on a hardcover….a day full of *girl stuff*, all to herself.

She was excited at the lazy day of Fourth-of-July self-indulgence. And as much as she first hated Cord for stealing Earl - she was still wildly possessive - she had come to enjoy the down time from him, as Earl did from her. It worked out, all around.

Cord had commissioned Marty's bike, since he didn't have his own. Earl stashed four bottles of *Vernors* in his bike basket and they hopped on, ready for a day trip; the destination was Earl's *big* surprise.

"Okay, where are we going?"

Cord asked within the first block down Water Street, knowing Earl wanted so badly to spill.

"You'll see."

Was all Earl said, holding the surprise inside.

They rode lazily down Water, up the small hill on Prospect Street, over the Pequest River bridge, taking a left onto Oxford at the big green Town clock. They were heading toward the High School, Earl in the lead. Cord wasn't sure how Earl's bike stayed together with that much meat on the seat; it had a carnival-comic look.

As they came upon the Cemetery, Earl suddenly hooked a left through the gate and stopped just inside the fence. Cord had been there just the one time last month, but every time he passed Carol's marker heading down Oxford, C would look and smile; most times he would mind-talk to her as he passed, nodding his head in acknowledgment. Cord made pretend she could hear him, but he never pretended Carol answered.

He felt like he knew her; he really liked Carol. How great it would have been to see Carol and Earl together, and Carol and Lilly together. He felt a twinge in his chest….melancholy.

Earl dropped the kickstand, as did Cord; Ay stood there, waiting for Earl to direct.

"Well?"

Cord proffered.

"I figured we would both say hi to my mom. She always liked the Fourth of July, it was one of her favorites."

Earl sported his famous toothy grin.

"Okay."

Cord said slowly, waiting for Earl to take the lead as to whatever came next.

"Well, go ahead."

Ay prompted.

"No, you go first."

Earl said.

"I don't know where she is."

Earl just kept smiling at him.

"What?"

"I *know* you've been here, I know you talked to her; you laid down right next to her!"

Cord felt the tiny hairs on his neck rise.

"How do you know that?"

C questioned, but Earl didn't change his face.

"Earl, Woody saw me here; so did that squirrely little guy you pushed down in front of the Post Office - what's that guy's name, anyway?"

"That's Jim-Bob."

"I mean his real name."

"That is."

C huffed a half-laugh.

"And I should be surprised, a *Jim-Bob* in Belvidere. Well, Woody and *Jim-Bob* saw me, and so did a couple of other people I couldn't really see on bikes, but I'm sure they know you. So, given that four people saw me, taking into account the Belvidere gossip-factor, you probably knew I was here in, I'd say, about thirteen minutes."

"Woody told me too."

Earl said deadpan.

"Too? In addition to whom?"

"You know who."

Earl whispered, although there was really no need to.

"Okay, if *she* told you, then what did we talk about?"

Cord quizzed, as they walked the short distance to her marker.

"Lots of things."

"Can you be a *bit* more specific, that's kinda broad."

C said sarcastic.

"She doesn't tell me the details, that's between you and her, she said; a secret....*your* secret."

"How convenient Earl, you sound like a priest, explaining the Almighty."

"But she did tell me, when you're ready, if you're ever really ready, she'll talk to you....she promises."

"Well tell her thanks."

By now, they were standing over her tiny marker.

"Why don't *you* tell her; she *knew* we were coming today."

Earl urged.

"Of course she did, you told her."

"I didn't have to tell her....she *knew*."

Earl said as he knelt down and gently ran his hand across her name on the ground, barely touching the spelter, *exactly* as Cord did the first time he was there, a mimic.

Maybe everyone did that, Cord thought to himself. Then again, maybe not.

Earl sat next to her, Indian-style and closed his eyes, smiling. Cord sat gently beside him.

Then, barely above a whisper, Earl started to sing Amazing Grace; the hair on Cord's arms rose to attention and tears welled in his eyes. He didn't know why he got so emotional, so quickly, but he did. It felt good.

Earl sang three stanzas and stopped as lightly as he started, his fingertips lightly rubbing her marker as he sang to his mother. Unlike Cord, Earl wasn't ready to cry; he was beaming.

"She *loves* when I sing to her, especially on the Fourth of July. But she doesn't want you to sing, ever….way too scary."

"Thanks Earl, thanks for the vote of confidence. I've been practicing you know, in the shower; I'm getting better….really."

"You have to get a *lot* better, so take more showers!"

Earl said. Then he smiled wide and put his arm around Cord's shoulders for a second, giving him a hug.

"But at least you're trying."

"You're a real motivator Earl; don't quit your day job."

"I don't have a day job!"

Earl exclaimed; C didn't answer. The two sat in silence for a bit, both with eyes closed, keeping their thoughts private. Then Cord asked the question.

"Earl, why didn't you two, or Frank, or Sam, or *somebody*, buy your mom a headstone? Why does she have this little shitty plaque - an advertisement for the Funeral Home, surrounded by dirt and mushrooms."

Cord got mad all over again, not realizing how what he said might sound to Earl. Then he did.

"Sorry, Earl….sorry."

"I have ten thousand dollars."

Earl said, matter-of-fact.

"What?"

"Ten thousand dollars - I have it hidden, in a box, in a secret place."

"Ten thousand dollars?!"

C exclaimed, to which Earl shook his head a single *yes*.

"A month after my mom went away, a man came into Sam's asking to see me, not Lilly….just me. He didn't look like a nice man; he was real big, like I am now, but not quite as big as me now, but close, closer than anyone else I ever met. But I was just a kid, so he was *way* bigger than me, with dark glasses and a dark jacket and dark pants – everything was black but him, he wasn't black. He was real white. He just walked into Sam's from nowhere; nobody even saw him come in, at least that's what Sam said. Sam was scared of him, I could tell. He wasn't a regular type of customer; he wasn't there to buy cucumbers!"

Cord looked at Earl anxious, waiting for him to finish.

"Anyway, I was out at the house, on Fourth Street, but just by luck, I had decided to ride my bike to Sam's to get a sandwich; it was a Saturday, I remember that, and I was *really* hungry.   And I walked in the store right when the man asked about me.   Sam took me by the hand; I was only fourteen, but I was already pretty big, you know, for fourteen, and he walked me over to the guy.   I remember he was surprised at how big I was; even though he had sunglasses on, you could just tell. Anyway, he told Sam he needed to talk to me in private, but Sam wouldn't let him.   By this time, Uncle Frank, even though he was more scared than Sam, came from behind the counter and stood on the other side of me; he still had a big butchers knife in his hand, I remember that, and his hand was shaking, just a little; he was trying to hide it, but I saw it shaking.   But the guy wasn't scared of Uncle Frank at all; he didn't even hardly look at him.   He leaned over and whispered in my ear, and pulled a small box, wrapped in string, from under his coat.   I took it and he turned and walked out the door. Just then a big black car pulled up, they must have really liked black, and he got in and left….that was it.   I never saw him again."

C stared at Earl, dumbfounded.

"What did he say, Earl?   I can't believe this fucking story; you and all your God-damn stories!   What did he say?"

"He just said *read the note*; that was it, then he left."

"Holy shit!   The note?   *The* note!   Your mom's note?"

"No, the note attached to the box."

"Oh *[C said, deflated, hesitating, then he finished the sentence]*; so, did you read the note?"

"Yeah."

And with that, Cord and Earl stared at each other for several seconds – Cord waiting for Earl to elaborate, and Earl not waiting for anything in particular.

"*Well*, what the hell did it say, the note, for Christsake?!"

C said, exasperated.

In response, Earl proceeded to recite the note, verbatim, just as it was written twenty-five years earlier, as if he had opened it just a moment ago.

Earl:

Your mother was a close friend of mine many years ago, and even though you don't know me, I know a lot about you. She loved you like a mother should love a son. Take the money and buy her a nice headstone.

"It wasn't signed or anything, it was typed and the envelope was blank. Do you think that guy knew my dad? He probably didn't."

Earl was hoping Cord said yes; yes he knew his dad, and his dad was a real nice guy. But Cord didn't answer Earl's question; there was no good answer to that one.

"What did Sam and Frank say?"

"Nothing. I didn't show them the note. Sam saw me read it and asked if I was okay....was the note bad. I said no. He asked if I wanted him to read it; I said no. So he said okay, but he told me Lilly had to read it, and if she wanted Sam to read it, then he would have to, cause, you know, Lilly said so. I didn't open the box till I got home; it was filled with hundred dollar bills, a whole hundred of them, wrapped in rubber bands – I know there was a hundred of them because I counted every one! Twice! I never saw so much money, ever! So later on, when Lilly got home, I told her the story; boy did she get mad! Then she read the note and got even *more* mad and ripped it up into little pieces, she kept ripping and ripping and ripping, till she couldn't rip it any smaller! And then she said to *never* bring it up again! Ever! And she meant it, I could tell, so I never did! She said I could keep the money; she said she would burn it, but I could keep it, but I couldn't tell anyone about it. She *grilled* me to see if I told anyone; she's relentless with the questions when she gets like that! I told her I didn't, and she told me I better not be lying! But I wasn't lying, I didn't tell anyone, that's the truth, until I just told you. So I guess it isn't true anymore. She said I couldn't buy a headstone; there wasn't going to be a headstone….*ever*. And she meant it! And she said she had better never see that money again, or *she'd* burn it. So I hid it in a secret place."

Cord never ceased to be amazed at the stories about this family….never.

"So where's the money?"

"Still hidden."

"Still hidden? For twenty-five years? How do you know? Does Lilly know where it is?"

"Nobody knows but me, and my mom."

"How do you know someone didn't find it? Didn't take it?"

"Because I know; it's still there."

"Why don't you just spend it?"

"Because it's for my mom's headstone."

"Then buy her a headstone."

"Lilly won't let me; but someday she will, and when she does, I'll buy it."

"Earl, your mom...."

He cut Cord off.

"She's okay with her little plaque; she doesn't mind it, really. And I kinda like it, hidden in the grass....and I *like* the mushrooms, I think they're nice too....I make sure I never step on them, *ever*. She knows Lilly's still mad; she's just happy when I talk to her, that's the best part of her day....and she's waiting for when Lilly will talk to her too, then she'll be *really* happy. She doesn't care about a stupid stone, or anything else, besides you, that is....she cares a *lot* about you."

Cord couldn't believe how much Earl really got the big picture, more so than just about anyone he ever knew; he loved Earl, he really did.

"Oh yeah, and why does she care about me?"

"I told you, she thinks you're an angel, or something special like that, and that you have something special in store for Lilly and me. She won't tell me what, I don't know if she even knows; but whatever it is, it must be *pretty* important."

Cord just stared at Earl, incredulous.

"Plus she thinks you're kinda cute."

And with that, Earl punched Cord in the arm, lightly, for fun. And even a light stroke still hurt.

CHAPTER 106 – INTO THE RABBIT HOLE THEY WENT

Earl and Cord had been traversing narrow back roads, more like country lanes, for a good twenty-five minutes once they got across Route 46 and the shadow of *Luigi's* Rancho, riding through intermixed woods and lonely farm fields, with nary a building in site for miles.

"How much further Earl?"

Cord whined, his legs burning from the ever-larger uphill climbs; the further they strayed, the higher they went. Earl, as usual, never broke a sweat nor changed his breathing. Cord wanted to smack him.

"It's just up about a bit on the left."

"How long's a fucking *bit*? You've been *just up about a bit-ting* me for the past half hour."

"Up that little hill, on the left….promise."

"That's not a little hill to me Earl; this better be fucking good."

Cord had to stop talking, the incline was eating all his oxygen.

And true to his word, Earl dismounted at the crest of the hill, across from a cow pasture, partially hidden behind a row of roadside brush. He pulled his bike onto the shoulder, waiting for Cord to catch up, which he did, eventually, out of breath and annoyed.

"I don't see anything but fields and lots of woods, Earl; I could've stopped to see woods a half-hour ago, just as good a woods as these."

"Not as good."

Earl whispered, as he smiled. He bent over amongst the pretty blue roadside chickory and picked a large white flower, a *Queen Anne's Lace*, and stuck the stem behind his right ear, grinning to himself as he did. He didn't explain why, nor did C ask; he was too busy catching his breath to care.

Without speaking, Earl hoisted his bike onto his shoulder and started to push his way through the thick tangle of brush.

"What the fuck Earl! Now I gotta carry Marty's bike through *that*? How far?"

Now, for once, Earl was starting to get annoyed with Cord's whining.

"I'll carry your bike Lilly."

Ow, *that* stung.

Cord pushed Earl's hand away in disdain, picked up his bike, huffed so Earl could hear him, and begrudgingly followed his friend into the bush.

Even though no one could see through the thicket a mere ten feet off the road shoulder, Earl carried his bike about twenty yards into the tangle, propping it against the back side of a group of slim cedar trees. Cord stacked his alongside.

And with that, Earl turned, flower still tightly tucked behind his ear, and weaved a jagged meander deeper into the thick wall of brush, picking his way left and right, as if on some invisible path carved in the understory that only he could see.

C stopped whining aloud, but he kept shaking his head and sighing to himself as he followed Earl into the abyss.

1005

The duo walked a slow, circuitous path in silence, obviously memorized by Earl, for close to half an hour. Cord saw no signs of civilization; no buildings, no log roads, no cell towers, no utility lines, no fences, no stone rows….nothing but thick, seemingly virgin wood.

Cord, simply following the traipse of the man ahead of him, was lost in thought, and paying scant attention, which is why he was startled by the meaty hand that slammed his chest, stopping him in his tracks, knocking his air.

"Be careful."

Was all Earl said.

"Of what? We've been walking through the same shit forever."

Cord said, annoyed.

"You'll see."

And with that, Cord was looking at an impenetrable wall of wild rose bushes; they must have been seven feet high, brambles and oversized pickers intertwined and woven into a lethal barbwire backstop. There was no getting through, no way, without being ripped to shreds. Cord looked to his left, and then his right; the wall of thorns went on in each direction for as far as he could see.

Earl shuffled a bit to his left, dropped to his knees, and pointed to a small opening, it looked to be the size of a fucking rabbit hole, that seemed to somehow sneak under the briars. The soil was bare at the entrance, covered in fine-grained tan sand, like beach sand, but darker.

Earl stared at it intently. It had faint striations in it, like the grooves on a record; but if you didn't look closely, you would never notice them.

"No one has been here; no one has ever been here but me. I put these tiny lines in the sand with a branch just to be sure, and they never get disturbed, never once, since I've been ten years old, when I first found this place. I learned that branch trick from Ken and Sandy; they do it, so I do it too, 'cause they're real smart about stuff like that.

Remember you told me about Panama; you said *every man should keep a special place to retreat, a secret-somewhere, to go and find himself, to heal....to be better.* For you, it was *Bocas Del Toro;* well for me, it's this place....this place is where I go when I want to *really* be alone. This is where I would hide out if I was with Ken and Sandy and the bad guys from Skeleton Island were after us!"

Cord was certain that was a direct Panama quote, of what he told Earl that night, months ago; Earl remembered every word....*everything.*

"But it's not a secret anymore Earl, you told me."

Cord mimicked Earl that night.

"Well, my mom knows about it too; now it's just the three of us. Okay, follow me; you hafta crawl on your belly for awhile, but if you stay low, you should be okay. Just don't put your head up, or your butt up, or it'll get pickered-up for sure, trust me."

"Great."

Was all Cord said, as the big man and his flower disappeared into the greenery, a belly crawl below the wall of thorns.

Into the rabbit hole they went.

CHAPTER 107 – THE LAST THING HEARD WAS A HIDEOUS LAUGH

It seemed they belly-crawled for eternity; all Cord could see were the soles of Earl's shoes in front of him, extra large and slithering slow.

Finally, he saw Earl emerge from the wall of thorns and hoist himself vertical. Cord was soon by his side, wiping dirt and dead leaves from his front. They were standing in a small circular clearing; in front of them lay more thick bushes….thankfully not briars.

"So what's the prize at the end of the rainbow, or is this it?"

Earl grabbed Cord by the shirt and slowly dragged him a couple steps forward, stuck his hand into the brush and pushed it aside, like he was opening the curtain to a stage.

He never let go of Cord's shirt; good thing….what a stage!

No more than three feet in front of them, was an eight-inch wide slab of exposed, weathered limestone, beyond which a sheer vertical cliff dropped a hundred-fifty feet, maybe more, to a jagged stone and gravel bottom, far below. A world away.

A couple more steps through that greenery and you had a one way ticket….down.

The limestone walls were creased and lined with cracks and fissures; plants clung precariously to the sides, trying to make a living. The sheer stone face extended to each side and slowly curved out of sight. The bottom of the quarry hole was filling-in with trees, but some had to be at least seventy-five years old, older even, stretching hard to reach the rim. And they weren't even close.

C could catch glimpses of large chunks of stone, some as big as trucks, lying at the base of the quarry, left when the last worker must have walked out a century ago. It was eerie and quiet, except for the sound of birds and the rustling of small animals, mostly squirrels, mostly unseen.

Unlike other abandoned quarries, this hole was dry, not a drop of water to be found, which is likely why this place remained hidden. Cord kept eying around, trying to absorb the scene. Earl just smiled.

"Follow me."

Was all he said, as Earl snaked his way along the rim, to the right, walking less than a foot or two from the edge like it was nothing, grabbing tree trunks and swinging around them, stepping over roots and loose rock. Cord was not nearly as cavalier, and soon was falling far behind.

"Hey, wait up, I can't go so fast."

C barked, but Earl didn't answer.

Cord kept walking gingerly; he couldn't move inland, away from the rim, because the vegetation was too thick and he'd end up veering away from the hole. He went another fifty feet and couldn't see nor hear Earl; there was no movement ahead of him.

"Earl….Earl! Where the fuck are you?"

Nothing; no answer.

"I know you didn't fall in, I would have heard the girlie scream, followed by a loud thud; come on and…."

"Hey!"

Came a yell to his left, and down, from inside the quarry. It scared the shit out of Cord, and caused him to lose his footing and stumble toward the precipice.

"What the fuck Earl! Are you trying to kill me?"

Earl was too busy laughing to answer.

"I got….you….good!"

Earl squeezed out, amidst his snickering.

"Funny, real funny; I could of fallen in!"

"I woulda caught you if you fell, and you wouldn't have gone too far anyway; come on down."

Cord peered gingerly over the edge, and saw a large rock plateau, about eight feet below the rim. The ledge was about fifteen feet wide, by twenty-five feet long, with a large crevasse running through it, small enough to hop across, but big enough to fall in, at least part of it, right in the middle of the slab.

"How'd you get down?"

"Right there! Grab that rock and stick your foot in there, and there; it's kind of like some steps….no, not there, over there, yeah, you got it, grab that root."

Cord scaled the wall and hopped down to the plateau; the view from down here was decidedly different….sheltered. You could see most of the rim from this vantage, and it was all ringed with the same thick bushes. The hole really wasn't that big after all, maybe a hundred or so feet across, maybe smaller. Looking into the quarry, Cord couldn't figure how the workers, the masons, got the stone out.

"Earl, there's got to be a way in from below."

"Nope, there isn't. It's like a big stone hole sunk in the ground and there's no way to get to the bottom, and I've gone around this thing a hundred times, more even, and this is as close as you get; you fall off this, and you're stuck! There's no getting back out, ever! Not on your own anyway."

"Maybe this *wasn't* a quarry; it isn't very big - it just might be a natural hole to nowhere....kind of strange. Who owns this property?"

"I don't know; no one *ever* comes here, not since I've been a kid. I've never been here except by myself; you're the first one, besides me."

"This is pretty fucking cool Earl."

Earl smiled, happy his best friend liked his secret.

"Hey, watch this."

Earl said, as he found a couple stones, the size of large pieces of gravel.

"Shh, listen."

Earl walked over to the crevasse in the plateau upon which they stood, and dropped the first stone into the darkness; not a sound for a count of almost six seconds, then a distant, faint kerplunk. The stone must have rippled unseen water, hundreds of feet below where they stood.

"Earl that has *got* to be pretty fucking deep, like football-fields deep, more than one, *way* below the floor of the hole; could you imagine falling in there? You probably wouldn't even fit Earl, you'd get wedged-in

1012

somewhere, but I think I'd probably make it the water. Christ, that's fucking spooky scary!"

Cord said aloud, as he stepped away from the blackness; it creeped him out, staring into the abyss.

"I call it the *Big Crack*; kind of like the *Big Hill*, you know, my scary story with the dinosaur, but this one's a crack. I've stuck just a tiny bitty part of my leg in once or twice, but then I got scared something was gonna grab it and pull me in, so I usually sit over there, way away from it.   It looks like a big scary Halloween pumpkin mouth, with a crooked smile, doesn't it?"

Cord stood back and looked at it, as he rubbed his chin slowly.

"You know, you're right; it looks like the mouth of a big skeleton head. Hey, wait a minute, I know what it is; it's the mouth of the puppet!"

"What!"

Earl yelped in horror.

"That's must be where the puppet lives! In the *Big Crack*; in the water at the bottom of the crack! Wait, did you hear that? I hear something laughing inside the crack!"

Cord turned around to smile at Earl, but he wasn't there. He spun around, full circle; the plateau was empty. He heard leaves rustling up on top of the rim.

"You coming?!"

"Earl, what the fuck are you doing? How the hell did you get up there so fast!"

"I can run fast when I have to!"

Earl yelled in a frantic voice.

"Well thanks for leaving me to get eaten."

Earl had no answer for that one; he guessed Cord was gonna get eaten then….he would sure miss him.

"Come on! Before he comes out! Now he knows we know he's in there!"

"Earl, I made it up; there's no puppet in the crack! I just made it up to get back at you for scaring me. Come on back down for Christ's sake."

"I've heard laughing in that hole before."

Earl said, suddenly vividly remembering something that actually had never happened.

"Look, I'll prove it to you; I'll go over to the crack, insult the puppet and nothing will happen, trust me."

"Don't do it C! Don't do it; that puppet is *very* sneaky!"

Earl pleaded.

And with that, Cord walked over to the widest part of the crack and laid down beside it. He had to admit, it was pretty fucking scary; he could feel a stream of warm air rising from the blackness, like a chimney.

Shouldn't that air be cold? he thought to himself.

C was keenly aware that if he mistakenly rolled a mere half-turn to his left, he'd disappear into the dark; gone….and not in a good way.

He laid his head beside the abyss, slowly slid his ear out over the void and listened; it was the sound of nothingness, just the light pressure of deep, alien air buffeting past his ear.

Or did he hear something after all?

Something was stirring in the depths; it was so faint, but he swore he could hear it....some strange sound mixing with the steady stream of warm air pushing against his cheek, like a long subterranean exhale, from something unseen, far away, watching him, flickering its tongue. He got a tinge down his spine....a flesh-creep.

He should have rolled away from the crack right then and there, and stopped playing games. But he didn't.

Instead, he craned his neck and dipped his head below the parallel, trying to get just a bit closer, to make out what he heard; it was *something,* not just air.

Yeah, it *was* something; he was sure of it.

"Hey puppet-head, come on out and play, you little piece of shit!"

Cord yelled into the darkness, which swallowed his words whole. There was no echo, the sound was hollow, absorbed into the void. A second tinge shot the length of his spine; now he was truly starting to scare himself.

He dangled his left arm into the pit, up to his elbow; it disappeared from sight.

Cord could feel the stone inside the void was noticeably colder, just a foot below the surface. And he thought again: *Why isn't that air cold? Why is it warm?* He spread his fingers and swept his hand along the face of the smooth stone, then swung it out into the open crevasse, lazily swinging it back and forth, like bait on a line.

1015

"Here, grab my arm, little man, so I can twist your tiny head off! You think I'm scared of you?"

"Stop! Don't say that Cord, you're gonna get it mad!"

Cord quickly spun his head and looked up at Earl on the rim and snapped his teeth together loudly and laughed, like the puppet always did.   Then he smiled at Earl, who was frozen in his tracks, with a look of spook in his eyes.

"Earl, take a breath, I told you, there's nothing…."

Suddenly Cord let out a blood-curdling scream, as his arm was pulled into the abyss.

The last thing heard was a hideous laugh.

CHAPTER 108 – AND THAT WAS THE END OF THAT

"Are we dead?"

Earl said, looking up at Cord, as he blinked his eyes and tried to focus.

"Not yet."

"Where are we?"

"*You* are laying right where you fainted; so much for your quick escape from the puppet; that little man could have belly-crawled and still caught you to eat for lunch."

Earl was trying to remember what happened last, but it was fuzzy.

"I didn't get pulled into the crack, Earl; I made pretend something grabbed me is all. I didn't think you would go down on me, but you did; you dropped like a rock. You didn't even take a single step, just thud, into the shrubs; it was pretty funny."

"There isn't a puppet in the *Big Crack*?"

"Nope."

"That wasn't very nice."

Earl said deadpan.

"You scared me first, remember? Payback's a bitch."

"Well, I'm not scaring *you* anymore, no way."

"Deal."

Cord held out his hand, then grabbed Earl's limp limb, picked it up, and stuck it in his hand to complete the auto shake. Earl slowly sat up, shaking the cobwebs.

"How long was I out?"

Earl asked.

"Just long enough for me to crawl back up here. I'm not as quick as you; maybe half a minute….you were groaning a bit."

"I always thought I would run fast when I was scared, even faster than I normally do. Guess not; guess I'm just a scaredy-cat."

"Earl, most people are scaredy-cats; despite all the heroics they think they'll perform, most just do the drop-in-place when they get scared….it happens. But hey, thanks for coming down and saving me though, I really appreciate that."

C said sarcastic.

"Sorry C, I was really scared; I didn't mean to faint. If I was braver, I would have come down and punched that puppet right in the nose!"

Earl exhaled a sigh and frowned, deflated and disappointed in himself.

So Cord told him a story to cheer him up.

"When I was a little kid, maybe eight or so, tops, my brother and I were watching a scary movie on television. It was just me and him home on a Friday night; my parents were out grocery shopping. It was about killer puppets chasing people around; I'm not kidding either, that's true *[Earl gasped at the horror – where did all these mean puppets come from – they're everywhere!]*.

Anyway, I didn't see half the movie; I was hiding against one side of the TV, and my brother was hiding on the other side. But you could still hear the puppet's voice, and I was scared shitless.

Anyway, the movie ends, and what does my shithead brother do? He gets up and runs out of the room, to hide on me. But I wasn't going to look for him, falling for that trick, so he can scare me, no way! So I just sat in front of the tube and didn't move; I flipped the channel to some corny show to make me forget about the puppet and waited for my mom and dad to come home, which they did, about fifteen minutes later.

I started helping my mom with the groceries, just to be near her, to feel safe; she was surprised at me helping out, but I didn't tell her the real reason. Anyway, I pretty quickly forgot about the puppet, and my stupid brother.

What was I scared about?   It was just a stupid movie, right?

[Earl shook his head in earnest agreement, but he didn't believe it, not for a second; he didn't trust that puppet one bit]

Now, it never dawned on me that my brother never showed up again, even after my parents got home. No help with the groceries, no *hi* to my parents….nothing.

Anyway, I told my mom I was going to bed, and went up to my room, feeling pretty confident; who should be scared of a stupid puppet anyway? It was just a dumb movie, right?

So I go upstairs to my bedroom, the same bedroom, by the way, that was in my puppet dream years later, the dream I told you and Lilly about. Anyway, I'm standing next to my bed, getting undressed. And as I raised my arms to take off my shirt, I happened to be *right next* to my closet, which had a sliding wooden door, which just happened to be barely open, a skinny little crack, which revealed a sliver of blackness in the closet behind the door.

Earl, I was less than three inches from that crack, and when I happened to glance into the darkness of the closet, into that vertical slat of black, and all I could see was this *huge white eyeball staring back at me*, the size of a cue ball, and it was shaking up and down, like it was dangling on a string, like it was going to spring out at me.

Now, I thought whenever I got scared I would run a mile a minute to get away; I was a pretty fast little kid back then. I'd be on the street in no time....safe. Well, it didn't quite work out that way.

I dropped like a sack of potatoes right in that spot, passed out cold. My brother thought he killed me. The stupid shit got in a lot of trouble for that one, I made sure of it....fucker.

You know why his eye was bouncing around in the dark like that, hiding in the closet? The asshole was trying to hold in his laugh; he had his hand over his mouth, trying not to laugh out loud....he knew he had me, but good. So you're not the only one who faints in a crisis; but then again Earl, I was only eight."

And with that, Cord smiled, squeezed Earl's shoulder, and helped him to his feet.

One part of C's story stuck with Earl, more than any other. He looked up at Cord and asked timidly, with an air of despair.

"You have a brother?"

Cord sighed.

"Yeah, I have a brother; I guess, technically, I have two."

Cord picked up a stone and lazily tossed in into the tree-filled hole.

"I wish *I* was your brother."

Earl said, head down.

Cord put his hands gently on Earl's chest.

"Earl, you *are* my brother; you're the best brother anyone could ever have. So I'm taking dibs on you; now you're officially *my* brother; I'll trade the other two for you and a *Snickers Bar*, deal?"

"*Really?* We can be brothers?"

"Really; done deal."

Cord said, as he brushed off his knees.

"And I promise, when the puppet comes, I won't go fainting on you; I'll stand by you, side by side. Maybe together we can beat the little fucker; what do you say Earl?"

"Yeah, we'll beat him together! I'll stomp him! I'll twist his head right off!"

Earl yelled. Inside he was jumping; he was so happy to have Cord as his brother - that was the best....*ever*.

"Now, let's go back down on the ledge, *away* from the crack, and drink the *Vernors* you've been lugging around, and stop thinking about stupid puppets."

Earl smiled; it was so cool to have a *real* brother! He knew his mom would be happy; he couldn't wait to tell her, but she probably already knew.

The two of them made their way back to the plateau.

"How the hell did you find this place anyway? Why were you all the way out here at ten years old?"

C asked.

"My mom and I went on a bike ride, on a picnic. It was the Fourth of July, just like today! Anyway, it seemed like we were riding our bikes forever! But I didn't mind, because I could ride all day with my mom! And all along the road, for miles and miles, were pretty flowers; they looked like big white umbrellas! I asked my mom what they were, and she called them *Queen Anne's Lace*; I thought that was just about the best name ever for a flower!

We finally stopped along the road, right where you and I stopped. There's a pasture across the street; it always had cows in it, and I liked to pet them! It's still there, and it still has cows; there were there today! I don't know if you saw 'em."

"Nah, I didn't. Too busy trying to breath."

Cord said. And then Earl rambled on.

"So when we stopped, I picked some *Queen Anne's Lace* where we laid our bikes and put it behind her ear. She looked so pretty; she was pretty anyway, but now she was even prettier. I asked her if that now made her a real queen; she said *sure, if I want her to be one.* And I said *of course! Why wouldn't I want her to be a queen?!* So she *was*, just like that! And my mom was a good queen too, very nice to me, which I really appreciated, because, you know, not all queens are nice....some queens, when they become queens, get a big head and stuff and act real snooty and snotty and stuff, like Lilly probably would, so I would never put that flower behind Lilly's ear and make Lilly a queen, no way! She'd probably lock me in a closet or something! Don't give Lilly that flower, *ever*; just saying. Anyway, not my mom, she was nice, even *after* she became a queen; she would still hold my hand and rub my back in circles and she didn't have to do that, you know, to a little, unimportant kid like me, because she was a queen….just saying.

So we had lunch on a blanket, then my mom said she was tired and was going to take a nap; but I wasn't tired at all! So I went and played with and pet the cows and patted their big bellies. You know, sometimes cows smell like cow poop, 'cause they walk around and poop a lot, right when they're walking – and they don't even care that you're watching them walk and poop! I like the smell of cow poop, you know – it reminds me of nice cows. Anyway, after awhile, I got bored of petting them and watching them poop; they poop a lot. So I went exploring, like a real explorer, and found this place. I don't know how I found it, I just did. I guess that's what explorers do, they find things; and I was a really good explorer that day!

Anyway, I was gone a pretty long time, and ran back when I realized I was probably getting in trouble. That's when I heard my mom calling for me, so I ran faster. Wow, did I get in big trouble! My mom never yelled at me, but she did that day; but you know, it wasn't because she was a queen and stuff, it was because she was a mom, and she was really scared. Sometimes moms can get scared too you know, not just little kids.

But then I started crying, and she said it was okay, she just was worried about me, and don't scare her like that anymore. So I never did, *ever*!

Anyway, then I told her I found a *big hole* in the ground; I don't think she really believed me, she probably thought it was a big groundhog hole, or something like that. She definitely didn't know it was a hole like *this*; she would have been *really* mad then, because I could have fallen in, and *never* gotten out; then I'd be in big trouble, for sure! Anyway, she said it was my own little secret, and not to tell anyone about it.   So I didn't, till you….till now."

And Earl took in a big breath and exhaled loud, now that his story was done.

"And did she tell you to tell me, you know, about the *Big Crack*? To bring me out here today, to see it?"

C said low.

Earl shook his head slowly in the affirmative, as if Cord expected any other answer.

"Why?"

C asked simple.

"She said it was for later."

"What's *that* mean?"

C said, confused.

Earl had no idea, so he just shrugged his shoulders; and that was the end of that.

CHAPTER 109 – A SLOW GRACEFUL ARCH OF BLOOD

They each drained their first bottle of *Vernors*, and cracked the second, laying on the warm limestone slab, eyes to the sky, soaking in the sunshine; making the most of a lazy Summer day.

"You know, Earl, you *are* brave, what you did with Loki; very cool, saving your sister."

Cord hated to remember, not because of what Earl did, but rather at the shame he felt, in standing frozen in the water, watching Earl do what he should have done. But Earl simply shook his head in the negative, the crew-cut stubble rubbing against the stone as he looked skyward.

"Nah, Loki's a good dog C, he really is. He just doesn't get treated right; they don't love him like they should….not like I would. You know, I go see him, bring him treats. I don't tell Lilly though, *no way*. He wags his tail when he sees me, a good dog wag. He doesn't ever get to do that, you know, except for when he sees me coming with treats. But I have to sneak them to him, so I can't do it as much as I want, which would be all the time."

Earl whispered the last part.

"Earl, the dog I saw that day wasn't a good dog."

Earl looked around for some clouds, but there were none, an endless cerulean palette.

"I asked my mom if I should let him out, you know, for good, let him go, let him run away from home; anything would be better than living there. Maybe I could keep Loki in the woods, maybe here, and take care of him, make him feel better. But she never answers me, not about Loki - never; I don't know why. She never talks about him."

"Hey, if Loki is *really* a good dog, then maybe the puppet is *really* a good puppet. Maybe he just doesn't get treated right, you know, no love. Maybe you can bring him some treats."

Earl sat up and pondered, giving the question due consideration. Then he reached a verdict.

"Nah, he's not friendly at all; I don't trust that puppet….no treats for him."

Earl got up and walked to the back of the rock plateau, where the shelf met the vertical wall. He bent down, close to the ground, and smacked the stone once, a good smack.

A bit of soil kicked up and a piece of the limestone shifted, enough for him to get his fingers on. He slowly slid out a uniform block of stone, like a brick, and stuck his hand deep into a black mortise. Out came a cardboard box, wrapped in gray string that was once white.

He walked back and gingerly handed it to C, like passing a delicate family heirloom. Cord carefully blew the fine stone powder off the box and looked curious at Earl, who simply upticked his head, as if to say: *go ahead, open it.*

C untied the string. He cracked the top; four neat stacks of bills, crisp and dry, lay inside. No creases, smudges or wear; clean long green, right from the bank. Cord didn't touch the bills.

"Pretty cool Earl; when's the last time you opened the box?"

"1981, when I got it; that's the only time I ever opened it, *ever*."

"Well, let's put it back then, until we're ready to spend it on your mom, okay?"

C whispered.

"Okay. Maybe soon? Maybe you can convince Lilly?"

Earl said with a smile, which Cord returned in silence; they both knew that was a slim proposition.

"I'll work on her, Earl, I'll get her to crack, promise."

Earl returned the box and sat Indian-style, next to Cord, who was still prone.

Earl's face turned troubled.

"C, tell me about Fred again."

Cord got mad, remembering the story. He was sorry he ever told Earl about Fred; it was something Earl didn't need to know.

"You don't like that story Earl; it never ends good."

"But I like the beginning."

Earl whispered slight.

"But with a beginning, always comes an end, eventually….it just happens. You know, that's how the story goes; and this one doesn't end well."

"You don't have to tell the end then."

Earl offered, weak.

"Yes I do; you always want to hear the end, *always*, even though it makes you sad."

Earl looked at him; Cord saw the tears start to pool in his eyes, like they always did, before C uttered the first word.

"Please, tell the story."

Cord frowned; deep down, he knew Earl had hoped that maybe, this time, the ending would change. But it never did.

"Fred was a cute little pink baby, only six weeks old, when Farmer Phil brought him home for his wife, for Christmas….a very special Christmas present. What do you think if Lilly gave you a pink little piglet for Christmas, Earl?"

"I'd love that piglet!"

"I know you would; and what would you name him?"

"I'd name him Fred!"

"Well, so did the farmer and his wife; they named their little piglet Fred. And for three years, Fred lived a happy life on the farm, eating his favorite food."

"Canned sweet potatoes!"

"That's right, canned sweet potatoes, lots on 'em! And the more he ate, the more Fred grew, till he became the biggest *sweet potato* Alabama ever saw; nine feet long and over a thousand pounds....that was some big pig!"

"Wow."

Was all Earl said; like he said every time he heard C tell the story.

"He's even bigger than you Earl, if you can imagine that."

"That's pretty big!"

Earl whispered in awe.

"Yeah, it is."

"And did he have any friends?"

Earl asked, prompting the answer he knew was coming next.

"Yes he did, the farmer and his wife would let their grandchildren play with him; and his best friend in the whole world, the one he liked to spend his days with, was…."

"A little dog!"

Earl yelled.

"That's right, a Chihuahua, if you can believe that."

"If he liked that dog, maybe he would like Loki too; maybe we can bring them both here to live; what do you say C?"

Cord didn't answer; he was hoping the story would end there, and Fred and Earl would be happy, forever. But he knew it wouldn't.

Earl looked at C and waited….and waited. He knew the bad part was next, so he hung his head.

"What about next?"

Earl breathed light, barely above a whisper.

"You know what happens next Earl, Fred goes away."

"He doesn't go away! The farmer made him go! He was sent away on a truck to be all alone, in a place where he had no friends!"

Earl started to cry.

Cord just looked at Earl with a look of utter sadness, wishing he never told him the story.

"They sold *all* their pigs, Earl, including Fred."

"But why? Why'd they have to make Fred go away? He didn't bother anybody; he just liked to eat sweet potatoes and play with the dog."

"I don't know why Earl, I don't."

Earl hung his head; Cord could see the tears drop, one at a time, onto the dry surface of the rock.

"What about next?"

Earl asked again.

Cord had argued with Earl many times before, threatening to stop the story, but Earl was relentless, asking over and again. So Cord, this time, just gave in without a fight, simply to get the sadness over with.

"He was sold to a farm and put out in the woods, all alone, in a place he didn't know. He only knew his fenced-in pen back at the farm, so he didn't know what to do, or where to go. So he wandered in the woods, all alone. And he got hungry."

"What about next?"

"This farm wasn't a nice farm; the farmer there let people come in to shoot the animals, for fun. Fred didn't know some people weren't nice, he didn't know he wasn't going to get any more sweet potatoes or play with the Chihuahua. So for four days, he wandered around the woods. The farmer didn't feed him, and no one came to see him; he was lonely, and hungry and scared."

"Don't finish the story."

Earl yelled, covering his ears, still crying.

So Cord stopped, like he always did, his own eyes wet, till Earl eventually said it again.

"What about next?"

"On the fourth day, a fat little boy and his fat father stepped into the woods, the kid carrying a large gun. And for the next three hours, the two chased Fred around the fenced-in enclosure, shooting at him. Fred tried frantically to get away, but the fence was too high for him to get over, and he was tired, and hungry….and scared. So it was easy for the fat little boy to shoot him, which he did….again and again and again. Each time, Fred tried to run away, but soon he was bleeding and too hurt to run away any longer, so he just laid down. The little boy shot him six times, and Fred died….scared and all alone."

Earl was sobbing, his head down, shoulders heaving quietly. Cord stood up and put his hand on his friend's shoulder, as he always did.

"Why'd they kill Fred? He didn't bother anybody."

"Like I told you before, because most people are weak. And many times weak people hurt things to make themselves feel strong; to convince themselves they're strong, or important, or clever. But really, they're none of those things; they mostly feel inadequate, and scared….scared like Fred was. So some redneck in bum-fuck Alabama lets his fat kid go hunt and kill a frightened pet pig who ate canned sweet potatoes, while he is confined to a pen in the woods, like shooting fish in a barrel, and they make the news as some sort of mighty hunters; pretty pathetic….fat, pathetic and weak.”

[Cord methodically hit his clenched fist on the rock beside him, progressively harder, as he shook his head. His mind was racing; nothing good ever happened when a loop ran in his head, churning, fretting….hot]

Earl spoke, just above a whisper, head still down, hiding his face from Cord.

“I would *never* hurt Fred; we could have brought him here and no one would have found him. He could have been friends with Loki, and we could have fed him sweet potatoes too, all the sweet potatoes he could eat, right C?”

“Right Earl, as much as he could eat.”

Silence passed between the two; Earl was still sniffling, even though the bad part had passed.

“You can’t save everything Earl; there are a lot of bad people, who do bad things. You can’t save everything Earl.”

Cord's words trailed off to nothing, as he closed his eyes and shook his head slowly in the negative. He was talking to himself more than he was to Earl. His hand was bleeding, the skin split where he pounded it into a sharp ridge on the surface of the stone.

“Man is just a come-lately parasite, Earl, all except you. If they *all* went away, every fucking one of them, it would be fine with me; I’d sign up for that plan. They will, eventually, just not soon enough for me. I'd kill 'em all myself, right now, if I could; but *you* can be the one tin soldier; you, only you, I'd let ride away."

"What about you C, you're good too; my mom says you are. Maybe you can ride away with me and Fred."

"I told you Earl, I'm not good, not like you, despite what your mom says....or wants to believe."

"My mom says you're better than you think; you have potential. She thinks you can be a great man."

Cord knelt down next to Earl, and spoke softly.

"*Great men are almost always bad men,* did you know that Earl?"

Earl shook his head slowly….no.

"You know who said that? Some dead English guy - Lord Acton; don't ask me who he was - I can't believe I even remember his name, another bit of worthless information floating in my head. But the saying is true, if you think about it."

"Yeah, but he said *almost*….didn't he?"

Cord smiled at Earl.

"You're right, Earl, he did say *almost;* maybe there's still hope."

Cord threw a small piece of limestone into the quarry; he didn't hear it hit the ground.

He sat back down beside Earl, both staring out into the quarry in silence. Blood still dripped from Cord's hand, slower now.

"You'd never hurt anything, would you C?"

There's a thin veneer between civilized and primitive in each of us, C thought to himself. Someone important once said that, maybe Freud, maybe not; who the fuck cares, really? Anyway, Cord didn't say that to Earl, he simply sighed, and closed his eyes.

"I would have never hurt Fred, *never,* that's for sure."

"You could help me feed him sweet potatoes if you want."

"*He's dead* Earl, he's not coming back, ever!"

Earl hung his head; he didn't want to think of Fred that way. He thought of him as being around, just in a different place, like him mom....a place where people are nice.

"Maybe my mom can feed him sweet potatoes; maybe I'll ask her to bring him a can to eat tomorrow."

Cord opened his eyes and smiled at Earl, who was looking for comfort from his best friend.

"Maybe, *sure*....your mom will absolutely look after Fred, and be his *best friend.* Don't you worry, Fred will be fine."

As Ay wiped his hand across the rock, in a slow graceful arch of blood.

CHAPTER 110 – SIT YOUR FAT ASS RIGHT ON MY LAP

The two were still sitting on the ledge; the Fred story had long come and gone, as did rambling talk of Carol, Lilly, Marty and Sam. The soda was spent, and the two looped back to the *List Of Ten*.

"So where are we again Earl? Count 'em down; I know you remember."

"No. 1 was *Go On A Date With Carol....And You.*"

"Nice try; it was go on a date with Carol *alone,* followed by lots of post-date headboard-banging."

Cord threw in a couple short pelvis thrusts for good measure. Earl turned red, didn't answer, and moved on.

"No. 2 was *Go To Panama,* to see Al's friends, and the pelicans and lobsters; when are we going C?"

"Soon, promise; maybe we'll go for Christmas, I like going down then."

"But you said you go alone; you're all alone for Christmas?"

Cord didn't answer.

"What are Nos. 3 and 4?"

Cord asked.

"*Go to Skeleton Island* and *Solve a Mystery*!"

Cord loved when Earl got excited. He didn't tell Earl that Nos. 1, 3 and 4 were well in the works.

"And what was No. 5 again?"

"No. 5 was *Get Real Mail*, and I did already! That one's done! Are you gonna come to Carol's party with me?"

Cord smiled and cracked his knuckles; the pops echoed against the limestone.

"Hey Earl, what did that letter say again?"

He knew Earl memorized it, word for word, even though Earl didn't know what half the words really meant. And he never got it wrong, no matter how many times C asked him to repeat it.

"Easy, it said *[pointing along, finger in the air]*:

Dear Earl:

The honor of your presence is requested at:

Actaeon's Annual Fall Bacchanalia

To thank our investors and celebrate another successful year.

Kindly accept this invitation for you and a revered guest to join me at a private, royal reception at:

L'antre du Lion

Our first venture into the woods, outside the confines of the venerable City!

- A black tie evening of pageantry and red-carpet events;
- Round trip limousine transportation to the *le repaire de lions*;
- Music by the *Loretto-Marigold Ensemble*;
- Live and silent auctions;
- Private commissions provided by on-premise *Premier Coup* artisans;

Followed by an agenda:

- 6:00 pm – *Aperitifs* and an artisan cheese market;
- 7:30 pm – *Haute cuisine*, epicurean delights from Europe and the Sub-Continent;
- 9:30 pm – Dessert, *digestifs* and cigar bar;
- 11:30 pm – After Party *Independent Film Festival Shorts*….to dawn; and
- ? am – After-After Party *petit dejeuner* for the rebel rock-ribs.

"You kill me Earl."

"What'ya mean?"

"I mean, how do you remember that shit, every God-damn word?"

"I don't know; so, you gonna come with me?"

"Maybe you'll go to that one *alone*, no guest, just you, so you can knock off No. 1."

"No way! I'm not ready yet."

"It's in October Earl! That's three months away, for Christ's sake; you're ready now, you just don't know it."

"You got that right!"

Cord laughed, then laid back on the rock.

"You know Earl, there's this place I think you'd like, it's called *City Park*, in Denver; a pretty place….quiet, especially on a Saturday morning, in the summer, on a day just like today.

Earl pulled his legs up to his chest and listened intently; he loved when Cord told him stories about places he'd never been, which was everywhere outside of Belvidere.

"Where's Denver, C?"

"Out west, *way* past Pennsylvania, where the land is flat as a pancake, as far as you can see. No trees, just open plains to the east, with a big blue sky, the biggest sky you've ever seen; it goes on forever, and wraps around you.   It's flat to the west too, until, all of a sudden, *boom!* You hit the mountains, the Rockies, snow-capped in the middle of the summer. They jump up to the sky; they don't even look real."

Earl closed his eyes and tried to imagine what a Denver looks like.

"Anyway, in this Park in the middle of Denver, there's a big fountain that nobody pays much attention to, with a reflecting pool around it. *Thatcher Fountain* they call it; some guy named Thatcher donated it to the City about a hundred years ago. Anyway, there are three sets of bronze statues around it, larger-than-life, of a handsome man and beautiful woman, and next to each one is a word chiseled into the stone, and each word starts with the letter *L*:

"Is Lilly one of them?"

Earl interrupted, to which Cord smirked.

"No, Lilly is *not* one of them. There are three simple words:

- **Love**;
- **Loyalty**; and
- **Learning**.

And the fountain doesn't say why those words are there; why this guy, a hundred years ago, donated a lot of money to build a monumental fountain to carve those three simple words.

So here's what I think, as I was lying in the cool grass, under a linden tree, on a Saturday summer morning, looking up at the fox squirrels running around in the tree top above me. I think to have a relationship that will last, a relationship that *means* something, that works, you need all three….you need the *L's*. I don't know if that's what Thatcher thought when he told someone to carve it - I couldn't give a shit if he did; it's what *I* thought, it's what made sense to me."

Earl just looked at C, trying to follow the story.

"The point of the story, Earl, is that *you have* them, you have all three, both you and Carol, you just don't know it. You *love* her, that's for sure; you're *loyal*, and would be to her, without question, and you love to *learn* and are willing to learn; you're a lot smarter than most people I know, trust me….and you listen."

"That's four *L's* C."

Earl said deadpan; Cord smiled.

"Okay, you have all four then, including a bonus *L*, for listening. Anyway, Carol is no dummy, and she knows you have the three, sorry, four *L's*, and for her, that's what will make her fall in love with you too. In fact, I think she already has.”

Earl’s eyes widened, and the blood ran from his cheeks.

“You think she has….*what*?”

“You heard me, and why wouldn’t she? You heard about all the loser boyfriends she’s had, all prima donnas or guys looking to spend her dough; you’re none of that, she’s never met anyone like you Earl, never. You’re a keeper.”

Earl laid back alongside C, eyes to the sky, with a smile as wide as the *Big Crack*.

“That’s crazy talk!”

Earl said aloud, but he wanted to believe Cord, so badly it hurt. He knew Cord wouldn’t lie to him on purpose, especially after the night he skipped out on *The Blob*. He sure wanted to believe him; Earl squeezed his eyes shut and wished as hard as he could that C was right.

Then Earl did something he rarely did, he tried to talk to his mom, talk to her first. She seemed to always show up at the right times without any help from him, but this time, she wasn’t here, and this was *super* important, about as important as important could ever be.

So, he concentrated, hard, trying to focus on that middle-something place behind his left ear, the part that always seems to tingle, just for a split second, whenever she talked to him. She would tell him if what C said was right; mom would know.

So he sat and concentrated, and then concentrated some more, willing her into his head. But she didn’t come, not this time.

Earl frowned.

"It must not be true."

He said, barely above a whisper.

"What? What Earl?"

C said.

"Nothing."

Earl whispered, dejected.

"Hey, remind me, I'll give you something when we get home."

"What?"

"I picked up a flower floating in that fountain that day, right below the word *Love*; it was a clover flower."

"Maybe it was a four-leaf clover?"

"Maybe; for you, Earl, it probably is. Anyway, I kept it, and I brought it with me to Belvidere, believe it or not. It was by mistake, tucked in with a bunch of other stuff; I found it unpacking. Why don't you give it to Carol? I think she would really like it Earl, especially if you tell her the story."

"But it's *your* flower, and *your* story."

"Not anymore, I gave them both to you; do with them what you wish, but my suggestion is to give the clover to Carol."

"Okay."

Earl said tentatively.

"Hey C, do you have the **L's** with anyone?"

Cord just smirked.

"Nah, those **L's** never really seemed to work for me."

"But your smart, and you like to learn."

Earl said, defending his friend.

"I may be smart in some things, sometimes, but one thing I never do, is learn. Enough about that."

C said as his voice trailed off. Then the two sat in silence, staring at nothing in particular.

"Hey, one last thing about that Park in Denver I know you'd like; there's a little lake, *Duck Lake*, just about a hundred yards from the fountain, and you'll never guess what lives in the trees on a little island in the middle of the lake Earl."

"*Ducks*?"

He said; Earl was sure he nailed it.

"There are about a dozen trees, with dozens of huge bird nests in each tree, and thirty to forty birds sitting in each tree; three to four hundred birds, *easy*, all in one spot; you'll never see anything like it. And you know what it sounds like?"

"Ducks?"

"Like hundreds of frog's croaking or pig's snorting, all at the same time!"

"I didn't know ducks croaked?"

"They don't! Who do you know who grunts at you all the time, catching fish?"

Earl's eyes widened.

"Al?"

"You got it! Four hundred Al's, all sitting in the trees, happily grunting away and fishing in *Duck Lake*; what a life in Denver."

"Really?"

"Yeah, you should ask Al about it, he's gotta have a relative in that bunch, somewhere, for sure."

Earl smiled. Everywhere C went was cool; there were always cool animals and cool stories. He wanted to go to *Duck Lake* too; he wanted to go to Denver and lay under a linden tree and watch the fox squirrels.

Cord interrupted the daydream.

"Okay, so *No. 5* is *Real Mail* – done. So what's No. 6?"

"I didn't tell you that one; the last time we stopped at No. 6 and I said I didn't wanna tell, but you already gave it to me, so we can cross that one off, kind-of."

"What'ya mean kind of? What did I give you? What's No 6?"

Earl put his head down, embarrassed.

"I wanted you to be my brother."

Cord smiled. No one ever said that to C before; he never had a *real* brother, not like the kind a guy should have, not like Earl.

"Why only kind-of? I told you it was a done deal."

"I kinda wanted you to be my brother in another way too."

Cord looked at him, stumped.

"I don't get it Earl."

Earl spoke, barely above a whisper, more of a mumble.

"What? I can't hear a word you're saying; just spit it out."

Earl raised the pitch a half-notch; C strained to hear the words.

"I was hoping, maybe, you'd marry Lilly, and be my brother that way....too."

"What?! Are you kidding? Lilly would never marry me in a *thousand* years, and I would never give her the satisfaction to say no to begin with, if I even wanted to marry her anyway, that's assuming I'm not *already* married."

Earl raised his shoulders, in defense of the vitriol.

"Sorry, C."

Cord frowned.

"I don't need to be married to Lilly to be your brother Earl, we already are; being tied to her is a non-sequitor."

"What?"

"It doesn't tie, it doesn't matter to you and me; we're a team regardless of how much Lilly despises me."

"But she *likes* you, a *lot*."

"Hardly."

Earl shook his head in the negative.

"You're wrong C; I know Lilly better than *anyone* in the whole world, besides my mom, and I know she likes you, deep down, trust me."

"Well, she has a strange way of showing it. And even if she does, like me, that is, *way* deep down, it's part-time at best; most of the time she would rather fillet me."

"*That's true.*"

Earl nodded in agreement.

"But she wants to do that to *me* half the time too, and I know she loves me more than anything, besides my mom."

Earl said, with a philosopher's air.

Cord smiled, knowing his friend was right. And if one thing was crystal, it was that Lilly loved Earl, without question, even when she showed it least, which was often.

And if Cord thought about it, he could think of a dozen times when Lilly was tender to him, a sweetness squeezed from God knows where. And it sure felt good when he got a taste, but they were teases, at best, clouded by a general sense of disdain.

"Yeah, but what about this Button clown, what's the story with him? What's she see in him, Earl? And why isn't he here if he's so great?"

Earl just looked at him and frowned, but didn't speak.

"Let me ask you something Earl? If that prick showed up tomorrow, would Lilly take him back?"

Earl couldn't answer any quicker, the question was that easy.

"In less than a second."

Cord frowned. That was not the answer he was hoping for; he hoped Earl would ponder the question, think about Lilly's struggle between C and Button, maybe even say that C would come out on top in the end.

But nothing doing, the verdict was clear, decisive; Button, hands down. Earl could see the disappointment.

"Sorry, C."

"Well why would you say she likes me then? Why not say she likes Button."

Cord barked in a general sulk, trying unsuccessfully to act like it really didn't matter to him.

"Because he's not around, and she likes you both; haven't you ever liked more than one girl at the same time?"

Earl smacked that one square on the head; C didn't touch that loaded gun.

"So, why isn't he around?"

"Something happened between him and Carol and Lilly. I don't know what, but it *wasn't good* – that's why Lilly hates Carol, or at least part of the reason, anyway."

C processed, and the thought came quick.

"Did Button *fuck* Carol, Earl?"

Jesus, that would suck on so many levels, C thought. The two girls he wanted to bang in Town in the worst way, the two best looking women by far, that probably wouldn't bang him, had both banged *this* jerk-off? He didn't think he could have liked this fuck any less, but he did, and it was painted in a color called envy.

Earl didn't answer at first, he just shook his head slowly....*yes*.

"I think so."

He said in a whisper.

"Fuck! Mother-fucker!"

Cord's voice trailed off, shaking his head in disgust.

"I don't want to talk about that jerk-off any more."

And they didn't; they both just sat there for a minute or so, in silence, looking into the pit beyond the *Big Crack*. Finally C spoke rote, still bitter at the thought.

"Okay, what's No. 7?"

Out of nowhere, Earl erupted.

"Hey! You were supposed to get me the next two books, after *Skeleton Island*! Did you get them yet? You lost the bet, remember?"

"Christ, where did that come from? Yeah, I remember. Geez, Earl, give me a break, I'll get the books; you don't have to ask me *every day*."

"I don't ask you every day; the last time I asked you was four days ago, at breakfast, when you and Lilly were arguing, and you said you would order them *that day [Earl poked C in the chest, for emphis]*. Well, did you?”

“No, I forgot! And stop poking me in the fucking chest – it hurts! I’ll order them when we get back; I’m not betting you anymore anyway, you never fucking lose! Whatever you bet, you bastard, you always win; I don't get it. What are the fucking names again?”

“*The Riddle Of The Stone Elephant* is next, then *The Black Thumb Mystery* - that one sounds kinda dumb. What’s a black thumb, and why is *that* scary? Ken and Sandy are *so* smart, I wish I could solve mysteries like them. There’s eighteen in all; wanna make a bet for the next two, after the next two you already owe me?”

“Forget it.”

“Hey C, what’s a stone elephant?”

“I guess it’s some kind of statue.”

“Ever seen a *real* elephant?”

“Yeah, I have; do you mean in a zoo, or at a circus, or in the wild, what do you mean?”

“I mean any kind, anywhere.”

“Yeah.”

“It’d be cool to see an elephant for real; maybe we can see one together some day.”

“Deal. And I know just where to bring you.”

Earl got excited, and pulled his legs up hard against his chest.

“Really? Where?”

"*Derdepoort*, in the *Northwest Province, South Africa*. It's right next to Botswana; that's another country in Africa. If we go see elephants, those are the ones I'll show you, lots of them, whole families living together in the scrub."

"Why them?"

"Because they're the only elephants I know."

Earl smiled. If C knew them, they must be nice elephants, from nice families, and he knew he would like them too.

"When?"

"After Panama, we gotta go to Panama first. Now what's No. 7?"

"I want to ride on a *Knucklehead*, you know, that Harley I told you about. But I want to ride on the police-type one, all black."

"Tell me again, I don't remember the *Knucklehead* story."

"Geez, you don't remember *anything!* I told you, you know, like the one that big fat guy had, with all the tattoos and curly white mustache parked in front of Carol's house last year, when *Rolling Thunder* came into Town….remember I told you? But his wasn't a police-type, it was just another *Knucklehead*, there are all kinds. But it was the first real *Knucklehead* I ever saw."

"It's vague, Earl, sorry; tell me again."

Earl grunted in frustration.

"Okay, but pay attention this time; you have to learn to concentrate!"

Ouch. Cord sat up and leaned into Earl, giving him his full attention.

"You should have heard it C, the *Rolling Thunder*! When they all come in and rode around the Park, there were *hundreds* of motorcycles! At least two hundred! I almost counted them all, but I got too excited and kept losing count. And it's so loud! The ground rumbles; I could feel it in my feet, my feet vibrate....*it's so cool*! The coolest thing ever! Could you imagine being in that? I think I would be scared, it's so loud. And they all wear cool black helmets, and neat jackets with all kinds of fancy patches; they come in every year for the war people, to say speeches about all the missing people, and the dead ones, over by all those big black stones at the Courthouse, with all the names on them. And they eat lots of hot dogs and drink beer and stuff. After about three hours, they're all gone, *all hundreds of them*, like they were never even there! I love that *Knucklehead*; I know it's called that because my mom told me about them, for real, when I was a kid. I didn't want to talk to him, the fat guy with the white mustache, too afraid, and of course he talked to Lilly too much and tried to be nice, but Lilly said he was a pervert, and she got mad and started calling him names, and then we had to leave, before she caused trouble; she was kinda mean to him."

"Big surprise there."

Cord said.

"I would *love* to ride on one of them police *Knucklehead*s, just once, and you know why, C?"
"No, why?"

"Cause I want to ride out to the levee rim road, right when the morning sun breaks the horizon, to see if I can

*beat the dust.   Right when the cloud edges are on fire
with sunlight, white hot embers, glowing across the
horizon, and I'll be listening to Sunset Grill as I climb
the crest of the levee."*

Earl sported a mischievous smile.

Cord smiled back; Earl had memorized and spit back
what Cord told him, verbatim, a month ago.

"You can *never* beat the dust Earl, that levee rim road is
too long."

Earl looked at C intently, like he was concentrating on
what Cord said, but his mind had wandered elsewhere.

Then Earl smiled.

"I'll bet you the next two *Ken* books, Nos. 4 and 5, after
the *Black Thumb* one, that I can; I'll beat the dust."

Ay looked at him intently. C knew it was a sucker bet;
Cord couldn't lose, Earl would *never* beat the dust. But
Ay still hesitated; Earl *always* beat him in bets, and Cord
always thought it was a sucker bet each time....the big
bastard."

Once again, C took the bait, eagerly offering an
outstretched hand.

"You got it, but you only get one shot. You're losing
this time, you bastard; you can't beat the dust Earl, you
just can't, trust me, even if I gave you a hundred shots."

Earl smiled a toothy grin.

"What are you smiling at, Snapperhead?"

C taunted.

"Ford Fairlane!"

Earl yelled, remembering the movie. Each of them quoted that one as much as *Neighbors*, both goofy, brainless films that pulled C and Earl closer together, the bond between two males over a nonsense topic; it was what made guy friendships special. The fact that nobody else got it, especially girls, that was the glue.

"Yeah, yeah; so what's the cheeser for? You know you're a loser this time, for sure....sorry buddy."

"I never bet you unless I get the okay, and I got the okay; you're gonna lose C, I'm gonna beat the dust!"

Cord knew *exactly* what that meant.

"What did you just say? You got the *okay*? No fucking way! Bet's off; I was betting against *you,* not you **and** your mother! Is *that* why you always win, you fuck? You ask her first? She's pretty good at beating the odds, like a hundred percent good; no wonder I always fucking lose! I shoulda figured she was in on it; is she still standing behind you? Let me talk to her."

Earl sported a pirate smile.

"She's gone. And no take-backs C! I don't wanna hear anything about take-backs from you, mister! I'm gonna have four new books on the way soon, five total. Hah *[Earl held up his hand high, five fingers pointing out in an open mitt]*! Holy mackerel, I'm gonna have a lot of mysteries to solve! No take-backs!"

Earl said a final time, just to be sure, as he pointed stern at C.

"Yeah, yeah. And when have I ever asked for a take-back, by the way? Even though you're a fucking cheater."

C said, disgusted at getting rolled yet again.

"I'm just saying, no take-backs. And I'm not a cheater; my mom never cheats!"

"She's not the cheater, *you are*! You know, now that I think about it, every fucking time we bet you always do that concentration-hesitation thing; you look right through me, off into fucking space, *then* you say you'll take the bet. I didn't know you were in a team huddle, you big, fucking, cheating bastard."

Earl just laughed at him; a shake was a shake, and C was always a sucker for a bet.

Cord knew he probably already lost, but he was stumped as to how Earl's mom thought he could beat the dust. If anyone could do it, if anyone was stupid enough to go fast enough to do it, it was Cord, and he knew he couldn't do it. So how was a too-close-to four hundred pound guy who never even drove a Harley ever gonna do it. This was something he would pay two *Ken Holt* books to see, for sure."

"I still don't believe it; it's a good bet. Earl, your mom's going down on this one. Sorry, you're a loser, whether you are my brother or not. The only one to beat the dust is me, and I'd probably fucking die doing it. You ain't doing it pal, unless, and this ain't happening, trust me, you sit your fat ass right on my lap."

CHAPTER 111 – JONESING TO DISMOUNT ON DERBY LANE

"How many more stops on the adventure Earl, I'm getting hungry."

"Just one."

"Slow down a bit would ya! Mother fucker, my legs are killing me."

Earl cut his pace, letting Cord catch up behind him on the bike. They got to the light, saw the lanes were clear and crossed Route 46, maneuvered through the A&P shopping center lot, riding the bikes up on the sidewalk. Earl leaned his against the wall by the front door.

"Don't worry, no one will touch them; they know it's mine."

Earl said, talking as he went inside.

"Hey Earl, I didn't bring any money."

"Don't need any."

He was already through the door and disappeared into the market.

"Why the fuck are we in here? Is this the last stop? *This* place? You know in the three months I've been in Town, this is the first time I'm inside; everything we need is at Sam's, food-wise anyway, and you two, well you actually, get me all the other stuff I need, so I don't need to come in here, besides, I…."

Earl cut Cord's ramble off.

"Were *not* shopping; it's a surprise, remember? You're not supposed to talk so much."

C was taken aback; Earl scolding him *again*, twice in one day. But he was right, Cord was rambling. So he followed in silence, Earl walking at a quickened pace, in a rush, right to the deli counter, where they took a left and headed to the small, non-descript seafood counter.

Earl stopped abruptly, with C practically running into the back of him.

And he turned, outstretching his arm, as if presenting a prize behind Door No. 2.

"Say hello to my good friend Louie!"

Earl waved at the lobsters in the tank, especially the biggest one, by far, tucked in the back right corner, with two other smaller lobsters climbing on top of him. The big one was the only one with the red rubber bands on his claws; all the rest were blue.

"Before you came along C, Louie was my fourth best-est best friend, behind Al and Marty and Sam; now he's my fifth best friend, but my mom said it's okay, Louie's not mad or jealous about that. Lobsters don't get jealous, it's a fact; did you know that?"

Cord shook his head no; he never read that one in the paper, for sure.

"Well, does he look familiar? Do his friends look like him, you know, in Panama? I wanted Louie to meet you, since we're going together to see the lobsters, you and me; I think he wanted to check you out first, even though I told him you were okay."

Cord stepped closer to the tank, to get a better face-to-face with Lou; he looked rather bored.

"I don't think he's too impressed Earl."

"Oh, he always looks like that; the other ones are always sitting on him. He's too big to sit on anybody else, and too lazy to move; he needs to get some exercise, but it's not like we can go for a walk, otherwise I'd take him."

Cord stared at Louie; his thoughts wandered to Lilly, with Earl saying Lillian would have been named Louis if she had been a boy. He thought about if Lilly had been a boy, she would be one scary guy; God knows what *that* temper would do in a man's body. Then he remembered the story about himself; that he didn't even have a name when he was born, he was just called *the baby*. Nineteen days without a name, and then he got one. He didn't share the story with Earl.

Cord focused back to the lobster in the tank. Lou was a pretty big lobster, C thought; maybe he *was* wrong, maybe Louie didn't get *sold* every week after all. That made Cord feel better, but not much, seeing him biding time in a glass tank, forever brightened by a harsh fluorescent bulb. Maybe a pot was a better end than this.

"Well, he doesn't look like his cousins in Panama, Earl; Lou is from up north, I'm pretty sure. I think he likes cold water; the water in Panama is bathtub warm."

"Oh, I know he likes cold water!"

And with that, Earl scooted behind the deli and thrust his hand into the icy tank, grabbing Louie and in one motion hoisting him out of the water. Earl didn't need the little step ladder to get at the lobster tank.

Lou instinctively curled his tail up and thrashed it back and forth in the air, spraying C with cold spoondrift.

"Wow, he's really excited to see you C! That's about the only exercise he gets!"

And Earl gently put him back into the tank, the other lobsters scattering for cover. Lou settled back into the corner, and just stared through the glass. C felt bad for them all, especially for the blue-bands….short-timers.

Then Cord felt it.

The feeling you get when someone is standing a bit too close behind you. He half-turned to greet a wrinkled old man gawking at the two of them talking to Lou. His cart was empty, save a pack of saltine crackers, a stick of butter and three cans of whole sardines, packed in oil.

"Can….I….help….you?"

Cord asked the old man, in a deliberately slow, sarcastic tone. The man's cart was just about pushed into Cord's rear-end.

The old-timer didn't say a word; he just huffed in the air. With that, he redirected his cart and shuffled toward Aisle Four, away from the two idiots talking to the lobster tank.

"Thanks, Earl."

"For what?"

Earl said, as he wiped his wet hands on his legs.

"For letting me meet Louie; I like him."

Earl smiled.

"I knew you would; you ready to go?"

"Sure, what's next?"

"Nothing! I wanted you to see my mom with me, my secret place and Louie on the Fourth of July; we did it all!"

"Cool, because...."

Earl cut him off.

"Oh, wait, there's one more place; we'll ride by quick. Marty can get us in, but not this quick, so we'll just drive by."

"How far is it, Earl?"

Cord whined, a bit annoyed, figuring he was set to make his side trip.

"Why?"

"Cause I don't want to ride another fucking hour; where is it?"

"Geez, it's right down by the river, off Water Street, by the bridge; it's on our way home, but I don't hafta show ya if you don't want."

Cord felt bad at snapping at Earl. It had just been a week, but he was getting used to a pretty regular taste, and he had been thinking about it ever since the whole Lilly and Button discussion earlier.

"Sorry Earl, it's your day; wherever you want to go, I'm in."

And off they went, pedaling slow into Town, Earl trying to make the trip last. Down past the huge DSM vitamin C plant on Manunkachunk Road, past the Town tennis courts and community pool, packed with people for the holiday.

They hooked a left on Market and a quick right on James Street.

"This isn't the way home, buddy."

"Just two blocks out of our way; we got to take this to the end, to the guard shack."

And in two long blocks, passing under the low, rusted, grafitti-covered train trestle, they were there, the end of the road, smack into the parking lot of a turn-of-the-century BASF paint pigment plant. The century-old buildings were all brick, with large windows and architectural accouterments.

Earl rode past the guard shack; the guy inside was less-than-interested in their presence. Earl stopped when his front bike tire hit the chain link fence on a roller gate, blocking the entrance to a driveway that seemed to trail off into the woods, toward the Delaware River, away from the plant.

Cord rolled up beside him.

"So? What are we looking at?"

Earl just pointed through the fence, to the left, into the thick greenery.

Cord stared, and didn't see anything at first.

Then the outline of what seemed to a brick wall formed between the branches of the understory trees and brush. C stepped off his bike and walked along the fence line, trying to fill in the line from spaces between the wall of greenery. It looked to be a massive brick structure, enveloped in the trees; it must be right on the banks of the Delaware, he thought.

He turned to look at Earl, waiting for an explanation.

1059

"That place is really creepy; I bet the puppet lives there!"

Earl said.

"You think the puppet lives everywhere that's creepy. What is it?"

"It's the old G-P plant, that means *Georgia-Pacific* you know; they used to make plastic stuff. Uncle Frank worked there when I was a little kid, and he brought me there sometimes after work, to run around – it's *huge*, like a football field long, but it's abandoned now. There are big holes in the ceiling and trees growing inside. When it rains you can hear the water running inside, lots of places, dripping, but you can't see it, because all the rooms are pitch black; the big machines and stuff are all rusted. There's mold and dead pigeons everywhere, and I bet the puppet too! Creepy."

Cord just soaked it in.

"How big is it?"

"Big! Like I said, the one big room is like a football field long, and so tall, like four stories tall; that was my favorite room!"

"Why is it sitting empty?

Earl just shrugged his shoulders.

"How do you know what it looks like inside? You sneaking around?"

"No! Marty lets me in; I only go in with him, otherwise, it's too scary! He has a key to the gate and he goes in about once a month maybe, to see if everything is okay. They pay him, like a guard or something, to do it. He sometimes brings me along; I think he gets scared too, but he'd never admit it like I do; there's never anybody in there. People say that's were Stinky-Steve lives, but I never saw him in there."

"Who's Stinky-Steve?"

"The little skinny guy who walks around Town, with the stringy hair, the beard, you know."

"*That* guy! That's Stinky-Steve? That's the guy that farted at me when I walked by him, that first day I came into Town….fucking nasty. I didn't know that was his name."

"I don't know what his real name is, I only know him as Stinky-Steve; nobody knows his real name."

"Well, that's it, time to go home; you wanna watch a movie or something? We could watch *The Blob*."

Now Cord knew Earl didn't want the day to end, and he would go through a litany of things to do with C to extend it. And normally Cord would oblige; he liked hanging with Earl. But not at this particular point in time; his dick was taking charge.

"Maybe I'll come over later; Mae asked me to come look at her flowers, you know, the ones for the Fair."

Earl just looked at Cord and snickered at his lame story.

"What?"

"You're going over there to *do it*; you're not looking at flowers - you're *doing it* again."

Earl snickered some more.

"What? I don't go over there just to fuck her Earl; I happen to like Mae, and as I said, she has…."

Earl cut him off, as he got on his bike, waving a dismissive hand in the air at C's lame story.

"You're gonna do it."

Cord was getting mad at Earl's mocking, but he didn't know why - Earl was dead right. Of course he was going over there to fuck Mae, like he did every week since that first time, like clockwork, sometimes more than once a week. It was the only pussy he was getting, and while Button apparently fucked all the good-looking women in Town at his leisure, Cord was trolling the retirement community. He felt pathetic, so he talked about flowers and the County Fair.

Actually that wasn't fair to Mae; she really was an attractive older woman, and to be honest, she had better stamina than him. But sixty-six years old? *Come on*; C needed to get some younger pussy, just to prove he still could.

But until then, he was once again on his bike, jonesing to dismount on Derby Lane.

CHAPTER 112 – IT WAS TIME TO TAKE OFF THE KNEEPADS

Her back hurt from bending over for hours, and she felt foolish wearing her new kneepads; she felt silly and insignificant….and old.

And he hadn't called all day, which frustrated her to no end, as she stabbed the ground in anger with her shovel, taking it out on the weeds. She knew he wasn't working; where was he?

She was on the far side of the house, buried in the perennial garden along the foundation, away from the driveway, so she didn't see nor hear him coast to a stop and lean his bike against the garage door.

He surprised her when he emerged from around the corner.

"Ahh!"

She let out a little yelp when she saw him.

"What, think it was Joe?"

"He's been over here three times already today, bearing stupid gifts, like usual."

She said, in an annoyed tone, stabbing harder now, little bits of soil flying in all directions.

"Why do you tolerate that little munchkin?"

"Because I use him, like you use me."

"Wow."

Cord said; then he didn't say anything else, he just stood there, watching her repeatedly stab the ground in silence, puffing a tiny grunt now and then. As usual, he was in trouble, so he tried to make light.

"Nice kneepads."

"I know; they look silly, and they make me feel as old as I am, which you remind me of all the time."

She never even looked up as she spoke.

"Jesus, Mae, what the fuck? I just came by to see how the flowers were coming, for the Fair, and all I get is grief; never mind, see you later."

"Oh, you came by to see the flowers? You didn't come for your weekly *fuck*? You know, the half-hour social visit where we don't talk."

She stabbed the soil harder.

"As a matter of fact, no, I didn't."

"Oh yeah, and why is that? Finally got one of the other half-dozen women your scoping to take off their underwear? Don't need the old lady any more?"

"No, I haven't *got* anybody else; maybe I'm just here to see flowers and say hi to a good friend."

Mae snorted a sarcastic laugh.

"Oh, so you *don't* want to fuck your *good friend*; that's what I am? A good friend with kneepads, who tends to the stupid flowers that you care so much about?"

She threw down her little shovel in disgust.

"What the fuck Mae? I came to say hi; I thought you would be happy to see me, and all I get is grief? I can get that anywhere."

"No, you get grief everywhere *but* here! Here you get treated like royalty, and get your dick sucked anytime you want, without strings."

"Sorry, I'm feeling strings; feels like lot of fucking angry strings to me."

She wasn't amused.

"I'm not a whore, and I'm not a charity case either."

"Fine, you're right, no whore, no charity case, no strings; sorry I stopped by. Happy Fourth."

Cord turned to leave, pissed that he wasn't going to bang her; he thought that was always a given. And it *was* the only reason he was there; well, the primary reason, anyway, the only reason….the primary reason.

"You're not leaving."

"Excuse me?"

"You heard me; you're not leaving till you apologize."

"For what? You get mad because you say I only come here to fuck you; I tell you I came to talk about the flowers you're growing for the Fair, and then you get mad because I *didn't* come to fuck you. So what am I apologizing for….fucking? Or not fucking? Or flowers? Tell me what to apologize for and I will, so I can go."

The last she thing she wanted him to do was go. She was upset all day that he wasn't around; him leaving, mad, would make it even worse. Who knows when he would show up again? She had this silly notion in her head all morning that he was going to show up early and surprise her, spend the day with her, spend the night….the whole holiday works. She didn't know why she thought that – they never talked about it, but she got it in her head and expected it to happen, even though she knew it wouldn't.

"It's been a shitty day; where have you been? I can't call you if you're not working, because you don't have a phone; I'm getting you a phone."

"I'm sorry you had a shitty day, but don't bother with the phone, I won't use it; I'll throw it in the toilet. If I wanted a phone, I'd get one."

He said, annoyed.

"I'll only call in an emergency."

"Was *today* an emergency? No phone; now, what can I do to make your shitty day better?"

"You know what; just pay attention to me."

Cord sighed.

"I do Mae."

But neither one was convinced.

She looked at him with hurt eyes; he saw them often.

"Okay, deal. But there are different kinds of attention; do you want me to make you feel good – that kind of attention, or do you want to talk about flowers? Whatever you want, Mae."

"I want *both*; I want you to treat me nice, and not just when you want sex."

"I *do* treat you nice; I don't treat you nice at the store? Didn't I come up here to say hi and talk about flowers, *not sex*, flowers; isn't that nice? I'm not a whore either."

"You're nice sometimes."

She said, begrudgingly. It was hard for her to stay mad at Cord; and as much she wanted to punish him some more, the effort was tiring, and she really just wanted to be happy with him. Being mad was simply too much work.

"But you are a whore."

She added, and cracked the smallest of smiles at him.

The storm had passed.

"Okay, I'll take that; I'm a whore. Now, what do you want to do? The table is yours to set."

"I want to go inside first, and clean up; my back is killing me. And then you are going to lay next to me on my bed and rub my lower back and kiss my neck the way I know you can, very lovingly and tender, for more than the fifteen seconds you normally do, before you start complaining that you're too tired. You'll rub and kiss till I stay stop, when my back feels better....I don't care if it's an hour. Then you'll have sex with me; and we are going to talk before, and during, and *after,* like we used to, when bedding me wasn't such a given. Then we are going to walk around the yard and talk about flowers and the Fair, and then you are going to have sex with me again, then I am going to serve you the holiday dinner I made especially for you, since I figured you would show up some time today to get your weekly fix, and then we are going to fuck again....all night, and I will make you breakfast in the morning. Then you can go home, unless you would just like to stay for good."

"That's a lot of fucking Mae; I only have so much endurance....I'm not as young and virile as you."

"Damn straight, and you better perform! No limp-dick syndrome excuses - you're too hot, or too tired, or not enough protein....whatever; I'm not in the mood for excuses."

He walked over and gave her a firm hug and a tender kiss on the forehead.

"Happy Fourth."

She collapsed in his arms, the final release of pent-up frustration.

"I'm sorry C, it's just been a crummy day, dealing with that idiot next door. And my daughter hasn't called in, I don't know how long, and, of course, there is always the issue of you."

"I know, you can't rely on *that* guy; he's such an asshole."

"On that, we agree."

She said.

"Maybe you should get him a phone."

Cord said sarcastic, as he held her close. She didn't respond – she just smiled, but he couldn't see it; her face was buried in his chest. It felt so good when he hugged her for real, not one of those fake hugs he sometimes gave, lately more often than not, but a heartfelt embrace, like he used to....like this one.

"Where were you all day? I thought you would have come by sooner. Which one of them were you out with? When am I going to hear that you are dating one of them, fucking them, and I get the boot? Today?"

She surprised herself by asking the question, since it was the one answer she didn't want to hear. She wanted a quick take-back.

Her kissed her gently on her forehead, right at the hairline again, and pulled away, looking her intently in the eyes.

"Would you relax, please? I was out with *Earl* all day; remember he had this big day planned, full of surprises for me? Well, today was the day, the Fourth of July; we were out all day on bikes, riding around the whole fucking county. My legs are killing me; you need to rub *my* legs, by the way *[he said sarcastic]*. I'm so tired I could just go to bed."

Mae *did* remember that story - Cord had told her a week ago; all of a sudden she felt a warm rush of relief, and the clouds lifted.

"You can go to bed all right, but I don't want to hear a word about sore legs or being tired."

As she ran her hand down to this shorts and traced along his cock with her middle finger, through the fabric. He had been thinking about fucking her all afternoon, so it didn't take much to get him going. The whole Button story – him fucking Lilly *and* Carol – frustrated him, and set him off, so he was more than ready to throw Mae.

"Well, let's go then; I've been thinking about that little pussy of yours all afternoon."

That's all he had to say; like clockwork, his words were hard-wired to her pussy, which immediately started to throb.

It was time to take off the knee pads.

CHAPTER 113 – SLIPPED INSIDE FOR ANOTHER GO

Since she was still a bit needy, Cord figured he would go with the role-play gig, rather than a short-cut to the fucking. It always bought him points. He vowed to himself not to fantasize about Carol or Lilly when he was pumping Mae; he didn't need those pussies anyway - no big deal that Button got both - he could get them to, if he really tried. He convinced himself as much.

She led him into the bedroom, holding his hand, like she normally did. But rather than going over to the bed, he told Mae to go into her closet; she knew that meant a game was in play, which she loved. It meant more attention, and more intimate sex; maybe she had to scold him more often.

She came out with his favorite, the short, mid-thigh plaid skirt and the white button-up blouse, sans bra. She had the Catholic schoolgirl look, which she was, albeit more than a few decades ago. Still, Mae's legs were killer.

"What's your name, little girl?"

C would ask her every time, as he stood close behind her, rubbing his cock in the crack of her ass and reaching around her front, slowly unbuttoning her blouse, as she faced away from him. He could see Mae's nipples through the fabric as he looked over her shoulder; they were stiff, as he knew they would be.

She would never answer him, only a low moan, as he ground his cock against her ass. But this time, she answered.

"Samantha, Samantha Pleasance; but I want you to call me Sam."

Just a few words, but what a turn-on; they both felt it.

After the blouse was unbuttoned, he would pull it out of her skirt, where it would fall partially open.   Cord would slide his hands beneath her mini, up the outside of her thighs, his fingertips barely touching her skin, till he stopped and rested them on her hips, at the elastic of her black lace panties; they were always black for this game. Then, in one swift motion, he would pull her panties right to the floor. Mae would always gasp when he did it, even though she knew it was coming. That was her favorite part; she felt so dirty, a total lack of control for the woman who controlled everything. Now she was simply submissive, just waiting to be violated, against her will.

She would step out of her panties and spin to face him, her blouse falling open, because that is what he told her to do. Cord would press his body against hers and push her back two steps, till Mae was pinned against her work desk, which she would shimmy onto, forced to comply.

He would grab her knees and slowly spread her open, the first step to take what was his, and she had no choice but to give in. If she struggled, she figured he would force her, but he never had to, because she wanted it, and she would open her legs for him, willingly.

He would then work his way down the inside of her left thigh, always the left, gently kissing her skin along the way, his lips barely touching her, following with a gentle touch of his hand to the inside right, spreading her open wider as he went down, till he got to the crease, and the prize…that little pussy, with just the right amount of fine, light brown hair, neat and trimmed.

Cord would purposely delay touching her; he would hover over her, a fraction of an inch away from the hair on her lips, breathing warm air on her pussy, which drove her mad. She would arch her hips to try and force contact, but he would pull away. Invariably, she would come within a few seconds of his tongue parting and licking her lips, running the length, from her ass to her clit, and back again, while his hands gently pulled her lips apart.

He did it every time, and she never tired of it; it was her favorite set-up. And Mae loved being a bad little girl.

She never wanted to leave that desk; he would fuck her there – first with her legs over his shoulders, then spread as wide as he could get her, his hands on her ankles. He loved watching her pussy while he did her. They would always finish from behind, her bent over the desk, hands stretched behind her, pulling her ass cheeks apart, so he got as deep a stroke as he could into her pussy. She called him *Daddy* when she came, he made her keep saying it while she was finishing, which always made the orgasm last longer. Mae felt juiced saying it over and again when they were fucking, and always felt a bit silly about it afterwards. But it couldn't have been that silly, because *Daddy* always seemed to join them.

They did have good sex; Cord seemed to get that part right.

Surprisingly, she let him get away with the one session on the desk; she came four or five times – she didn't keep track. He came once; he was only ever good for one.

A half-hour later, they were back in the yard, looking at flowers.

"Hey Mae, I know I shouldn't ask this, God knows what taboo story is behind this one, but who joined us today? Who's Samantha, that dirty little Catholic girl I just hard-fucked?"

"Nobody, I just made her up."

"Uh huh; come on now, remember who you're talking to? Now, who's Samantha?"

Mae knew he wasn't going to let it drop.

"She's the niece of one of my neighbors, two streets over. She comes up to visit her aunt some weekends during the summer; she comes over to see me sometimes with her aunt. She's a cute girl, college kid; kind of reminds me of me when I was younger, although I was much better looking, of course. Next time she comes up to visit, I'll point her out if you happen to be over; maybe you need to come over more often to meet her.

Cord smiled, and Mae quickly qualified, knowing she may have just opened the barn door.

But she's just for our sex stories! I don't need another one in the mix. Anyway, when I'm playing a schoolgirl, it's easier to be her than sixty-six, if you know what I mean; it helps make it feel more real. I've been using her for awhile, just never mentioned it; do you mind?"

"I guess I can live with it."

Cord said, with an air of mock sacrifice.

"Call me on that phone you're gonna get me the next time she's up; you know, emergency call….I'd be happy to meet her."

"I'm sure you would, and I'll be sure that doesn't ever happen. Sorry I mentioned it; no more Sam, you can color her gone."

"Too late, even if you don't say it, *I* will. And I know we'll both be thinking it."

C said, smug.

"Jesus, I should have kept my mouth shut."

Mae whispered, as they walked side-by-side. They made their way around the foundation, mixing with the plethora of annuals and perennials; Mae was an amazing gardener.

"So, give me the updated tour; which ones are going to the Fair?"

"Well, I haven't decided yet. It'll probably be the roses and gladiolas, but I may also put in some dahlias, marigolds and zinnias, since I have them all, and they all look pretty good this year. People from Belvidere, in Town, seem to win most of the flower groups pretty much every year. Nuts, now that's another story; there's a hard-core nut group in Stewartsville who *always* win the pecan and filbert divisions."

Cord just looked at her, eyebrows raised.

She ignored the look and continued.

"Flowers are it for me though. I don't have any nut trees and the fruit tree I have is nothing special. And for some reason, I just can't grow show-quality vegetables; now *those* guys, that's a whole different mindset. The vegetable competition is crazy! Last year, the winner squash, *Best of Weight Category – Adult Division*, was a Blue Hubbard - 23.61 pounds! Can you believe the size of that ugly sucker?! The guy was carrying it around like an Olympic medal, doing an Irish jig.

C's eyebrows raised higher.

"I never pegged you for getting involved in this kind of thing, Mae; sounds kind of, I don't know, pedestrian….colloquial. Kind of queer."

"Well, if you said to me ten years ago I'd be fighting for a piece of plastic ribbon for flowers with a bunch of old ladies, and men too, at a bumpkin fair, I would have laughed my ass off, calling it pathetic. But, you know, the competitive juices do get a hold of you. The competition out here in Brookfield is pretty crazy; some of these women, *friends*, won't speak to each other after the competition, for months, over who had better cinnamon buns or lemon meringue pie. And there is *no way* that Arlene Schelling is going to beat me in the roses and brag all around the Community Center for another twelve months; I've seen hers – nothing compared to mine - nothing - she's gonna get crushed. She's the defending rose champion, you know – *Class 16 – Perennial Category.*"

"*Class 16,* really? You're scaring me, Mae."

C said sarcastic.

"That does sound a bit scary, doesn't it?"

She said, with a chuckle.

"Regardless, she's toast."

Mae let out a huff.

"What were those cut flowers in the vase, on the table?"

"Gladiolas – aren't they beautiful? Salmon-colored are my favorites; here come look at them."

Mae slipped her arm into C's and continued their leisurely tour of the gardens surrounding her small yard – the variety she grew in such a small area was stunning. The entire yard was bathed in sun, since Brookfield had no mature trees to speak of, just typical new-development saplings here and there.

And Mae pointed out beds of tulips and jonquils, daffodils, zinnias – both dwarf and large, marigolds – a sea or orange and yellow, and hyacinths; she knew the Latin names, the hybrids, the history of each.

"Here, you should know this one; this variety blooms in the autumn."

"Sorry, don't know."

"It's a narcissus."

"Funny. Hey I know these."

Cord said, as he walked over to a thick patch of peonies, well past their flower.

"I have both pink and white; they're beautiful in the spring."

"When I was a kid, I used to flick the flower buds, when they were still in a ball, like a jawbreaker; they were always crawling with little ants, and I used to launch them through the air."

"Hey, talking about ants, can you do something about this big anthill over here? What should I spray to kill them?"

"Leave the ants alone Mae, they aren't hurting anything."

"You just said you launched ants?"

"Yeah, when I was eight and stupid; I don't launch ants anymore. *Leave the ants alone.*"

"I'll get Joe to take care of it."

C got a bit testy.

"Mae, please, just leave the ants alone….*please*?"

"Why?"

"Because I *asked* you to, simple as that; please, just leave them alone, and drop it."

"Fine."

She said, not really being sure what that was all about.

"You know what kind of tree that is?"

"Nope."

"It's a plum; it'll be loaded with fruit soon. Not Fair quality, but they still taste good."

"I'm impressed Mae; when did a lobbyist learn so much about gardening? When you weren't a lobbyist anymore?"

"I'm still a lobbyist, I'll always be a lobbyist, it's in the blood. Nah, I grew up with a grandmother and grandfather who had amazing green thumbs – I inherited it I guess. Whatever I plant grows, I'm just good at it. Maybe I should plant you."

"I doubt that would grow very well; how do we always get back to that topic?"

"Because you're stubborn, and never give me the answers I want."

"Wouldn't that make *you* stubborn?"

"I suppose we both are. By the way, I notice you conveniently ignored my offer earlier."

Cord knew exactly what she was talking about.

"What offer?"

"The offer to stay."

"I have a place Mae; it's close to Earl, and…."

"And Lillian?"

"I wasn't going to say that; I was going to say that Earl would be upset. Also, although you never want to acknowledge it, we had the discussion about you and me….fun, remember? Nothing more; well, not nothing more, I enjoy being with you, a lot, but we are not dating Mae, and moving in here would send all the wrong messages….*way* wrong."

"To who, all your other girlfriends?"

"I don't have any girlfriends, *any,* including you."

"We would just be roommates; it would save you some money."

"I don't need the money, and we wouldn't be just roommates, you know that; let's just drop it, before we start fighting again."

She started to sulk.

"Mae, I know you don't want to hear this, but I'm forty-three, and I've been in this Town for three months; I've been lots of places before, and I'll be in lots of places after. I know me; I'm not staying here. We're all on our way someplace else; I'm just passing through."

Mae got a sharp tinge of anxiety, mixed with panic, which showed in her voice.

"Are you leaving? When are you leaving?!"

"I'm not leaving; I have no plans to leave, but I will, I always do. Things will happen, they always do, and I move on; it's just the way it is. I've told you that from day one."

"You never said you were leaving!"

Mae yelped, exasperated at the conversation turn.

"Yes I have, you just choose as to when you want to listen."

They both circled the balance of the yard in silence; she dropped his arm as part of her sulk. They ended on a small wrought iron bench, set amongst the beds, aside two terra cotta cachepots, brimming with geraniums and petunias. He put his hand on her left leg, cupping her knee.

"Mae, I do care about you, a *lot*, maybe not in the full commitment way you want, but in the best way I can. And it's not just about getting sex; I like talking to you and being with you, I do. You're smart and sarcastic….and fun. I'm a mixed bag; please believe me on that and just enjoy our time together, no matter how long it lasts; it could be another day, or another ten years….I just don't know yet."

"Why are you even here? In Town, I mean; it would have been better to not even know you."

"Really?"

"No, of course not really. But why?"

"I'm not going to lie to you, so don't ask me that question."

"Why?"

"Because if I answer that question, I will lie to you, so I'm being honest, I'll lie."

"That's ridiculous, just answer the question."

"Well, here's an honest answer; I thought I knew why I came here, but now I'm not so sure. Things have happened here that aren't supposed to happen, and that complicates things. That's as good as it gets."

"What things have happened? *Me*?"

She whispered, hopeful.

Now he would have to lie.

Because what had *happened* had absolutely nothing to do with Mae; there was a Mae just about everywhere he went, and it never ended well. No, what *happened* was Earl, and Earl's mom, and dreams, and talk of angels and kindred spirits; none of *that* was supposed to happen....none of that *ever* happened. No matter where C found himself, he does what he does, what happens, happens, and he moves onto the next place, and the game continues....simple. But he guessed maybe every game sooner or later comes to an end; it has to end somewhere, right? It can't simply go on forever. Maybe it was going to end here; maybe that was what this strange place had in store for him. And he was okay with that. But all that had absolutely nothing to do with Mae, she wasn't even the smallest part of what was important in the mix, so he lied.

"Maybe; you're part of the mix Mae, aren't you?"

And that fib did the trick; it was the little bit of sugar that made the whole conversation taste better. Much better.

She slipped her arm back into his, and rested her head on his shoulder, looking up at him with doe eyes.

"So, did I tell you my name? My name is Samantha, but you can call me Sam. Do you want to see my bedroom *Daddy*?"

She cracked a goofy, mischievous smile.

Good God, he wasn't nearly ready for another round, but C knew he had little choice in the matter; and with that, they slipped inside for another go.

www.ingramcontent.com/pod-product-compliance
Lightning Source LLC
Chambersburg PA
CBHW051005180726
48291CB00006B/1981